In memory of my Roski. I miss you.

CONTENTS

Stitched up

CHAPTER ONE: CAN I SLOT A MURDER INTO MY SCHEDULE?

"I'm going to kill the Queen!"

It was beyond annoying that the doors to Magda's chambers didn't burst open with a dramatic flair to match my storming of her rooms. They were too heavy for that. Life is unfair in such ways. Instead, I had to force the one on the left open and wiggle inside. I straightened up once through, letting it slowly creep closed again being me. Taking a deep breath, I repeated my murderous intentions to Magda, putting every ounce of frustrated certainty into the declaration.

The woman didn't even look up from her book.
"Good afternoon, Nina, how lovely to see you. Do come in for some tea."
"I don't want tea! I want vengeance!"
"It is the Rhean blend."

Hmm, that was something to pay attention to. She somehow always had the best tea in the whole castle. I was knew that she made half the blends herself, putting old skills to new use, and the others were sourced from various trade connections without the usual tax addition. In fact, I am pretty sure that she billed it to the kingdom in expenses.

She gestured with one foot from her sofa to the glass pot full of something faintly red. It did smell rather good now that I was paying attention to it.

"I mean it- I am going to kill her with my bare hands." I kept speaking even as I crossed the room.
She at least glanced at me for that, one eyebrow raised. "That sounds rather unhygienic."

I scowled, even as, taking her at her word, I poured out a cup from the pot on the low table in between our chairs. A heaped spoonful of honey would no doubt do wonders to sweeten my temper. Mags wouldn't mind. She didn't even like honey, only kept it around for visitors.
"Fine I will use my teaspoon." I brandished it to make a point, narrowly avoiding speckling us both with the honey. A raised eyebrow had me setting it back down gently. That would be the stupidest way to die.

She nodded, accepting the apparent surrender, and turned another page. "Well that will give the guards something to talk about on their lunch break."

Huffing, I threw myself down into the deepest armchair in her room. I loved that chair; it was like being hugged by puppies. Slurping my drink down despite the heat, I caught the biscuit she threw my way without having to look. It was an old game of ours. And alright, I knew I was being melodramatic, but sometimes there is just no place for reason.

For a few moments there was relative silence as I let my temper simmer down and she leisurely kept flipping through her story. When she reached the end of whatever chapter she was reading, a piece of ribbon was placed within the tome to mark her place, and she finally turned her full attention to me.

"So... I believe you were planning a murder?"
"Yes. And at least I know you won't rat me out." I gestured with the biscuit, ignoring the fact that I was getting a fair few crumbs on my shirt.

Magda eyed them distastefully, for all that she seemed resigned to letting me be childish for a little while longer. "Of course not. So, you are going to kill..."

"Clarisse."

"Of course."

"Using a spoon."

"Fantastic." There was a beat of silence as she seemed to mull over my idea. She shook her head as if suddenly struck by a thought. "I would remind you that regicide is rather frowned on. After all, if the queen is dead that is highly inconvenient for royal portrait painters, and the mint will have to restrike coins, it will be a logistical nightmare. People will be highly annoyed at you for committing a murder with so much logistical fallout."

I rolled my eyes to high heaven in the face of her overwhelming sense. "Fine, I will make it look like an accident. A tragic teatime incident. Such a dangerous way to spend an afternoon. Or even better: I kill her and then we replace her with someone who looks identical. But is less annoying."

For all that my tone was still on the acidic side, I could feel my irritation shedding off my shoulders. It was why I had come here in the first place. It is sometimes beyond difficult when you are tasked with being the Queen's bodyguard. And who else would understand better than the person who used to have my job?

In this whole country, there is one person who I personally value above all others. For all that it is probably treason to say, that person is not the Queen. Don't get me wrong, Clarisse is my priority, the person for whom I would lay down my life. She is the embodiment of the country's history, the physical form of centuries of divine and secular existence. My life and honour have been sworn to her defence through oaths which to break would damn my eternal soul.

She is also, in my humble opinion, a bit of a bitch. And not in the fun way.

No. My favourite person is Her Imperial Eminence, the Duchess Magda of Increstia. It is such a fantastic title, and she takes great pleasure in making pages announce her fully at every single event she attends. The best part is that as a title it doesn't actually make any sense. Increstia doesn't even exist. It is a land from a story told to children. If you have lost something, you say it was sent to Increstia. She takes great enjoyment in regaling visiting dignitaries with detailed explanations of her country's customs. And her targets either don't realise that she isn't just talking about an obscure dukedom, or figure that she is someone's troubled relative.

She was the bodyguard to the previous Queen, staying by her side until the day she stepped down from the throne to let Clarisse take over. With her charge no longer being queen, it meant that Mags was no longer needed in the same capacity. Having reached the end of her service, alive, it was considered a good idea to thank her for her many, many, many years by giving her a real position. You know, rather than the half acknowledged 'commoner amongst the ladies' vibe which tends to be our lot in life. Even if that is as regent of a make-believe country.

Only fair. And in all honesty, if you think of a Duchess, you will probably have the mental image of someone remarkably like Mags. She just has that presence which lends weight to whatever room she walks into. I swear she looks the same as when I was first brought to the castle. I truly believe she was born with steel grey hair. Seriously- you can see it even in the paintings and tapestries from the early days of the previous Queen's reign. At the same time, her face is one which doesn't seem to weather no matter what she has gotten up to. And ours is a profession not known for being kind to a person's complexion.

In the general storm of craziness and crap which has been my life since I was trained for the 'illustrious honour' of being a human shield, she has been my rock. Occasionally a rock used to crush parts of me which were deemed unnecessary, but a constant nonetheless.

I had asked her once, how did she make it as far as she had? The question had been partly from curiosity about what wonders she must have lived through, more from wanting to know that longevity was a fluke. In my defence, it had been a particularly hard week when I was getting my ass handed to me at every training session and the doses of poison I was growing immune to were shredding my guts. Part of me hates her for what she made me into. It was a day when I was sure that I would never forgive her choices. That being said, she had never lied to me.

At first, she had just laughed, a rough sound far from the tinkling bell notes that you would expect from a lady. Years of yelling, and drinking various toxins no doubt, would do that to your vocal cords. She patted me on the hand and claimed that the Pantheon simply found her too amusing to kill off, so the gods kept her alive for their amusement.

My facial expression must have hinted that I did not share that opinion.

With a wry smile, she had told me, "Dearie, when I was your age, I figured I would die before I got old. Is it so unreasonable to plan by average life expectancy? Although if I had died young, as is traditional, I would have missed all the fun of my decrepit schemer years." She had cackled, and politely not commented as I turned three shades paler and threw up into a convenient bucket. Repeatedly.

Instead, she pushed the hair back from my face and handed me a cup of tea when I could finally sit up again. "Ooh the things I can get the young fools around here to believe. Honestly, I could have been a world-famous bard in a different life. My position these days is a great cover as well for when things need to get done around here. Someone pushed the asshole ambassador down the stairs in the night? How tragic. A poor, old woman such as myself could start to feel unsafe in such troubled times." She had looked me up and down, quirking her lips into a thin smile, "and I thoroughly expect you to that part of my legacy when the time comes. So don't die until then, as I would hate to have to train a new accomplice."

So, you know, there is hope for me after all. At the very least it serves as a pleasant daydream of what chaos I can cause should I reach my twilight years. Not to mention, Magda is a great excuse for dodging certain members of the royal household who like to try and get me to do things for them due to my lack of station yet proximity to the Queen. Mags delights in being my alibi, provided I either let her be directly involved in whatever scheme is going on, or at least tell her every juicy detail.

Considering all this, it was only natural that her chambers were my first stop once I had been dismissed from Her Majesty's presence. I had been at Clarisse's side during the council meeting where the delightful news was shared that 'Empress of Intari' is apparently going to be the next title bestowed when she gets re-sworn to the throne. You know, what with the invasion of the closest small neighbour resulting in a swift and noble victory. Her brave forces had risked life and limb to annex the next closest trading partner. The Council told her this morning. I may have not controlled my facial expression as well as I should have. Remarks were made.

And now here I was eating biscuits and trying not to spit venom.

Mags had been like a sister to the previous Queen, or at least so everyone seemed to say. Judging from some of the stories that she herself has let loose after a few too many glasses of wine at parties, I reserve my own conclusions. There are so many different forms of love after all.

In comparison, Clarisse and I don't really get along in the best way. As you may be able to tell by this point. I mean I am trained to notice behaviour, to analyse potential threats, keep a low profile until it is time for me to act. So I should be better at hiding the fact that I don't necessarily like my monarch. The animosity doesn't half make my job harder in some ways, as she is adamant on getting a break from my presence. I don't even try to antagonise her, she just...

I even offered once, when she had spent a whole week purposefully making my life miserable by refusing to cooperate with anything I asked her to do, to leave the court entirely. How could she trust me to watch her back if she apparently thought so little of me? She said that she reckoned I would save her life just out of spite so that I could hold it over her forever after. It wasn't far off the mark. I had still driven a fist through the wall of my room. Mags must have gotten involved at that point, since the next day Clarisse agreed to some of the precautionary measures which we had been pushing for an upcoming state visit. The bitterness still lingered.

Of course, these days we are older, and whilst not necessarily wiser we can both see the benefit to existing alongside each other. And, for the record, I stopped keeping track of how many times I had saved her life by this point.

I can still remember a time when we used to be closer, although it really hadn't lasted all that long. When I was younger, about fourteen I guess, and Tabitha was still at court as one of the Maids who could double as the Queen when needed. In the year that I had been living at court I had learnt a lot about friends, enemies, rank and duty. Then I got sick, really sick, the sort of sick which had Mags staying behind to care for me whilst the others travelled to the Summer Palace. I don't remember much of what happened during those weeks. Just Mags looking grave and concerned, someone who was probably a doctor, and then the Queen visiting and sitting to read to me despite her Councillor's protests that it was too dangerous. Apparently, part of the reason why they left me behind a week later was out of fear that whatever I had could pass to the others.

When I finally came out of it, able to stay awake for more than a few minutes, to keep down water and gruel, when the doctor announced I wouldn't die after all… that was when they figured I was strong enough that they could tell me.

There had been an incident at the Summer Palace. Somehow a fire had started in the residential wing, trapping the Queen and her Maids. By the time that the guards managed to beat a path through the flames, they say that none of them could even scream from the way that the smoke had scorched their throats.

Thankfully Her Majesty was relatively unharmed. In shock, slight burns to her arms and hands, but otherwise in one piece. Tabitha hadn't been so lucky. In protecting the Queen from the blaze, she had taken the brunt of the flames to her face. I never saw her again. They returned to the Castle without her. It seemed the wounds were terrible, the scars anticipated to leave her face all but destroyed, and she hadn't been able to be moved. Some say that she eventually healed, only to refuse to return to court. Can't say I blame her. Others insist that she quietly died not long afterwards.

After that, well, the dynamic within the court was definitely changed. I can't help but think that Clarisse thinks it was my fault. For not being there. It should have been me to take that damage. It is literally my job after all. Even then, that would have been my responsibility. And I had failed. The circumstances don't matter. The outcome was unchangeable. And as a result, the distance had grown between us. She just never had the same warmth to me as before, and didn't acknowledge my overtures of peace.

I gave up eventually. I didn't have to like her in order to protect her, and I have friends amongst the other people at court, so it is not as if life is unrelenting misery. Mags reckons that as Queen she is allowed to have a bitchy streak. In her field that is called having grit. On the flip side, it does mean that I get a bit of time off every now and again when Her Majesty is secured and would rather have no company. Or at least not mine.

Mags flicked an apple seed at me to draw me back to the present. A knock at the door interrupted my imminent revenge. A shame. The amount of harm I could do with the remaining half of my biscuit. It would have been a fate worthy of record in the histories of the land.

Serafina stuck her head around the door jamb, getting a fond smile from Mags as she waved her forwards. The girl has been at court for her entire life, the daughter of one of the cooks who just so happened to run into Clarisse when they were both small children. They had remained friends over the years, with Sera getting promoted when Clarisse assumed the throne to become the main attendant for the Maids.

It was certainly a coveted spot, at least by anybody who didn't have to deal with all the regular nonsense. I swear, Sera has the patience of a saint. And everyone feels bad if they happen to upset her- she just has the best puppy eyes. I am of course immune. Such a weakness would be beneath contempt for someone in my position. And I most certainly never covered for her when she wanted a break from the Maids' mania. Not once. No way.

She was a friend. A good friend. One of the people who wouldn't report me in for treasonous talk. She got that when you spent so much time catering to the whims of a single person you had to fantasize about their graphic murder in order to remain vaguely sane.

Considering how quickly she scarfed down the new biscuit I passed her, I could guess that her day had been as frustrating as my own. Magda put her book to one side, sitting up properly so as to give a bit of space for Sera to rest even though she waved away the offer of a seat, preferring to just perch on the arm of my chair instead. She did accept the teacup which was pushed into her hands, inhaling the fragrant steam with a sigh of satisfaction. We had joked once that we could create a society of some sort, a 'Refuge from Royalty' perhaps. Then again, no point in risking being accused of organising a coup.

That had nearly happened to the Woodcutters Guild over a truly unfortunate series of misunderstandings. According to castle gossip, they had meant to be running a teaching evening on 'thorn thrashing' for their apprentices to stop them getting shredded by brambles. The man in charge of spreading the word had been truly appalling at spelling, putting out pamphlets for 'throne thrashing'. The fallout had almost been disastrous. Since then, private clubs had lost a bit of their appeal, and the benefits of editing had been firmly recognised.

The crunch of another biscuit being demolished brought me back to the present. I really had to stop going off into my own thoughts so much. From the look on Serafina's face, I knew that I wasn't going to like what she had to say. Sure enough, she washed down the biscuit with her tea despite it being so hot the steam was still curling over the edge of the cup. Putting the crockery down, she immediately began pulling me up out of my chair. I dug my heels in on principle alone.

"Come on, come on, we have places to be."

I let myself be dead weight, getting some amusement from how she couldn't find a way to make me move. It was petty, true, but it still made me smile. I get my kicks where I can. A few seconds of fruitless struggle and she let go, Huffing in irritation as she fixed some of the hair which had come loose from her cap. The glare she fixed on me would have been more effective if, as already stated, I wasn't already immune. My decision to get up was entirely separate from her expression.

"Thank you." Sera took a moment to brush the crumbs from my clothes, tutting quietly to herself as she did. "Now go! We were meant to be in the throne room five minutes ago. Clarisse has to meet with heads of the temples about the re-swearing ceremony and then she has another meeting with the Diplomatic Corps over which ambassadors are lined up to be welcomed over the next few weeks." There was barely a breath between the words.

Yay. Both those options were going to be so much fun. There was no containing my excitement. Annoyingly Sera had already hurried us both towards the door. Mags was absolutely no help, simply waving us goodbye with a smug smirk as she picked her book back up. She did at least throw me one last biscuit, not bothering to look as I caught it over my shoulder and shoved it straight into my mouth.

Sera was already charging ahead, gracefully of course, muttering to herself about the next chore on her list as her skirts swirled around her legs. The girl really was a force of nature, one to whom anyone with half an ounce of sense would defer to when it came to the background running of the castle. It could be pretty amusing when servants of visiting nobles tried to lord themselves over her. They inevitably ended up being won over by her personality, terrified of her temper, or begging forgiveness when everybody else made their lives a misery until they got over themselves. Or all of the above. In truth always all of the above.

I lengthened my stride until I could overtake her, making sure to brush any remaining crumbs from my face as we reached the doors to the throne room. She ran a critical eye over me, straightening my collar slightly, before giving a small nod and a pat on the shoulder.

Busy as she was, she barely waved goodbye before heading off. I took a deep breath, fixing the belt of my scabbard to sit more comfortably on my hips. One of the privileges of my position was that I was one of the few who was permitted to be armed in the presence of the Queen. After all what use was a bodyguard without a weapon on her person? As you may have guessed however, the main thing I considered using the sword for on a daily basis was to fillet the queen.

Perhaps I should stop thinking such things. Thoughts become words, words become actions, actions become who you truly are. Or so Mags has tried to tell me before. I am pretty sure she got that from one of her books. After hanging up her own blades she became rather fond of philosophy. I think she just liked finding a new way to basically eviscerate people without leaving a mess on her rug.

That being said, the sword was honestly a bit more for show. I mean true, I could use it, no point in carrying the extra weight if not. And it served as a reminder to the court as to my position. But in general, I preferred my smaller blades, the ones I kept on me at all times and made sure that people didn't notice until it was far too late.

It was a good day when I didn't have to use any of them. I kept a chart of how long it had been since the last attempt on Clarisse's life. I was very proud of the fact it was still in the double digits.

The streak was one which I refused to break myself. That was the thought I decided to hold onto as I took a deep breath and opened the doors to the throne room. Time to go to work.

CHAPTER TWO: GET THIS BALL ROLLING

Clarisse came careering round the corner and almost crashed straight into me. She was flushed, half laughing and genuinely looking half worried. It was always the same when she had the night off from being Queen. Considering general stress of the last few days, she had taken the chance to have one of the Maids take her place for the reception. The event itself was simply to acknowledge the success of a recent trade negotiation, so no actual queenly duties were required other than her presence.

These sorts of calmer celebrations were ones which even I could enjoy. The background music was kept at a lower volume, people's discussions were more easy going, the crowd in general more comfortable with each other. And the food was less fancy than at full on banquet nights. All in all, it was a level of social which I could be part of and still do my job without excessive stress.

I wasn't the only one who enjoyed these types of gatherings. Clarisse had leapt at the opportunity to take a step back. It'was a tactic which usually helped when we had potential suitors visiting, as it allowed her to interact with them as someone other than the queen, to test the waters of how they really were when they thought that she wasn't looking.

On the flip side, she did tend to see it as a chance to let off a bit of steam which in her daily role of Queen would be frowned upon by the council. The last time we had switched for a Maid, Clarisse had ended up swimming in the moat at dawn after losing a dare.

Sera had almost had a fit when she found out.

At least the shift in dynamic meant that she was much more positively inclined towards me. I swear her shifts in mood are going to give me whiplash one of these days. This time, her eyes lit up when she saw that I was propping up a column, drink held loosely as I kept watch over the rest of the guests. "Oh shit, oh shit, you have to help me!"
"What have you done now?"
"It wasn't anything I did."
I raised an eyebrow, "Uh huh."
"But I am your queen and as my guard it is your duty to protect me!"

I watched the wine swirling in my glass, pointedly not looking at her. "Is it indeed? But I thought the Queen was due to be dancing..."
She slapped me lightly on the arm, "not funny. Dressed up or dressed down I am still the monarch of this realm, the leader of my nation, and I command you to hide me before my Maid spots me!"

It was a hushed plea, and even from where I was standing, I could hear the approaching footsteps of our monarch's understudy. Across the room Mags was shaking her head at us with a fond smile as she clocked our antics. No doubt she remembered times when her Queen had pulled similar stunts. Although those instances ended up with Mags going missing from parties as well. No doubt to keep extra close watch on her charge.

Ah the joys and follies of youth. Or at least that was what she would usually say when I went and vented to her later.

I turned my attention back to Clarisse who was looking over her shoulder with wide eyes. "What happened?"
"I had a bet with Jeremy about one of the councillor's sons who kept trying to dance with me, and I kept turning him down as he really isn't my type."

"Right..."

"And then we got talking about what was my type, and he said that the reason why I haven't chosen a Consort yet is that I am dreadful at flirting."

"Don't tell me." I downed my drink and set the glass aside.

I made a mental note to have a word with Jeremy later as well. He is a guard who has been part of the castle for longer than Clarisse has been alive, so of course he would notice that she was in disguise for the night. Even so, it was always worth checking if there had been anything particularly noticeable as off with the ruse. No deception is ever perfect after all.

She shrugged with a half guilty little laugh. "Yeah, so I ended up making a pass at one of the dukes. And he spat out his drink. All over an earl. And they may have started fighting. And now I am on the run from Delilah because she was tasked with making sure tonight went smoothly and..."

"Oh for the love of the gods." There was a small ripple of bows at the other end of the room, no doubt heralding 'the Queen's' arrival.

Clarisse's eyes were comically wide and desperate. "Please!" it was a rare enough occurrence for her to use that word. And it is only logical to reward desired behaviour. How was it possible to so often feel that I was in charge of toddlers?

"Alright, duck behind this curtain."

The most powerful woman in our land heaved a massive sigh of relief as she slipped behind the drape. Just in time as well, I had barely resumed my lean against the wall before Delilah came storming over to my chosen corner. I always found it rather funny when she was standing in for the Queen. With her makeup done, and in that dress, she was an almost perfect copy of Her Majesty. Almost. For those who knew them as well as I did, it was obvious that Delilah was ever so slightly too short to be the real queen. The heels usually made up for it, but when she was covering at a ball, she tended to wear slightly flatter shoes so as to be able to dance. Just because it was her job to play the part of the monarch, didn't mean that she couldn't enjoy herself at the same time.

Everyone in the room bowed or curtsied as she moved, forcing her to remember her rank of the evening and just about manage to slow to a more regal pace.

"Ah, Nina."

"Good evening, Your Highness." I inclined my head, managing to hide the twitch of my lips.

"I don't suppose you have seen one of my Maids come through here?" her accent was perfect as always, a flawless rolling of vowels as only those trained from birth to talk like a queen could manage. They used to sometimes get me to try and mimic it, but what with my already speaking in a second language, my own accent had been too hard to shake.

"Indeed, I did, Majesty."

"And where, pray tell, did she run off to? I wish to have a word with her about the progress of her diplomacy lessons. It is rather important." There was a tension in her jaw from slightly gritted teeth, for all that rye amusement hid in the corner of her eye.

I made a show of nodding, completely earnest in my answer, "I see. Well, she came through her not a moment before yourself, I believe she was intending to take a turn around the gardens. A bit of fresh air to cool down perhaps."

She hummed a little at my response as we shared a knowing look. Delilah knew that the queen was hiding somewhere in this room; that I was giving her an out. For all that we were playing roles tonight, that didn't mean a Maid could berate the real queen. If anything, I think Delilah would have passed out if she had been told to do so. To anybody watching, it would simply appear that I was taking pity on a friend to protect her from her queen's displeasure. An act to be written off as peace keeping at court. Respect really was such a delicate balancing act between genuine feeling and performance for the sake of external expectation.

With full regal poise, she inclined her head at my statement. "Well, when she comes back this way to return to the dancefloor, do remind her to have a touch more caution in future. Spilt drinks are such a hazard after all."
"Of course, your highness." I curtsied as she moved off to take a turn around the room, greeting the various dignitaries and courtiers before she could return to the main ballroom.

It was always fascinating seeing the Maids portray the Queen. They each did so in slightly different ways, composite actresses both of them. Even those most often at court didn't seem to notice the difference as they interacted with Delilah rather than Clarisse. Amazing what expectation and belief can do. That and a highly effective use of makeup.

When the coast was clear, Clarisse came edging out of her hiding spot, managing to snag a glass from a passing server and taking a long drink. I watched her from the corner of my eye.
"So, I take it you are having fun this evening, My Lady?"
She lifted one shoulder in an elegant shrug, "Certainly more than if I were playing my usual part."
I hummed in agreement, "Yes, so lucky that a small win could be had at the end of such a trying week."

I could feel her eyes boring into my head as I pointedly examined my empty glass. "Yes, what a strangely fortuitous timing."
"Indeed. The delegation from Rhean was so polite as well."
"Right. Almost miraculous with how rumours had been circulating that they had been originally unhappy with the slight decline in relative spending between our nations."
"Exactly."
"But I hear that they had a most delightful interaction with a couple of tea enthusiasts."
"Well that is a relief to hear. Amazing what a bit of personally applied diplomacy can achieve."

No matter how much she prodded I would not admit my part in

any of this. I wasn't being nice to her, it was a present to myself. If she didn't burn off some steam now, she would be frankly unbearable during the upcoming ambassador's stay. He was due to arrive in the next couple of days and there was already some bad blood there from his last visit. Clarisse at least cared enough for her Maids' sanity not to inflict the bastard on any of them, so she was due to be stuck with the prat for the foreseeable future.

That was my story, and I was sticking to it. Purely self-preservation that I may have hinted that she be allowed to be a Maid for the evening. And in fact, it was a part of my job protecting her. By making sure that she would less insufferable, she was at less risk of being throttled by me over her breakfast crumpets.

At least she knew better than to try and thank me. And I knew better than to expect her to.

By Inar's tits we had a weird relationship.

CHPATER THREE: MAIDS AND MELEES

"So, does someone want to explain what happened?"
"Honestly? No." Delilah's sweet expression was somewhat undermined by Serafina face palming hard enough that I worried it would leave a bruise. The others didn't even blink at the noise. I tried not to snort as I heard her mutter under her breath, "she may not be the biggest idiot in the world, but she better pray that the winner doesn't die."

The Queen eyed the little group critically. Delilah and Lizzie were doing their best to hold a strong front, neither looking at the other for help. I mean, let's be honest if they did, they would probably start giggling. The number of times they had set each other off and gotten into trouble... even when it was pretty damned important to keep a straight face.

Clarisse was less than impressed, seeing as how she had been called out of one of her social engagements by a panting Sera with a report that her Maids had gotten into a fight. I think it was the fastest trip we had made to the training fields, the apparent location of the brawl. At least the courtiers had the sense to not follow. Even so, no doubt there would be gossip flying within minutes.

We had reached the grounds to find a pair of flushed Maids, some wary guards, one apparent casualty and an entire platoon of men doing an admirable job of pretending to still be focussing on their drills. No doubt they would be capitalising off the story to get free drinks for the next couple of weeks at the local pub.

"Lizzie." The girl all but jumped to attention. "You are the erstwhile historian of my inner circle, the one who holds truth above all, the one who I trust to give an honest report." Her tone hardened ever so slightly, "the Maid in fact who was today tasked with making sure that the next level of embroidery was an accurate depiction of our nation's noble history and the righteousness of my reign." As the girl in question did her best not to squirm, I couldn't help but look over what sewing they had managed to accomplish. It was about half of the battle of Narden.

It was a period of history which I always did my best not to get in debates about. According to the intentions of the official historian weavers, the records would depict the defeat of my home nation and its subsequent annexation. I had soon upon my initial arrival to Tartyn given up trying to remind people that 'the battle of Narden' hadn't taken place. My people had never had a standing army. True, Tartyn's troops had managed to put down a few defensive guerrilla groups, but for the most part they had contented themselves with torching the oasis camps where most took refuge when the weather was too harsh to continue roaming.

Those who hadn't been able to melt back into the sands on the caravans which were so firmly part of our culture, had since been heavily 'integrated' into Tartynian society. At least in my case, it had seen me ending up literally watching the back of out conqueror. You have to admire the audacity of the political statement which my position made. Especially with the official story being that we were a proud culture of nomadic warriors. Never mind that according to our goddess Inar, war was frowned upon. True, we believed in calling down Anar's wrath, but that was only as a last resort. At our core we were simply survivors, which mostly meant the path of least resistance.

Alas, I guess that is the trouble when my people rely on oral tradition whilst our 'conquerors' have a record that they can literally throw in our faces. Or, given the medium, wrap around our necks and choke us down until there were only whispers left.

But, like I said, it was a debate I really didn't try to get into that much. The one time I did, after yet another poisoning attempt on our sovereign had left me somewhat loopy, the councillor I was arguing with gave up after an hour saying we should 'agree to disagree'. I told him to live with whatever made him more comfortable so long as he recognised that he was not telling himself the truth. Funnily enough he decided not to speak up again when I got involved in courtly arguments.

However, at the current moment, I was busy focussing on exactly how the record keeper of the Maids intended to present events. It was particularly telling that Sir Gavin, who was in charge of overseeing the day's drills, was very clearly sticking to the opposite side of the field for the time being rather than trying to put in his opinion.

As Lizzie cleared her throat and clearly tried to come up with a palatable version of whatever the hell happened, I took the chance to do a proper scan of the area. Just to the right I could see the physician's apprentice was very clearly dealing with one of the squires. The boy was prostrate on the training field and yet still being mostly ignored by the others running drills all around them as if they were vaguely embarrassed about whatever had happened. Which meant it was likely to be a pretty good story no matter which way it was told. I smirked a little if only to myself, suddenly enjoying my day just a bit more.

I gave a small wave to where I saw Jeremy was standing oh so subtly between the casualty and the Maids. From what I could tell he was ostensibly acting as some sort of deterrent for whatever fight had broken out continuing. That being said, he didn't seem to be making too much effort to stop people jostling the squire. At least the boy was still moving so there probably wasn't much wrong, and the medic looked more irritated than concerned.

Considering that they tended to be much more empathetic than their teacher, I was reassured that the squire was at best lightly maimed. The medic was in fact the same one who often ended up giving me a hand if a suspicious accident had led to a slice or two being taken out of a hard-to-reach spot. Magda refused to deal with things like that anymore, always pointing out that she was retired, and blood was a nightmare to get out of velvet. I waved jauntily at the medic, getting a set of rolled eyes in response. Not fair.

Hanson, a kid who insists on trying to hang around my shadow and pick up training tips, even 'accidentally' stepped on the injured man. I would have to talk to him about that later. You should of course always kick a man when he is down, else they might try and kick you back, or worse. The thing was to only do it where no one else could see.

Delilah cleared her throat, stepping despite her companion having been asked the question. "Well, Your Majesty, we were diligently sewing here as instructed."
"Intent on taking advantage of the sunlight to best match the thread shades." Lizzie piped up, definitely not hiding bruised knuckles behind her back. If I squinted, did one of the marks on the squire's face match to the pattern on one of her rings?

"Right. Anyway, one of the newer squires was overheard making a few choice comments about our activity." Delilah flushed a little as she said it, and I could tell that was the result of barely restrained temper.

I couldn't help but frown at that. There was no way that any recruit would be commenting on the sewing activity itself. It was one which all were taught- partly as a useful life skill so they could at least fix their own clothes after any training accidents. Further, it was supposed to promote attention to detail; build patience. You could tell the merit of a knight by how his cloak was embroidered- it was each their own responsibility to depict their personal story in thread and add to it over the years. Part of me wanted to pointedly suggest at the next inspection they have to present their cloaks. That was normally not supposed to happen until their knighting ceremony, but a bit of fear might not go amiss to remind them of their duty.

As to whatever had gotten Delilah and Lizzie so irked, I was waiting to hear what nonsense he could have spouted. I mean, sure, they had doubtless chosen the spot to watch what was going on, but that was probably to keep an eye on the latest techniques being taught. Ladies had to defend themselves after all. Often Magda had mused that one day we would discover where exactly men kept the audacity which let them believe that they could act in whatever way that they liked. When that happened, they had best run because there is a generally a lot hiding behind sweet smiles.

Lizzie took up the report again, "He seemed to be under the assumption that we had chosen our spot solely to have a better view of the training grounds. To ogle the knights." She glared pure murder at him as she spoke. Those blatantly listening in all had the same vague look of discomfiture. That was not the sort of comment which a trainee should have ever been heard to make. Let alone to address it within earshot of the Maids themselves. That was a special sort of stupid.

Frankly, it was a demonstration of a potentially dangerous level of ego for someone aspiring to be a knight. True, they could be arrogant asses, but they respected where the lines were drawn in terms of courtly behaviours. Making insinuations about some of the highest ranked ladies in the castle was social suicide.

To be frank, even if they had been wanting to check out the assorted men at arms, to call out the Maids was to in effect call out the Queen herself. They were the favourites, her chosen sisters, her closest allies.

Basically, whoever had been making those comments was quite possibly too stupid to have any hope of lasting as a knight. It was no wonder that the others were all trying to have nothing to do with him. Especially within sight of Clarisse.

Delilah coughed slightly awkwardly, "Well, in light of such a heinous accusation and aspersions upon our honour, and by extension yours, we made it abundantly clear to the squire in question that we had simply been monitoring technique."
"Right." A raised eyebrow, "And how was this argued?"
"We helped to instruct him on his own shortcomings in terms of the lesson as had been laid out to the others in his group." Never let it be said that she used one word when five would do. I could just see Sir Gavin shifting around, looking uncomfortable in the background.
"He did not like this." But judging by Lizzie's poorly hidden grin, she had.

No doubt they had decided upon a practical demonstration. Which would explain the wounded squire, irritated medic, and wide berth which the other trainees were giving to them when we first arrived. Jeremy seemed to be half choking from trying not to laugh at the memory of whatever he had witnessed.

"Indeed, and he then proceeded to make further rather ungentlemanly remarks." Which would suggest he was not just stupid but also downright rude. Never backchat once you had been fairly bested, especially with the number of witnesses around. Whichever way the rest of the story went, there would no doubt be one less squire come the morning. Whether he was allowed to stay on in a menial position or got sent home in disgrace was yet to be seen. Still, better that such a character flaw be revealed now before he had any form of real power or influence.

Clarisse was rubbing lightly at her temples by this point. "I am going to tell you now that my patience is at a remarkably low ebb by this point. Please wrap this little narrative up soon."

"Of course, Your Majesty. Well, to cut a long story short, we realised that he must not have understood his practical lesson the first time. As such, we kindly decided to re-demonstrate what we had been saying."

"Actions speak louder than words after all."

"Right. So… we asked ourselves… what would Nina do?"

For a moment, all those in earshot flicked their eyes over to me. I did my best not to growl at the Maids. The sound of Jeremy choking on his own spit as he tried not to laugh was startlingly loud. Clarisse herself could only just keeping herself from snorting. Sure, the knights would never dare to comment on it, but she still worried about her reputation should she lose control so thoroughly.

I leaned in close to Delilah as Clarisse did her best to not lose it, hissing loud enough for everyone to hear. "In the future, you will stand at the edge of the grave which I dug for your gods, weeping, and I will be the only creature for you to answer to. You will beg for an end, but due to your words here today, I will deprive you of that luxury." Alright, it was strong, but I bloody well hate having attention drawn to me in that way.

The queen turned to me with wide eyes which in public was her equivalent of cackling like a drunken witch. "… and that is why I ask you not to make public speeches."

Lizzie hummed, "I don't know- let her at the ambassador from Namet on his visit?"

The queen took a deep, if shaky, fortifying breath as she visibly willed her facial expression under control. When she could

finally look me in the eye, it was with a calm reminiscent of oh so thin ice beneath a nervous skater. "I feel the sudden need to scream into the void."
I nodded in understanding, making a show of thinking, "Hmm, I regret to inform you that the void is becoming rather full. Might I suggest a cushion Your Majesty?" the look I got in response could work as a declaration of war in other situations.

Taking advantage of the brief break in interrogation, the physician's apprentice came scurrying over to give their report. It seemed that the squire only had a broken nose. And two bruised ribs. A fractured finger. And would be unlikely to bear children for a time. By the end of the list, the blatantly eavesdropping bystanders looked both vaguely impressed, and in the case of Sir Gavin almost turned on.

Clarisse ignored them all, merely smiling at the apprentice in thanks and patting them on the shoulder to send them off. They almost split their face with grinning as they retreated back to the castle. No doubt they would be politely mobbed when they got inside. If they played their cards right they could probably earn a tidy little profit from those wanting first dibs on the latest incident.

The Queen was now openly rubbing her forehead with one hand, eyes closed in irritation. "So, what I have gleaned from all this, is that one of the squires, who I was supposed to knight in little under a month, currently has a broken nose. Amongst other ailments." She fixed the Maids with her hardest glare. "Give me a damned good reason for why I shouldn't be angry with you for going so far by the time I count to three, or I swear I will start screaming."
"Listen, we-"
"One."
"The thing is-"
"Two."
"In our defence..."

I am proud of the fact that I was the only one to not jump when the Queen of the realm of Tartyn threw her head back and shrieked like a toddler denied their pudding. On the training field, I saw the trainees falter, whipping around to find the source of such a piercing yell. A couple made as if to head our way when they saw that their sovereign was in apparent distress, only to be waved off by Sir Gavin. He just gave us the most unimpressed look possible without actually committing treason. In fairness, he did motion a guard over as a token response, and I grinned ever so slightly when I saw Jeremy all but jump at the opportunity to get a little closer to the drama. At least he had the sense to stop at a supposedly respectful distance.

"Alright, you know what? I do not have the time to be dealing with all of this." She threw her hands in the air. "The squire was injured in a training accident. Such things happen. Hopefully his wounds will heal easily, although I will of course consent should he request to return to his parents' estate to recover. Knighthood is not the path destined for all."

It was as close a warning as the boy in question would receive before he would face truly serious consequences for his foolishness. Run now or be run off later.

"Now, I require the presence of my Maids. With all of this nonsense we are running rather behind schedule. We are to receive the court in the throne room, to discuss the petition regarding the airship incident. Lord Arner will be presenting his case, and that is something for which I need support to judge fairly." She fixed them both with a hard look, "and then they will of course finish the work which should have been completed this evening. Candlelight will have to suffice for judging colours."

We could all read between the threads on that one. Clearly relieved at having gotten off so lightly for their actions, Delilah and Lizzie swiftly stowed the cloak back in its' special bag, falling into step behind Clarisse as she headed back up and into the castle. Serafina was waiting for them just inside, already waiting for the hand off. The servant would take it back to the treasury where it would be stored until it could be worked upon again.

It was one tradition which I could respect. Just as with the knights, each Queen's cloak was a living record of her reign, hand stitched only by herself or those closest to her. The triumphs, the losses, the times of wealth and poverty... all were told in those stretches of cloth. A couple of the historians had explained it to me once: how it wasn't just the images picked out oh so carefully which supplied their people's history, but the quality of the thread used, the amount of time which was able to be dedicated to the stitching. All helped build a truer picture of what their nation had achieved and endured.

As we entered the throne room, the chosen stage for this latest farce of courtly life, the cloaks of generations before stirred softly along the walls. History's eyes were ever upon us. I couldn't help but wonder, sometimes, if Clarisse felt the weight on the back of her neck every time she took the throne.

CHAPTER THREE: THE REAL CRIME IS HIS AUDACITY

There was a notable level of tension in the air of the council chamber. Clarisse was sat on her throne, spine perfectly straight and face impassive even as the fingers of one hand tapped out a steady rhythm from her nails against the lacquer. She was wearing her serious dress, the one in the dark red and black lace which made her look ready to shed blood if necessary.

It was a stark contrast to Delilah and Lizzie in their far gentler hues, apparently carefree and at their leisure. There was no indication that they had been in a fight not half an hour before. At least to an untrained eye. Anybody with half of their wits would have noticed how their eyes tracked all in the room. There was a definite smirk playing around Delilah's lips. I was in my customary spot just to the right of the raised platform so as to best be able to access all points of the room.

It had been argued for years that body-guards should be allowed on the same heights so as to better oversee the crowd. Such a concession of rank was only granted to those who shared the joys of being Royal Consort. Mags liked to boast about how much easier her job had been at her queen's side. It was a perk that I was more than happy to do without and compensate for.

No matter whereabouts in the crowd you were, it was clear that there were high expectations for how this meeting was going to play out.

Perhaps the tension was more anticipation. Blood sports went of fashion many years ago. Of course. So uncivilised. It did make a metaphorical evisceration far sweeter to savour.

I could see Hanson way in the back, bobbing up and down from his position behind Sir Gavin to try and see better. No doubt he was here to see what happened to the Arners, although arguably with more care for the outcome than the other spectators. One of his best friends was the Lord's nephew, a boy called Samda who was nothing short of a genius. Many was the time that they had decided to sit near to where I was training and discuss the latest advancements in various scientific fields. Sometimes I even had the chance to correct their assumptions based on my own life experiences. Their discussions about how to prevent injuries due to falls from high places had left them both vaguely horrified at how often I had apparently found cause to drop from such heights. The trick is in the tuck and roll.

The fact that Samda had gifted me a new climbing winch of his own design, which provided a significantly better emergency braking feature, most certainly did not make me fond of the boy.

Councilman Arner approached the throne, walking far too confidently and apparently blind to the way that both of the Maids' gazes sharpened on him. Perhaps he did feel it, and completely misunderstood the reason for their baited attention. The joys of hubris I suppose. Perhaps those few seconds extra of confidence and belief were worth it.

The thing was, we all knew why he had requested the audience. He had been attempting to slip legislation which granted extra leniency for his own interests into the council discussion for the better part of a month. So far, he hadn't appreciated the subtler hints which had been dropped up to this point. Namely that he was coming off as rather single minded in the face of the numerous issues plaguing the country. There were many things which councillors were able to get away with, behaviours which could be excused. But with how much he had pushed the limit on acceptability?

We all knew that Clarisse's patience was rather less than infinite.

He probably would have stood a better chance if he hadn't been insulting the collective intelligence of the Court. He hadn't exactly been careful in his dealings, and through some rather less than scrupulous speculations he had managed to alienate even his most staunch supporters. Courtiers could smell blood in the water, they had been eagerly circling for some time now. All it would take was one slice of the Queen's claws to start the frenzy.

Hell, a papercut would be sufficient for this lot. There are few things more terrifying in this world, than well bred Lords and Ladies being given an excuse to air their savagery.

Arms spread wide to try and throw his robes into a striking swirl, he bowed low before the dais. "Your most gracious Majesty. I thank you for allowing me to bring my humble business to your personal attention."

More fool him. She had been wanting to vent some frustration for a while. Even the knights had been commenting on her sharp edges when she joined them for training. The fact that she had been breaking up a brawl not long before had shifted her mood even further away from benevolent.

One hand gestured elegantly in his direction as a cue to speak. It quickly resumed its sharp tip tapping.

Arner bowed again. At this rate he was going to make himself seasick. "As you are aware, my nephew and I have been making the valiant effort to establish an airship company to rival that of our neighbour to the north."

I swear, Hanson and Samda have been driving me crazy with all of their talk about the air ships. I keep reminding them that barracks exist, or pubs, or hell even an empty square, where they could go and talk rather than constantly bothering me. They had laughed and blithely carried on. We ended up arguing over what the limits of human endurance really were. Samda was convinced that we could last at higher altitudes and speeds than currently deemed safe. I had been inclined to agree on some of his points but pointed out the fact that such resilience required training, and therefore incurred short term costs beyond what the average merchant team would be willing to cover.

Of course, then we started on the possibility of air ship racing, and the entire thing got completely derailed. I had told them off for almost making me late to my duties. They took that to mean that they should find me at the end of the day to carry on the argument. Cheeky pups.

I truly think that if Hanson hadn't been so keen on becoming a knight, then he would spend every day with his best friend in the research and development section of the Arner company. Samda had tried for the squire training course... it had not been a particular success. He had been far happier during his apprenticeships to the various trading guilds, most particularly the shipwrights.

I will always remember when he had made a tiny clockwork mouse for the amusement of the Maids, one winter day when it was too cold to venture outside. He had been only a child at the time, but far more interested in his inventions than the various pursuits preferred by his social circle. Hanson had been the one that he had best connected with really, and the pair of them had combined their brains to schemes ranging from amusing to downright dubious. If anybody asked, I had no bearing on their choice of targets. At all.

Come to think, it was rather odd that the kid wasn't here as well. After all, if Lord Arner had been summoned to apparently discuss the company business, then surely his main apprentice should at least be present to witness it? Unless he was more aware than it seemed, and had intentionally placed his nephew out of the possible line of fire.

My attention was drawn back to Lord Arner as he somehow

managed to fold himself lower into his next bow. I really hoped that he cut it out soon- it was like a form of unnecessary punctuation at this point rather than a marker of respect. "I am pleased to report that progress has been good so far, with our research and design department already putting together a new form of ship. One which will change the face of air travel."

Lizzie discreetly hid a scoff behind the bolt of fabric she was oh so carefully working tiny blue flowers into. We all knew how those 'advancements' had really been achieved. It was the whole reason why this meeting had been called, so publicly, so intentional a demonstration of exactly where the monarchy stood on the issue being raised. No doubt reports would be winging their way back to the concerned parties as soon as the court was dismissed. Basically, it had been discovered that Arner had been using some less than honourable contacts to steal plans and designs from rival companies and neighbouring kingdoms. And now his little bit of dabbling in pursuit of more money was rapidly spiralling into a diplomatic incident. Somehow, he hadn't yet realised just how badly he had fucked up. He was about to be informed by the Queen.

From a purely professional standpoint this little farce was vaguely insulting. If there was one thing I had learned from my time amongst the aristocracy it was that if you are going to indulge in espionage it is better to pay more than your competition or have fanatics under your banner. This man had neither advantage, so when his little spy had inevitably been caught, the story had come spilling out in record time.

"Lord Arner," the queen's voice was devoid of any inflection, but the very sound was enough to make him stutter into silence. At least he had a speck of self-preservation, otherwise this show would be over far too quickly. "It is true, you have made many promises regarding the development of the air freight sector. A veritable gold mine I believe you called it."

His mouth spread wide into what he probably imagined to be an enigmatic smile. "A flying gold mine, if you will."

She continued as if he hadn't spoken, "I would ask though, out of concern for such a worthy enterprise you understand, what steps you have been taking for the safety of your research?" He looked genuinely confused. She cut him off before he could form a sentence, holding out an expectant hand into which Delilah placed an unfolded letter. Clarisse made a show of running her eyes down the contents.

"I state this concern, as I received a most troubling report from our friends in the northern kingdom of Namet. Apparently, their main airship development facility was broken into a month ago."

He had the audacity to look shocked, "how heinous!"

The queen's lips thinned, "Indeed. Naturally the King himself took an interest. Family is so important after all." A raised eyebrow at the way that the Councillor had frozen, a slight frown between his eyebrows. "Oh, were you unaware that the owner of the airship consortium is the King's cousin? A lovely lady by all accounts, and one on whom he does like to dote."

The end of her sentence was sharp enough to make a few of the more nervous onlookers wince. I saw his throat bob in a hard swallow. Clarisse's nostrils were flaring as she clearly caught the motion as well. There was a slight stirring in the crowd. The first slice had been made; it was only a matter of time as to the result.

He coughed into a fist, "while that is a worrying turn of events, I thank you for informing me of what occurred. I will of course increase the security at our own factories in case this spy attempts to infiltrate one of them."

A hand slamming onto the arm rest of the throne made his jaw shut with a click. "Unnecessary. The spy was caught. And after some little persuasion was most helpful in identifying their employer."

The statement was intentionally vague. It was always better when a person was in trouble for them to imagine what exactly had happened, whether they had been caught out, what fate could befall them. Generally, people were far more imaginative when scared, and no doubt his brain would be conjuring images of what his informant could have undergone. It was nothing so drastic, at least in this case. When confronted they had surrendered their information and employer. They had stated that they were not paid enough to hurt for the cause.

And so, the same lessons are repeated over and over for those willing to learn.

It was almost a shame really- with how much he was sweating, his fine outfit was going to be ruined. "I do so hope that no aspersions were cast upon my character. Or that of my nephew, who was placed in charge of this most vital project. Such an underhanded trick would be almost expected from contemptable competitors. I would of course not sully my endeavours with such foolish and disrespectful conduct."

Was I the only one who remembered that his nephew, being so expertly thrown as a sacrifice to social wrath, was only seventeen? So much for the idea that he had been trying to protect Samda by keeping him out of this discussion. It seemed rather that he was a convenient scapegoat who couldn't protest the thinly veiled allegation. Was he hoping that any wrongdoing would be laid at the feet of Samda's youth and inexperience? If so, it was a tactic that wouldn't bear fruit. The boy had far more friends at court than his mentor.

I was almost impressed by how he seemed to genuinely believe that he could argue his way out of this. Most would have had the sense to grovel by this point. That was something which a lot of people never understood- that sometimes breaking was a necessity, a tool in your arsenal to ensure your survival and consequential ability to fight another. Most believed that there was dishonour in such a surrender. I have always failed to understand how that can be. Surely the one person you ultimately owe allegiance to is yourself, and so there is no shame to be found in protecting number one.

In truth that was a point of view which if I had ever voiced would result in some pretty severe issues for me. I was sworn to the Queen, to the protection of the monarch. My role in this grand comedy which we call life was to be subservient to the will of another. I did not exist in my own right. I hadn't since I was brought into this country, and at this point to be a truly free agent was a paradigm for which I had no real reference to image. For me to say that self-preservation was a virtue could in a certain light be called treason.

But then, I have so often been accused of selfishness that they can't have all been wrong.

"While I appreciate you speaking up with your recollection of events, there seems to be some confusion on your part regarding the situation. Allow me to provide you with some clarity. According to our records, and correct me if I'm wrong, you did in fact pay a young lady to acquire the plans of your closest competitor. In more precise detail, your agent was tasked with infiltrating Namet's research and development sector with the express intention of illegally taking advanced research materials. This was despite their being private property and protected under an allied nation's laws, a fact of which you were well aware. She proceeded to return these to you for you to then try and pass off as your own. In the spirit of striving for clarity in this matter, if you still feel that there is a disconnect, please feel free to explain your version of events, Councillor."

Lord Arner stood at the foot of the dais, openly gaping now. The level of cold fury on Clarisse's face was pretty terrifying to behold. It is always the way with her, she either goes full, devastating, explosion of temper, or the complete opposite. The former can be weathered. The latter will surely destroy you and all who make the mistake of trying to hold onto you.

Lizzie leaned forwards when the Lord seemed to be frozen in place, clearing her throat, and speaking with her friendliest tone. “She means: you are a dirty, stinking, inbred, sycophantic liar with delusions of grandeur. Now: off you fuck.”

He gaped at her for both the audacity and the language. A brief glance at Clarisse showed that she had no intention of reprimanding her Maid. To be fair, it was not the first time that she had acted as a sort of anger translator in such situations. For all that Clarisse herself couldn’t say certain things, it didn’t mean that others were incapable of making those sentiments clear.

A round of tittering broke out among the gathered witnesses, even if it was subdued by the prevailing sense of danger. Perhaps it affected me less because I knew that part of her ire actually stemmed from the fact that we would now have to host an ambassadorial visit from the north to reaffirm our alliance, and the ambassador was rumoured to be a complete pain in the ass. And this time he had a legitimate reason to give us a hard time.

Amazing what a bit of perspective can do for how you approach an issue.

I couldn’t help but wish such clarity upon Arner even as he finally rallied enough wits to fold himself once more into a far stiffer bow in the presence of his sovereign, with whatever tattered dignity he could hold in his pockets. Clarisse narrowed her eyes at the man, barely leashed anger tightening the lines around her eyes.

He held the position as a flick of Clarisse’s wrist sent the rest of her court from the room in a rasping of silks on stone. Even as the Queen and her Maids left through the side door which connected to one of her personal chambers, he held his position. The sound of the doors closing seemed to almost echo in the room.

I stayed behind, leaning against one of the support pillars.

When he was sure that everybody else was gone, Arner stood tall once again. He sneered as he looked me up and down. “You here to make sure I don't do anything reckless?"

"Too late for that. I would say you might not have burnt your bridges yet, but you certainly seem determined to fan the embers at your feet."

"I don't need to hear this from you." If he were one of the hounds he would be snarling with his full fury. Human teeth aren't as effective when bared. At least not for him.

It was my turn to bow now, sweeping my arms wide. "Of course not. My Lord."

He took a jerking step towards me, as if his muscles had moved without the conscious decision being made. It was my turn to smirk. Pushing off from my overly relaxed pose, I began to stalk closer to him. I let the tension fall from my shoulders, being replaced with the feline grace which had been beaten into me over many years. Art is pain in so many ways.

There is a power in such assured movement. And something in the smile- having just enough teeth showing that it couldn't be mistaken for friendly. Now that was how to have an intimidating expression. His own settled into something far less defiant.

"I won't warn you against trying to harm Her Majesty, that isn't your style after all. You are all about survival, seeing how close to the edge you can walk so that those below can marvel at how you shine in the sun. But we both know the risks associated with burning."

His eyes flickered to the side for a moment, and I wondered if he was remembering what had happened to Tabitha. It had been an incident seared into the memory of the court, especially when rumour had started going around that it had been a deliberate attempt on the Queen's life. The hunt for culprits which followed caused more than one noble house to quiver to their foundations.

I was close enough now to smell the expensive cologne which he had imported from too far away and applied with a remarkable

lack of subtlety. Perhaps it is an inherent risk of basing your daily interactions on bullshit- you go a touch scent blind. I made a point of wrinkling my nose as I stepped past him. "I will remind you though that you have people depending on you. Your nephew for one."
Now it was his turn to properly snarl, a far more honest expression of restrained rage. "Don't threaten my family."

So apparently he did have an element of humanity in him. I was actually a bit impressed. In my mind he had been categorised as a money grubbing bastard. Which he was. But it seemed one with layers. I could find a small measure of respect for that.

"You mistake me. I am not threatening you with his safety. I am reminding you of your responsibility."
"Why do you even care?"
I scoffed a little, half laughing at myself. "He is a pain in my ass, a regular pest, and a friend of someone I keep an eye on. I am simply watching out for those under my protection as is my prerogative."
He hummed a little, looking at me calculatingly. "I think we understand one another."

There was an assumption in that gaze, of knowing, of having finally quantified something that had long escaped him. That was unacceptable. To be known in such a way by someone at best neutral and more likely an enemy? Unforgivable.

I laughed, lightly, tinkling bells in morning dew.

Between one blink and the next I had him pinned to the floor with a blade at his throat. He half choked, almost turning purple as he tried not to let his skin convulse any closer to the cold steel. Another laugh. The same at first, worthy of any lady of the court. It dissolved towards the end into something far more unbridled and genuinely amused.

And there it was. The flash of fear deep in his eyes. The realisation that he had stepped far too close to an unstable cliff edge- one which could collapse and take everything with it.

Because that was what I truly acted as. Lightning in a bottle, the reminder that the monarch has both the monopoly on violence and the ability to keep her own hands pristine. Her protection, in all ways, was my only purpose. It's a hideously twisted form of devotion. But at least it allows me to use aspects of my reputation to benefit the others who I claim.

I left him there. No doubt he got a bruise or two from the rough landing. I didn't do him the honour of looking back as I slipped out of the throne room.

CHAPTER FOUR: QUESTIONABLE TASTE

I hate mornings. Truly. If someone wanted advice as to when to assassinate the monarch of this realm, I would recommend making a try for first thing in the morning. It's not that I would be unaware of what they were doing. Professional pride never sleeps. No, I would simply be petty enough at the ass crack of dawn to let them have a decent go at taking her out.

Perhaps the most annoying thing is that I don't really hate it anymore. Not in the way that I used to, right back when I was first being made into what I am, when I still remembered a different way of existing. By this point my own body wakes me up at stupid o clock. It is a curse. There is no escape.

At least in the summertime the moat is somewhat warmer. Doing my regular swim laps in winter is the closest I get to letting myself drown. It's been slightly better the last few years since Hanson started joining me. The kid is crazy, more than I ever was. He chose this lifestyle.

I mean, I can sort of see where he was coming from at first. The bastard son of a minor earl, having just been accepted as a squire, he had a lot of eyes on him. There was a hunger in the kid, a desire to prove himself more than anyone had anticipated. I could have sworn during the first few months that he burned a circle of warmth into the very ice of the moat each morning.

At first, I had pointedly ignored him. Stupidity of youth often saw boys and girls during their combat training years make overly dramatic assertions of their dedication to drills and fitness. It seemed like there was a group each year who figured that following after me would help them improve their skills by proximity or something. They would try to match my regular pace, or if they were really gluttons for punishment ask for a demonstration of fighting techniques.

I never blamed them, just found a grim level of vindication as they each inevitably gave up after a few mornings of hell. Frankly, the mornings were my time to myself. I spent all day in the company of someone who I didn't particularly like even after all of this time. I needed my escapes like anybody else. Whether that helped motivate me to keep at an extremely high level just to discourage visitors is something you can speculate on for yourself.

Hanson? He had showed up one morning as autumn was starting to dye the trees, wordlessly did his best to keep pace with my stokes around the moat, failed miserably, and been coming along ever since.

I had thought he would finally realise his own idiocy when, one winter morning during his first year of the ridiculous regime, he came down clearly already suffering from an illness. It wasn't my place to comment. If he was old enough to be learning how to kill another man, he was old enough to die. It sounds brutal, but that is the reality I live with. Sometimes lessons need to be taught with harsh methods so that they stick. That includes making it abundantly clear where someone's limits truly lie and getting them to acknowledge that they are out of their depth. Literally, in his case.

When he cramped up, dipping below the surface and drifting beneath the edges of the ice sheet... when it apparently hadn't occurred to him to shout for help... when I pulled him up the bank and breathed my own icy breath into his seized lungs... well.

The medic had sworn at me in four different languages when I carried Hanson into the infirmary and dumped him in their care. It was pure coincidence that I had to stop by there that evening to pick something up. He had been back to his usual colour, waved at me from his cot, and declared that next time he would pace himself better.

Maybe after that I took a shade more interest in his rise through the ranks. Just monitoring my investment.

Once he was released from the physician's chambers I thought that would be it. He showed up the next morning at the same time as always. He did realise that he needed to dial it back a bit, not pushing to match me stroke for stroke anymore. When we climbed out of the water, he handed over a measure of warm tea from the flask he had left on the bank. He told me how his friend Samda had designed it to keep things warmer for longer.

To this day, Jeremy occasionally drops hints that the reason why Hanson tends to win in combat drills is that the boy seems to have found himself a tutor. I have no idea what he is talking about. And the fact that I have a partner in sparring sessions before I head into my daily duties? That is purely a coincidence of good fortune for helping me stay supple even as I grow older. A useful warm up routine after a chilled dip.

At least during the summer by the time that I arrive at her Majesty's chambers, the sun has long since risen. In winter that doesn't happen until she has managed to roll herself out of bed, partaken of breakfast, and already started listening to the drivel of court.

Thank whatever gods are listening that this was late summer. Autumn would soon be pulling at my bones, sinking its teeth into my mortal shell of skin. For now, Hanson wouldn't actually be torn apart when he practiced his parries in the morning dew as I endeavoured to generate enough heat not to freeze.

On this particular morning, I knew that I had a little bit of extra time before I had to resume my place at Clarisse's side. The

Queen was adamant on having the morning off every now and again. Her advisors were vehemently against it- stating that as the spiritual leader of the nation she was forever on duty. Heavy is the head which bears the crown, after all. She told them to sod off unless they wanted to feel the edge of sleep deprived wrath. The crown in question may have taken a short flight across the room to emphasise her point.

It had been a rather leisurely morning in truth. Hanson had been talking my ear off between bouts about the buzz going around regarding the upcoming re-swearing ceremony. Word was that Lord Arner's nephew had been working on some special secret to make the event even more memorable. Considering what a thin line his family was walking at the moment, anything that Samda could come up with to resecure their position at Court would be beyond valuable.

And perhaps I had a bit of insider knowledge as to what exactly this grand new invention could be by dint of the fact that they both seemed to like hanging around me like a pair of shadows. I had grown reluctantly interested in their experiments. Hanson had clearly that morning been trying to put a brave face on when talking about his friend's relative position in the whole mess. I didn't try and offer any condolences. There wasn't anything that I could really say. So... perhaps I let him get a little bit closer to winning one of our matches. Not just handing him the victory of course- that would spoil the whole experience. But I may have let his swing cut a tad nearer to my throat than he had managed before. The gleam of triumph in his eyes was well worth the small sacrifice of pride.

Long story short, it meant that I had made it through my regular security checks with a bit of time free to swing by Magda's rooms. Considering the situation, it was extra fortunate. In truth, if not for Sera having spotted me weaving my way through the castle corridors, I probably would have taken significantly longer to reach my destination. She hadn't bothered with any questions, just ducked beneath one arm to help me stay steady as we made our way to Magda's chambers.

The night before I had made sure to do a spot check of the Queen's Holy Regalia- considering that we would soon be heading into the Springtime festival calendar, she would be required to attend certain public appearances. Most importantly, it was going to be the re-swearing of the throne in a relatively short amount of time. It was one of the biggest events on the courtly calendar- happening every five years of a monarch's reign when she had to reaffirm her vows and duties as Queen before her people. I could appreciate the sentiment at least of wanting to remind the person in charge as to what they were responsible for. Even if it had become somewhat of a pageantry situation, as anything remotely connected to royalty tends to.

If everything wasn't exactly right, then it could spell serious headaches for all involved. Most notably when her resulting fit of temper resulted in significantly raised voices. And of course, there was the small matter of in previous points of history a botched re-swearing had been grounds for a rebellion and regicide. No pressure then.

Bearing all of that in mind, I was making sure to do even more regular checks of all the different aspects relating to that event. Last night had been allocated to inspecting the holy water source which is said to be the birthplace of the country. It will be central to the ceremony: her reviving herself in the waters and so reaffirming her connection to the lifeblood of her nation. It is rather poetic really. A truly solemn moment which can move the most pious to tears.

I had naturally downed a cupful of the holy sacrament of blessed water. It stems from an ancient spring, the shrine for which has been protected since before the birth of the nation. Only the Monarch is allowed to actually partake of this most holy right. And I had slurped a hearty handful. A heinous crime, for which punishment according to the ancient texts was that the perpetrator was to be trampled to death by a congregation of the faithful.

I honestly wondered how that was supposed to be coordinated. I mean, that is a lot of effort for a single punishment. And to be honest, the average citizen would probably object to potentially ruining a pair of shoes or something.

All of that considered, someone in my position had an ever so slight measure of unofficial leeway. For all that the officials of the Pantheon would froth at the mouth at the thought of my touching the sacred pool, they would probably be more upset by their monarch dropping dead mid ceremony. It would completely ruin the atmosphere and frankly I doubted that any of them would be strong enough to move the body.

As to why I would even consider sullying such a rite? Come on- a place that only the monarch is supposed to go along with a thing which only she is supposed to ingest? It's the perfect set up for an assassination attempt. A concept which I might have extremely recently proved.

I poked my head around the doorway, being sure to make plenty of noise to alert the occupant of my intentions. I didn't much fancy a dagger to the face, and some habits die so hard they must be actively murdered. "Mags? You free?"
"Oh, Nina! This is a lovely surprise. What are you doing visiting an old lady at this point in the day? And... what is with your companion?"
"Heh, funny story really, all told. Thanks Sera, you head back to the Queen alright? Tell her I will be back on duty in a couple of hours, and not to fall out of a window or something before I get back."

The girl looked at me, unsure, even as she helped ease me into leaning against a convenient table. I couldn't afford to sit down, not then. The pain would strike like lightning as soon as I relinquished my tight reign. From somewhere deep inside my chest, I managed to dredge up a smile. Sera's eyes flickered briefly across my face and no doubt picked up on the strained lines around my mouth. She wisely chose not to notice them, instead just rolling her eyes at my apparent stubbornness.

There are things you just don't mention in polite society. When a courtesan is seeming to change shape over the course of a certain number of months. When a servant is spotted stealing out of his master's chambers before the moon has fully set. When the bodyguard to the Queen herself apparently takes sick after the night before illicitly tasting the most holy and protected representation of the gods' blessings to the Nation.

We all learn the complex realities of life according to our relative stations. Including exactly when words would do more harm than good. At times, a blind eye aids more towards healing than a light ever could. Especially for people such as Mags and myself. The shadows are the greatest opportunity to apply balms of many kinds.

Mags watched Sera exit her chambers with an ever-keen eye, finally turning back to me as the door clicked shut. "She is such a nice kid."

I snorted "Everyone is a kid to you." And in comparison to Mags and I, most people would probably qualify as nice. No part of me paid attention to how deeply the edge of the table was pressing into my palms.

"True. The joys of my dotage. It lends such a measure of perspective to things."

"Right."

Mags very pointedly did not look at the shade on my cheeks, paid no attention to the faint tremor which had begun stealing through my hands. Instead, she stood across from me with straight spine and challenging smile. She was waiting for me to break first. This was the game which we had so often played. "So? I highly doubt that you chose now for an informal visit. The royal schedule would not leave you enough space for such a frippery."

I almost didn't hear the words, my ears taking a moment to

catch back up to the conversation as the distinct sense of pure fire licked its way up from my belly. Perhaps if I had less pride, or more sense, I would have ended the little dance we did a bit sooner. Or simply not met up with Hanson that morning and just come straight to Mags.

Then again, in my defence, I hadn't felt ill first thing this morning. And as I have said before I am not as young as I used to be. The years take a toll on the body which could have been the reason why my hands had felt cold even in the morning sun. Chronologically I may have only been in my late twenties, but by Inar's tits I often felt as ancient as the hills. Living too much too quickly will do that to you.

In an ideal world I would have gone straight to aid as soon as I felt the least bit off. In such a world I would have registered the sense of wrongness far sooner since my base line wouldn't have included pain.

But that couldn't happen. It simply wasn't the way that things were taken care of. If I wanted help, I would have to abide by the forms, the manners, the expectations, and rote replies. Such had always been reality for all those close to the nexus of power.

Instead, I inclined my head in deference to Mags. I would have bowed, but then I would have probably started puking all over her expensive rugs. That would have just been embarrassing. Especially if I had been upchucking blood as I felt like I wanted to. That would be a nightmare to clean out of such expensive furnishings. "Fair. You are as sharp as ever."

"So?" there was an edge to her tone, an expectation that I wished for once I could disappoint.

"Well, I don't want to inconvenience you, but... well I seem to have been poisoned."

It was strange. I could never quite pin down what the expression which ran across her face was whenever I staggered or was helped to her chambers in such situations. Some people would say I was mad to go to her for help. After all, surely a poisoning could be better dealt with by the Court Physician? If there was one thing which I had learnt over the years, it was that nobody knew better how best to heal a poison than the person whose job it was to make sure they were lethal. In truth, the only real difference between us and the Court Physician is that we *intend* for our concoctions to be deadly. On the other hand, he might be the best accidental assassin.

In terms of my currently needing a bit of assistance to get out of my predicament? This was most certainly not the first time. No way it would be the last. Unless the world happened to end rather abruptly or Inar herself stepped in to put an end to human foolishness.

In the back of my mind, I couldn't help but think the very fact that it was affecting me to this extent was a clear indication of just how serious the incident was. There was a form of bitter satisfaction in that. You know, if you are going to be poisoned on behalf of someone else, better for it to be dramatic rather than embarrassing. At least that was the mentality I had adopted over the years.

When I had been but a child, fresh from the sand and barely old enough to understand the concept of what I was to become, poison had been introduced as a staple of my life. There had been days when I felt as if the flesh were melting from my bones. When a mouthful of food or drink, denied to me for long enough that I couldn't bear the thought of refusing its consumption, would leave me hating my own weakness and begging for death. Yes. Poison and the development of resistance had been one of the few constants in my life.

To this day in fact. I do my laps, spar with whatever squire may have completely randomly appeared to train at my side, and then take a tincture of distilled death in my morning tea.

I have long forgotten what it feels like to consume something without the expectation of pain. Such is life.

Mags brought me back to awareness of where I was, sighing

and wrapping an arm around my shoulders to support me to sit down. "What have you done now, foolish child?"
"Hmm, I think someone tried to kill the Queen."
"I thought we had purged you of the tendency to state the bleeding obvious. At least I know it wasn't you despite your many proclamations of intent. No apprentice of mine would be stupid enough to poison themselves as well as their target."
"Unless I was trying to divert suspicion from myself by making sure I was mildly affected."

I chose that moment to finally loose the fight against my own body and cough up a mouthful of blood. At least I have an element of comedic timing. And aim. It only caught my clothes.

"I'm pretty sure it was Talan berries."
"Hmm, unusual sweetness?" even as she spoke, Mags was opening up the small chest which she kept by the window. It was possibly the most valuable item in the entire damned castle. At least in my opinion. The contents had saved me too many times already.
"Yep- before I never really got what the Priests would drone on about the spring being the purest nectar of the heavens. Further proof the various Pantheons hate us mortals I suppose."
She hummed, handing over a vile of something which smelled remarkably like a dead rodent. "That's blasphemy."
I coughed harshly as I downed the contents. "And that is disgusting. Besides, not my gods so not my problem."

I couldn't help but wonder if their Pantheon would be angered by the fact that spring was going to need to be drained and cleaned before it could be used for the re-swearing. It would no doubt be done with absolute secrecy and the most holy of scrubbing brushes. They would have to make it pretty damned quick as well, what with the ceremony in question being insanely soon.

For a moment I was completely distracted as the light caught the edges of the bottle which had held the antidote. It's always been one of Magda's quirks- she keeps all her various potions and poisons in the most beautiful bottles. Some of them could probably be several hundred years old, others made specifically as pieces of glass art which she has put to use. They are all fantastic and no two alike.

Their contents tend to be pretty awful to consume.

Magda's gaze all but burning a hole through my head brought me back into my body. I responded to her unasked question with my best careless shrug, the epitome of nonchalant attitude. Never mind the fact that antidotes had the habit of hurting almost as much as that which they were fighting. Even if they were supposed to do some good, nothing could magically make the damage done by a poison vanish into the ether. I would have to stay where I was for a little while to make sure that the cure took, and that I wouldn't end up doing something stupid like throwing up on the queen when I returned to duty.

Balance in all things I suppose. Besides, if healing was so easy everybody would be going out to get half killed if only to have a story to share over dinner.

CHAPTER FIVE: IS THIS REALLY IN MY JOB DESCRIPTION?

I was enjoying a brief detour through the gardens, taking a moment to breathe deeply and so dispel the lingering smell of Magda's potions, when a pair of fiends in human form came barrelling across the grass. I swear, Lizzie and Delilah can dance like feathers on a breeze, but when they run the very foundations of the castle tremble. They were moving at a fair clip this time, skirts plastered against their legs.

Delilah reached me first, grabbing onto my arm and heaving for breath. "You're a bodyguard- guard our bodies!"

"What have you two done this time?" I tried to fold my arms to look more intimidating, but her grip was like iron. I am pretty sure it was to stop herself from keeling over as she caught her breath. Lizzie at least was able to still form sentences. "We may have executed an ill-timed prank. And Clarisse may have gotten caught in it."

For a moment I just looked between the pair of them, trying to put together what she had just said. That it took me so long to connect the dots I place solely at the feet of being recently poisoned. These things take a toll on how much of your brain can be rallied at a given time. That said, I clearly had more sense than both of them put together, whatever state I was in. "You planned a prank whilst the Queen of the realm is in the midst of a fasting induced hunger rage?"

There was the distinct sound of a shriek of monarchic fury from within the castle. No doubt anybody within hearing distance was suddenly remembering important duties elsewhere in the castle. The back passages would likely be facing a bit of crowding in the near future.

Delilah refocused her attention on me, giving her best puppy eyes as she continued to cling to me. "Please save us!"
"Seriously? Did neither of you think this through?."
Lizzie actually seemed a bit indignant at the accusation. "We did, then decided to do it anyway. We calculated that the risk was minimal." Her expression turned slightly more contrite, "It just turns out that neither of us is particularly good at math."

I heaved a sigh, finally shaking off the limpet. "I am surrounded by children."
"Hey! I am older than you."
"Nope. I have lived centuries. Just not in corresponding chronological years."

Anything she could have said was cut off by another shout from inside. "Where the hell are they?!" The words were getting clearer, she was no doubt drawing close. Time was of the essence if they didn't want to face the very real chance of being thrown in the dungeons. I made the mental note find out exactly what they had done once the current crisis was past. If it was amusing enough I might even be persuaded to forgive them.

Lizzie latched on this time, all but clinging to my shirt. "Pretty please! Just don't tell her where we are or that you saw us pass this way."
"I will give you my desert for a week!"
There was a slight look of triumph on Liz's face as something clearly popped into her head. "I won't tell anyone about how you stop to pet the hounds every time you walk past the kennel."

That was suspiciously close to blackmail. I narrowed my eyes at their falsely innocent faces. How had she even heard about that? It was one of my few guilty pleasures, and the main reason why

I would walk a certain way back to my quarters when dismissed for the night. Not that I minded her knowing, but it would do damage to my image of untouchable hard ass if the word got around. I can't help it that dogs are the best. Far better than humans.

From the corner of my vision, I could see Clarisse storming her way out of the side door which connected to the gardens. A heavy sigh, and I hooked a thumb over my shoulder to tell them to hide. They grinned at me for a split second before simultaneously diving into the bushes. The laundry was going to kill them when they saw the grass stains. There was an element of bitter satisfaction in that at least to me.

The thing is, I have known Lizzie and Delilah for longer than anyone, aside from Magda of course. I mean, when I was first brought to court, they were all very careful to keep me at a distance from Clarisse. For all that the intention was that I be a symbol of the apparent harmony over the recent invasion, they were all still wary of letting me get too close to the heir until it had been proved that I wouldn't bite the hand feeding me. Even if the food was toxic and my teeth blunt.

That, and Clarisse was busy learning all she could from her mother about the responsibilities of being queen. As such, why would she spend time with some bodyguard in training who might not even survive to stand at her side?

It didn't help that I didn't even understand much of their language in the beginning. For all that I had picked up basic words and phrases from passing groups of traders as a child, it was very different being in the heart of a strange land's capital. The learning curve had been steep, and often edged with pained confusion.

Lizzie and Delilah on the other hand were fascinated by my very existence. Clearly, they had been brought up on too many bedtime stories of the mysteries of the desert lands. Whenever they found me out, they would beg for stories of my homeland.

I never obliged. Or at least not at first. I was too angry, it was too raw, they had no right. I tried to stay silent. Ignore them. Hope they would lose interest. After a couple of months, when everything hurt and I could feel the edges of the callouses growing over my soul, I snapped. I told them in my broken Tartynian that they should fuck off, leave me alone, grow up already. I remember shoving Lizzie away before I ran on my aching legs until Magda tracked me down as I tried desperately to scrabble up the garden wall.

The next time we crossed paths, they had stared in morbid fascination at the purple and black stripes trailing down the side of my face. Neither of them asked me questions about home after that.

It is strange though, how proximity forces people to adapt. You can't hold onto hate forever. Not when far more energy needs to be funnelled into survival. I became faster, tougher, my immunity grew. I guess so did my tolerance.

I suppose the main change came when I finally started looking at them as just girls like me. At least deep down. They weren't the enemy, or at least not mine. They were simply too naïve to realise what they had been doing. They didn't have a frame of reference for why I was that way. So I began to talk to them, and they helped me find the words in their language, to place stitches into cloth. In return I showed them how to make paints which would hold on fabric. We learnt to understand one another.

It was then that I realised I recognised the way that Delilah acted towards one of her uncles. She would get this look in her eye, a stiffness to her shoulders, and if I saw it from the corner of my eye I could have sworn I had walked past a mirror. I didn't ask. She didn't talk about it. We both knew.

On a sunny afternoon, when I was finally free for the day on a rare bit of time off, I found her shivering in the shadows by the guard house. I passed her a vial. Just one of the plain ones, nothing like the gems from Magda's collection. Not for such simple contents.

Delilah had stared at me with the widest eyes, and when she went to speak I simply shook my head before walking away.

It was at least interesting to see the difference in funeral rites between our cultures, although apparently the affair for her uncle was one of the smaller ones seen at court.

When we next passed in the hall, she gave me a cerus fruit tart. It was delicious.

A year later and Clarisse ascended to her throne. As part of the celebration, she welcomed new members to court, including Tabitha who had won favour to become part of the Maids. For all the good that did her in the long run. She only ended up being around for a couple of months, and in that time it seemed the other two weren't as keen to spend extra time with her. Such is life, and death, I suppose. But I guess death doesn't discriminate. At least one entity holds to true equity.

But philosophical ruminations on the futility of existence would have to wait. For now, I was in charge of damage control.

"Nina! Have you seen my idiot Maids?" I half expected the Queen to burn the foliage with her glare alone. Damn, she always got beyond cranky when she had to fast before the re-swearing ceremony. It was part of their traditions, something about needing to only be nourished by the heart spring of the land. The fact that after partaking of the waters she emerged visibly revived was surely due to a touch of the divine. Not just that she could finally stave off dehydration. Even more of a reason why that being the point of poisoning would be highly awkward. With nothing in her stomach it would take her down in record time.

Her raised eye and tapping foot demanded that I give her an answer. The hedges trembled slightly, remarkably subtle to be fair- considering that there were two women crawling through them. No doubt trying not to laugh. There was a faint squeak and then the sound of someone swearing as they splashed into the moat just on the other side of the shrubbery. Oh yeah. They were dead meat when the servants got hold of them. I made a mental note to tell Jeremy to hang around the laundry with snacks for when they got caught. He loved a good bit of gossip.

I kept my face resolutely set. "Umm... they are not in the garden." A second splash and some poorly muffled shrieking. "But perhaps your Majesty should move to a different area. It would seem that the mice in this part of the grounds are particularly rowdy this afternoon."

That at least got me a snort. It was the most amount of humour that anybody had managed to draw from her since the night before.

I let her lead the way as she took my advice and began to wind her way through the gardens. This was one of the most pleasant spots in the castle grounds. It was set on a terrace which overlooked the town sprawling over the surrounding planes. The castle had originally been built as a fortress of course, and as the seat of the capital it kept those practical aspects of its layout. The elevated platform on which the keep had been built, the moat which had been constructed by diverting the nearby river into a constantly running defensive line, the high walls surrounding the outer courtyard.

With years of general peace, or at least violence outsourced to other country's lands, some alterations had been made for the enjoyment of the court. The gardens had been probably the best of those changes. The blossom trees which grew here shed their petals in the spring until they rained down like perfumed snow on the general populace.

Clarisse folded her arms as she leaned on the dip of the battlements. Tipping her head back, she breathed deep and soaked in the warmth of the late morning sun. When it looked less hazardous for my health, I briefly stepped next to her. A quick flick of my hand, a smooth step back, my mission was complete.

She looked down at the bun which I had placed next to her on the stone, before turning her renewed glare my way. "And what the hell is this?"
"I have no idea, Your Majesty. Perhaps a gift from the gods? I saw no other explanation for how such an item could have materialised next to you." As I spoke, I kept my eyes firmly fixed on the horizon. If I focused hard enough, I was almost sure that I could see one of the air ships slowly drifting at the edge of the sky. Hopefully despite recent dramas, it was a sight which would become more common.

When I did finally chance a look back the bun was gone.

Clarisse flicked her eyes sideways, a faint hint of embarrassment tinging her cheeks. "Was I really being that bad?"
"Ma'am, my job is to protect you from all threats. Consider this a preventative measure to quell an insurrection."
She finally broke, chuckling ruefully, "in some circles that could be considered treasonous talk."
"From my lips to Inar's ears."
"That is not one of the Pantheon." The tone was mild with her observation. It was true- the Goddess of my people was not recognised by any of the religious tiers in her Pantheon.
"Indeed, so you need not fear Her interference in your reign."

CHAPTER SIX: IT COULD HAVE GONE WORSE

"If it's not one thing it's another."

"That does tend to be the way that reality unfolds."

"I really don't have time for your attitude right now." Clarisse raised an eyebrow as she looked me up and down, "and if the colour of your face is anything to go by, neither do you."

"Oh please. It is nowhere near that bad. Just a scratch." It was true- a couple of stitches needed but nothing drastic. I wouldn't even have to go track down Mags with this one. Although I would of course seek her out later, to thank her for helping out with the immediate cover operation.

Part of me got side tracked thinking over whether it would be possible to get hold of a small gift. Then again, my lack of medical need was a gift in and of itself… no, there was no way that she would go for that. Perhaps the kitchen would be able to provide me with some of those little cakes which she was so inordinately fond of.

Thankfully my ceremonial uniform had done its job, the red colour not allowing anyone to see that there was a couple of cups worth of blood leaking out of my body. I mean, it is literally the reason why I have to wear that specific shade. Some bodyguard, somewhere in the depths of history, had no doubt pointed out the benefit and so the tradition had stuck.

And the silk absorbed the blood really well so the cleaning staff wouldn't even be able to have a go at me for dripping on their floors. They can be pretty vicious about such things, and they were already facing an unreasonable amount of effort after such a big event. If I had made people play a game of 'follow the bleeder' they would have dispatched me with far more ruthless efficiency than the official executioner.

In this instance, I would probably even get away with having ruined yet another set of ceremonial robes. With the entire court working their way through a costume change as we spoke, the laundry would be far too preoccupied to notice anything short of the castle burning down around their ears. Hell, even then they would probably thank the gods for the clothes drying faster, as they cursed the ash in the same breath. All of which was to say- anybody who came across my ruined outfit would have far more to worry about than speculating on the source of the bleeding.

At least no one in the crowd seemed to have noticed. That would probably have been far more dangerous than the assassination attempt itself. Come to think of it, there was even a cloak on the wall which depicted the Tragedy of Harna Square- when an attempted assassination had resulted in a panicked crowd all but rioting as they tried to escape from the perceived danger. Fourteen people had died, and according to some witnesses at least three had been on the end of the guard's own swords as they tried to forge a path through for the Queen.

So yes, it was rather a relief that this time I had been the only one caught out.

If anything, I was almost professionally offended by the apparent lack of effort which went into the actual attempt. The entire plot seemed to have consisted only of a bolt being fired from a pre-rigged crossbow hidden in the back wall. Pretty unimaginative to be honest. Not to mention inefficient. If they had wanted to have a greater chance of hitting Clarisse, they should have set up their little device from further into the hall.

Disguising their trap with one of the cloaks would have been far easier than trying to blend it with the wood panelling of the walls. Not to mention the angle would have required a bigger response in order to protect the queen- one which would have been noticeable enough to at least disrupt the ceremony.

All I could think was that the perpetrator didn't want to chance the cloaks being hurt. But that made less sense, at least to me. But then again, I tend to be highly mission focused. Unless the unknown assailant placed greater value on their historical significance than on the life of the current Queen. That in itself was a possibility, and a pretty sobering one if truth be told. Because frankly the only people who generally cared that much about such artifacts were the ones who were represented by them. As in- it would have most likely been a member of the court. The nobility to be precise. And that was a less than comforting thought.

I mean, plots against the monarchy are pretty much a prerequisite of life at the castle. But there is normally an entire school of etiquette around how they were conducted. This had been out of the ordinary.

As a result of all the background drama, the main event of the day had seemed almost surreal to me if I am honest. Re-swearing of the Queen was a concept which I most certainly agreed with. It just seemed logical to me to ensure that the head of a country was reminded periodically of her responsibilities to those who she claimed as her subjects. The fact that she had to fast beforehand, as I may have mentioned, did wonders for ensuring that the lesson stuck.

Magda had tried to explain to me once about how the fasting was supposed to serve as a reminder to the monarch that she was in fact human. That she could feel hunger the same as any of her subjects, that she should desire to ensure that those under her rule never had to feel hardship. I had only scoffed at the time, replying that whoever came up with the idea seemed to have conveniently made the period only last for a day. Perhaps their Queen had taken to the task as kindly as our own.

The court at least seemed to lap it up. The ceremony began at the sacred pool, and they had watched with shining eyes as Clarisse had cupped her hands into the water, bringing it to her face to drink. The refreshing effect was pretty instantaneous for her, eyes brightening, muscles easing. The nobles seemed to breathe a sigh of relief at the apparent evidence that their Pantheon still blessed their leader. I echoed the relief that she was finally hydrated and would hopefully be less bitchy.

Delilah and Lizzie had stepped forwards to drape the Queen's cloak around her shoulders, symbolically once again conferring the mantle of leadership. It was all very poetic, the richness of the hundreds of hours of embroidery against the relative simplicity of her white dress. Whoever had initially planned the tradition had certainly had an eye for the details.

Then had come the procession to the throne room, the entire route being lined with her adoring subjects. That was the part which I hated the most. It was always the point of weakness in terms of security capabilities. True, there were guards lining every inch of the path, but having that many people around just put my hackles up. Even Jeremy pulling a face at me from his point along the way did nothing to ease what was no doubt a firm scowl on my face. I wouldn't apologise for it either. Lizzie and Delilah were supposed to look beautiful and capable as they flanked their queen. My job was to keep them all alive. Who knows, maybe some even approved of my apparent attitude as reassuring- a reminder that there was an element of reality to the day.

Entering the throne room had in truth been pretty spectacular. Samda Arner had put his genius to good use in so far as trying to redeem some favour with the Queen went. When Sir Gavin gave the smallest push to the massive doors, they had swung open smoothly on silent hinges. At the same time, baskets upon baskets of flower petals hidden in the rafters had tipped out their contents to rain down upon the procession. Taking their que, the ranks of waiting musicians struck up their instruments to play the national anthem, even if it was a somewhat extended and embellished version.

As we moved through the room, so too did the waves of petals, becoming mixed in with scraps of shining paper which caught the light from the windows until the very air gleamed and shone. It really was beautiful, and as Clarisse spread her arms wide in benevolent blessing for a moment, she looked like one of the goddess statues in the town's main temple.

And it was naturally at that moment that it almost all went to shit.

Air full of floating distractions aside, I am good enough at my job to notice when something is off. And a panel at the back of the room sliding back on a hidden mechanism was certainly off. Luckily, with all eyes on the star of the show, nobody noticed as I flicked a small blade from sleeve, to fingertips, to the string of the rigged crossbow.

Talk about your timing. It was just fast enough to prevent the trap from fully firing, as well as managing to knock the bolt off course. Instead of punching through the Queen's back, out her front, and coating the nearest spectators with something other than petals, it lost momentum and only managed to sink an inch or so into my flank as I twisted into its path. Thank Inar that my uniform included a red leather jerkin. For all that it was highly decorated with imprints of various flowers, armour was armour. And this set did its job well.

The music covered my brief curse, the confetti pretty much hid the movement. For a split second it was as if time had frozen, or that I had been plunged underwater. I was there with a bolt in my side (not deep, thank Inar not deep) as Clarisse had her moment of triumph. There were only rapturous faces in the crowd. Nobody seeming disappointed. I breathed out in slow increments. Sounds came rushing back into my awareness.

Almost nobody noticed. Magda seemed to materialise at my side between one blink and the next, having slipped through the jubilation without leaving a trail, and pulled the knife from where it had sunk into the wall before it could be spotted. She deftly slid the panel back into place to hide the trap from sight. Coming to stand at my side, she must have looked nothing short of a proud mentor surveying the continued triumph of her Queen. Nobody would have known that from her position she was able to pull the bolt from my flesh and hide it in the pocket of her gown.

All I could do was mentally chant a thank you that the damn thing hadn't been barbed. That could have been messy.

A pat on my shoulder and she was returning to what was supposed to be her place in the festivities. All she received were indulgent smiles from the few courtiers who spotted the deviation. Who could fault an old woman for briefly breaking ranks when emotion overcame her after all?

There were no further moves made, no traps triggered, not one toe put out of line. I stood in my place, keeping my expression flat even as I could feel that I was leaking. Blood seeping down your back is a really uncomfortable sensation. It was hard to resist the urge to scratch.

The rest of the re-swearing went off without the slightest hitch, until at last everyone was dismissed after the final speech. There would be a ball tonight of course, so the court were keen to have enough time to prepare themselves. It had been then that I finally let my posture drop, along with the string of curses which I had been holding back in a hissed bout.

Lizzie had almost shrieked when she realised what had happened, and only Delilah giving her a warning thump on the arm had stopped her. I was glad for that. If she had made a fuss, then I couldn't be sure that I wouldn't end up snapping at her. Delilah at least had the wherewithal to pass me her handkerchief so I could press it against the wound as a bit of a bandage. I have always appreciated her practical nature.

A swift retreat to the Queen's chambers so that she could be made ready for the ball had also allowed me to get a better look at the damage. It was pretty bad if I am honest... the laundry were going to have my head. It may even be a better option to burn the evidence. At least it was expected that we would all be in different outfits by the evening. If there was anything I had learnt from all my years of service, it was that grand events required an intimidating amount of costume changes.

Delilah and Lizzie were taking turns in helping Clarisse change even as they switched their own dresses. At least the fact that the Queen's wigs were already prepared saved a massive amount of time on hairdressing. Because that was the priority.

The rest of the room averted their eyes as I threaded the needle which I kept in the emergency medical kit in the chamber. Sewing really was a life skill. There was an awkward silence for a few moments, broken only by the rustles of cloth as the others shifted around the room. They knew better than to try and talk to me, to distract me from either the pain or the reality of what I was doing. I wouldn't have responded if they tried. For at least the immediate moment, I felt as if I were actually two paces to the left of my own body, like I was watching myself go through the motions without being actively involved.

It wasn't until I snipped off the excess thread that Lizzie finally approached. Her hands were gentle as she helped to secure a proper bandage and then assisted me in getting into my own outfit. At least the lacing of the stays would help keep pressure on the wound. At least I wouldn't be expected to do any dancing. At least the contact helped to draw my awareness back into myself. Even if I still felt as if my skin wasn't quite my own, that my muscles didn't really belong to me, that everything was too damned bright through these eyes. I realised that I was running the fingertips of one hand over and over the texture of my skirt.

Clarisse had finally dismissed the others to finish getting ready and check on the preparations for the ball. She would only appear once everything was perfectly in place, the guests ready to be struck speechless by her graceful entrance. It was all so carefully planned, and if anybody saw her before the appointed moment it would ruin the whole effect.

It thankfully meant that we also had a bit of time to discuss what had just happened. And now here we were.

"So what do you think?" She was watching me in her mirror even as she adjusted the lay of her jewellery.

I hummed a little, taking a moment to recheck my blades as was my want when thinking things through. "It had to have been done by someone smart. Someone who knows their way around engineering and devices if I had to give my guess."

Her hands froze, "Someone who had access to the throne room to rig up a variety of other contraptions for today?"

"You mean Samda?" I kept my tone deliberately light, "Admittedly he was my first candidate, but I genuinely don't see him wanting to kill you. Does he have the brains? Sure. But he has no motivation. He is still only really a child, remember, for all that his uncle makes eager use of his talents."

Clarisse turned to face me now, kicking up her feet to rest on the edge of her dressing table. How she managed it in that gown was an art in and of itself. "So, what about Lord Arner himself then? He does have skill with devices even if it is not true genius."

"He would be able to rig up a trap like that." and it was possible that he cared enough about national treasures to try and protect them. Out of the Arner options, I could see Samda being simply more efficient if he did ever try to assassinate someone, damage to cloaks be damned. The nature of the problem would demand a more elegant option than what had been done. His uncle could have some more hang ups about historical preservation though.

I shook my head a little, "But again that doesn't entirely make sense. Why would he take such drastic action? He has nothing to

gain from it."
"Unless it was not his whole idea. We all know that he did not take kindly to his previous unsavoury actions being brought to life. Perhaps another kingdom offered him enough incentive to take some bigger risks. He knows he is on thin ice, who's to say he hasn't decided to cut his losses?"

There was nothing I could say to that. It was a possibility, sure, even if I couldn't really see it being the truth. Something about the concept just didn't sit right with what I knew about him.

No doubt Magda would already be working on her own investigation. It would not surprise me if there was a sudden rash of odd tasting drinks and suddenly honest courtiers. That was one great thing about social contracts and civility. It would be beyond rude to refuse a cup of tea from one of the most established dowagers in the castle.

For now, it would have to wait. We had a ball to attend.

CHAPTER SEVEN: A LITTLE PARTY NEVER KILLED NOBODY

If there is one thing I love about a ball, it is that there is inevitably some level of dramatic fall out. Whether a cheating scandal is revealed, or someone gets snubbed on the dance schedule, it is like watching a real-life play taking place. That, and I get to watch Lizzie and Delilah do what they do best. That is, be ridiculously vicious, dance like angels, and generally make the rest of the court fantastically jealous of their closeness with the Queen.

It is always mesmerising to see how their skirts swirl and sparkle in the lights. For all that I technically rank just below the maids, but higher than a minor noble, I stay in my uniform of a split skirt. It is rather fancier than my now ruined ceremonial version, although still in that same shade of red. The bodice is lined with linen glue armour, so as to seem normal without losing any of its protective qualities. When I stand still, the legs hang in just the right way to look like I am wearing a full gown whilst still letting me move far more freely if necessary to defend my Queen.

One day, somehow, I will be off the clock and prance around in a proper ballgown which has all the practical features of a cake.

The other benefit of my evening dress uniform was that it had the biggest pockets possible without altering the fit. There were at least two vials of headache reliever hidden in there, just in case they were needed. Or rather, for when it all inevitably got to the Queen or her maids. It was Mag's own recipe, so was guaranteed to be effective without compromising your ability to think. That stuff was a lifesaver. Literally on a couple of occasions.

I had already downed the slightly stronger version and was enjoying the fact that there was only a dull ache radiating from my flank. It was all about appearances. Talk about performance art.

Anyway, this evening had the potential to be even more hilarious than normal. There was an ambassador at court. Namet's ambassador to be precise. As in, the country that we were in a precarious trade dispute with.

It was made worse that we knew the man who had been sent. This wasn't his first trip. Most prayed each time that it would be his last. He seemed to have some sort of infatuation with anybody in power, which meant anyone in a close enough radius would be witness to a thinly veiled series of attempts to try and woo Clarisse.

I mean, that alone was a pointless endeavour. Even were she to fall madly in love over the course of a single evening, there was no way even the greatest miracles of several deities combined would allow for the Queen to match with someone of such a relatively low station. I genuinely don't know why they kept trying. The best anyone could ever hope for would be a vague 'favoured' position, which courtly jealousy would deem a death sentence. The level of hubris tended to make everyone close to Clarisse rather fractious. Even more so when we were all keenly aware that there were far more important plots playing out.

If I ended up taking a second hit in the same day I would be royally pissed off.

We would have had longer to brace for the impact of the Nametian visitor, but it turned out that he and his entourage had been closer than anticipated. In fact, they had already been at court for two days, but thankfully due to the preparations for the re-swearing Clarisse had not yet crossed his path.

Normally, Namet would have likely wanted to send an air ship, since that way only took three days capital to capital. Considering the reason for the visit, that was probably deemed either in poor taste, or simply dangerous when technological theft was the order of the day. Using horses, that journey was roughly a two-week venture, provided you weren't desperate. If you were, that could be cut to nine days. Unfortunately for the relative sanity of the court, the ambassador's party had been investigating one of the trading towns on the border. It had taken them only a week to reach the castle. As ever, life proved itself once again to not be fair.

Frankly I was sick and tired of nations sending their ambassadors whose intentions were of the more amorous variety as if they expected a star-crossed romance to unfold in the space of a visit. I had asked Magda about it once, and it turns out that the ploy had worked exactly once in the course of recorded history. It was apparently enough for nations to keep taking a stab at the policy.

Truth be told, the only time that sort of plan had a vague level of success in living memory, was when the Republic of Rhean sent Lady Alara a the year before last. Now she had been what is universally recognised as a stunner. Biggest doe eyes you have ever seen, the ability to pull off any outfit, and a frankly wicked sense of humour. I don't think anybody has won general court approval and hatred in equal measure so quickly. Even the most bitter had to admire her clarity of purpose and dedication to the pursuit of her country's aims.

Clarisse had almost choked on her own tongue during their introductions, and for the entirety of the visit she had sported a rather flushed look. I spent the entire time trying not to laugh out loud at the sheer level of fluster. Turns out she most definitely has a type. To be fair, out of all the dignitaries we have to host, Lady Alara was one of the ones who actually treated *me* as something more than a piece of furniture.

So maybe I had accidentally left the pair of them alone on balmy summer nights in the rose gardens.

Strangely enough, Rhean had recently been granted use of a large proportion of our forces to help them with their ongoing pirate problem. Anything to help a friendly nation.

Truth be told, the council have been somewhat pushy lately in reminding her that a consort can be a valuable commodity in diplomatic relationships. And they do have a point. However, they really need to do better at choosing potential matches. Their latest offering was... well... frankly he was a he so that was automatically not going to work out.

And no, damn it, here we were dealing with another absolute prick. Like, out of all the possible nobles available in Namet, they had to go with the King's brother, Alastair.

Now, don't get me wrong, the King of Namet is actually pretty chill. We went to his coronation about four years ago, and although there was some inevitable tension, he was rather nice as far as I could tell. He even made a point of checking that I was comfortable with the arrangements which he had come up with from a protection view. That sort of consideration gets my vote.

Unfortunately, his brother is a complete and utter twat. I don't know what made him think that he is the gods' gift to humankind, but dammit whichever deity responsible is going to get a strongly worded letter from me. And an in person visit when I give up the ghost.

When we visited his country, he almost made poor Lizzie cry with how obnoxious he was being when hitting on her. Not taking 'no' for an answer and getting offended when the rest of us closed ranks in her defence? It wasn't an endearing quality.

And that was who had been sent to court our Queen and smooth over a brewing international shit show.

Since his arrival, he had crossed paths a few times with various ladies. Even in a castle this big it was nearly unavoidable. Their subsequent reports throughout the day had been extremely vocal. During those interactions he had: commented on one having muffins for breakfast, attempted to explain to another why she had been shooting wrong her whole life during archery (then lost their little competition), and tried smack one of the dogs. In response to the last, I had 'stumbled' into his side and sent him tripping into a flower bed before he could follow through. Perhaps it was universal punishment that I was wounded a few hours later.

As if that wasn't bad enough, his protection detail were pretty obnoxious as well. As a king's brother, although apparently not recognised fully as a Prince for whatever reason, he was entitled to having his own protective escort whilst in a foreign court. Fair enough. Whenever we visited elsewhere then I would be on high alert the entire time with Clarisse. That is normal. What is not expected is that Alastair's bodyguard is highly aggravating. Honestly, rather than assassinate the ambassador I am regularly tempted to aim for his protection detail.

To be fair, the lesser knights who are part of his entourage aren't too bad. Sure, a couple of them seem particularly keen to show off on the training grounds against our own men, but I am pretty sure that at least for the youngest one it is his version of flirting. If the kitchen maids are to be believed there is a lovely little star-crossed romance blossoming between him and Lord Grinshaw. Good luck to them both.

No, for me the main problem is Alastair's escort head. Sir Enhani seems certain that he is the be all and end all of knightly virtues and skills. My teeth are actually aching with how hard I have been gritting them since the start of the visit. The man has opinions on everything. Literally. And seems to believe that he should share his 'expertise' with me. To be fair, no doubt he must have at least some skills or else he would not have achieved his rank. But he should give that same level of courteous respect to me.

Then again if he is actually useless the King may have assigned the duty in hopes of an accident to his brother... it is not outside the realms of possibility.

Anyway, the long and short of it is that if I have to hear Enhani point out the bleeding obvious then I might just snap. He just had no respect for the fact that I had also earned my position. I have been trained for longer, and in far harsher ways, than he could hope to comprehend. I know what I am doing. And if anything, I amuse myself when Alastair is present in figuring out how I would go about killing the man. Just hypothetically. Although if Clarisse were to order an unfortunate series of events to befall the ambassador, then I would seriously consider the weight of my oaths to loyalty. I must obey my queen after all.

So yeah. None of us were excited when he came striding into the hall. Late as well, which is so phenomenally rude that I can't help but wonder who the hell raised him. Like, damn, there are rules!

The youngest member of their party almost immediately diverted towards Lord Grimshaw, a faint pink dusting his cheeks as the knight in question automatically pulled him closer and flagged down a drink. Any fondness which the sight might have inspired was swiftly crushed as Enhani stepped into my personal space. He flashed what he probably imagined to be a charming smile at me, eyes flicking up and down my uniform.

"Fancy seeing you here."
"Hmm." I didn't want to interact with him, instead making a point of keeping my eyes on the nearest guests to our respective charges. It didn't help that I could feel the dull ache radiating from my flank every time I shifted my weight.
"You know, whilst my Lord and Her Majesty are occupied, how about you and I get to know each other..."
"No. I am on duty." I raised an eyebrow at him, keeping my most unimpressed expression on my face. "As are you... Sir."

He chuffed, taking a moment to very deliberately survey the

room. I had the sense that he was not so much scanning for threats as heaving bosoms. I got the distinct impression that he had an inflated sense of his own appeal. A sadly common affliction amongst visiting nobles it would seem. And now he was leaning closer, as if we shared a sense of camaraderie, of shared ambitions. If only I had been able to get my hands on a stronger pain reliever then I could have been high enough to have more patience.

"You know how it is for us. We have to find a way up the social ladder." He didn't even look at me as he spoke. If I were one of her Majesty's dogs my fur would have been bristling. I still had to resist the urge to snap my teeth at him.

"Will you pray tell me, sir," damn my speech was slipping. A sure sign of my fraying temper. But then, it is hard to remember grammar rules in you second language when you are trying not to spit venom. "What do you think it means to be a lady?" I didn't let him get a word in edgeways. I didn't want to hear it. "You must of course know it is not bestowed solely through blood?"

That was an irrefutable fact. Considering the inherent dangers of childbearing, many women chose not to risk their lives and lineage on such an undertaking unless they were entirely sure of their decision. Rather, most inheritors were adopted into the family at a young age so as to be trained into the traditions of their new station. There are merits, there are draw backs, and none of them are mine to go into. At the very least it means that there is rather less of a blood-based prejudice amongst the Court. Although anyone who takes a jab at a person's family name will be, likely literally, eviscerated as the others look on in manic glee.

I found my lip curling of its own volition as watched the peacock out of the corner of my eye. "A lady must be skilled in the political arts, languages, music, multiple cultures. She must know of the world and see it for its true nature so as to shape it to her will. She must understand not only how to please others, but when to do so."

There was no denying the slight smile which stole across my face as I watched Delilah flirt beautifully with one of the councillors. It holds true across creation it seemed, that the brighter the colours and display put on, the more dangerous the animal. "And a maid? Well... she must have the strength and sense of self enough to trust another with those skills." I finally looked at Enhani directly, "obeying orders is no excuse after all for the way which someone acts."

Alastair was apparently done with various introductions to some of the nobles he hadn't met yet and was starting to make his way through the crowd. Seriously- his 'security detail' had left him wide open. I could take him out with one well thrown dagger from where I was standing. And I never threw poorly.

Enhani scoffed a little. He seemed to be amused by my continued disdain. It was beyond frustrating. I made to move closer to my Queen as she began to move across the room. Probably plotting her own course to try and avoid interacting with Alastair. A hand on my arm. It took all of my self control not to punch him in the face on sheer instinct.

"Then how about after this you explain it all further to me in a little, private, get together? We could..."
Had he heard nothing that I had said? I let my expression fall like a rock in a well and just as hard on impact. "Remove your hand or lose it."
He at least had the sense to recognise a pissed off predator, pulling back sharply with a small laugh which did nothing to hide the slight flash of brief fear in his eyes.

My lip curled of its own volition as I stepped around him to retake my rightful position at Clarisse's side. Taking the hint at last, the unwanted pest mirrored the move to fall into place behind his Lord. I did my best not to acknowledge his existence.

It always got under my skin when people flirted with me. I mean, I didn't mind a bit of positive attention (I was big enough to admit that- if only to myself) but when someone can't take the outright statement that I am not looking for that? They always seem to take it personally that I am just genuinely not interested. I never have been, in anybody really. For a while I had thought I must just be attracted to men and women alike, before I realised that I actually had an equal amount of apathy for both. Gender means nothing because there is no attraction to begin with.

And yet for some reason the maids often asked my advice with their romantic pursuits. According to Lizzie the fact that I just genuinely didn't get a lot of what they were talking about (why would anybody enjoy the feeling of butterflies in their stomach? Surely that would just lead to indigestion?) made me a better impartial judge.

Whatever. At least this time I wasn't alone in failing to find any form of appeal in Lord Alastair.

As he made to approach the Queen, my barely repressed snarl was only enough to make him hesitate for a moment. Alas for the fools who believe themselves brave.

He bowed before her, barely deep enough, before straightening and fixing her with an oily smile. "Your Majesty, your radiance lights this ball as if the sun itself were made human for a night." In the corner of my eye, I saw Delilah making an exaggerated gagging motion only to get punched on the arm by Lizzie.

Alastair continued, "might you enjoy a dance with me?" he leaned in closer, apparently not noticing how I shifted my stance as he crossed into her personal space. "We could take a turn or two in each other's arms..." it was probably meant to sound alluring, and if the leer on his face was anything to go by, he truly believed it to be a tempting offer.

A small round of tittering went through those closest as Clarisse very deliberately took a step back. "Lord Alastair, alas that will not be possible at this time."
"Ah, is my lady already engaged for this number?"

"No."

The expression on his face soured for a second, before his eyes alighted on Lizzie. I guess there are downsides to looking so much like the Queen. "Then may I escort one of your maids to the floor instead?"

Anyone with eyes could see how unenthused Lizzie was by the prospect, however there were at least some diplomatic niceties which couldn't be ignored. Where the Queen was well within her right to refuse a dance, she couldn't very well begrudge him from interacting with everybody else. At least with it being Lizzie we all knew that Sir Gavin would be keeping a close eye. Honestly, the way that those two were so nearly together, was maddening. They just needed to kiss already.

For the moment however, Clarisse could only graciously wave Lizzie forwards even if it was with clear reluctance.

Grinning triumphantly, Alastair led her to the dance floor where the musicians had just struck up the opening to the next dance.

After that, things seemed to go well for a few hours. Even if Enhani dared to ask me for a dance when I was doing a circuit of the room. My flat refusal was once again met with an attempt to hold me in place long enough for him to press his case. I walked away with my head held high whilst he nursed his trembling fingers. They were only slightly cracked from being yanked backwards. He had exited rather sharply after that, firmly convincing me that he was not in fact a professional security officer. What exactly he was doing as part of the ambassadorial party I could not fathom. Perhaps he was a noble's son trying to earn some favour from the King?

Whatever, it was none of my concern so long as he left me and mine alone.

I smirked to myself when I noticed the youngest member of the group discreetly exit with Lord Grimshaw later in the evening. Perhaps it would turn out that the ambassadorial party would return home with one less member than they arrived with. I supposed we could always request that the man remain in his master's place as a continued point of contact since surely the King could not spare his brother for a long-term assignment.

The night continued, and I found myself wishing for another round of painkillers. It seemed the night wasn't going to be as amusing as other times, but then I hadn't been starting from the best point.

There was one close call a couple of hours into the whole tiresome evening. It's not that I actively hate balls… it's just… for a moment there was so much noise, too many people talking whilst the music was just loud enough to be distracting but not enjoyable. I could feel how hard I was gritting my teeth, the tightness in my muscles which in turn tugged at the stitches in my wound. There was a thrumming across my very skin which just refused to settle. I wanted to hit something, to yell at everybody to shut the hell up for more than five seconds so I could pull pieces of myself back together and pretend at still being human.

The temptation as strong to sidle up to Jeremy where he was guarding a window, lean into his side until he got the hint, and let him hug me hard enough that the soul would be pressed back into my body. He never judged me whenever that happened, just said I was a cat in a previous life and waited until breathing didn't make my face twist in pain.

I settled for digging the nails of one hand deep into the palm. Mags had taught me once to look around the room and identify five things I could see, four I could hear, three I could smell, two I could taste, one I could touch. She called it an awareness exercise to keep me in tune with my surroundings. I reckon she knew what it was to have to force yourself back down into reality.

On a more positive note, the buffet was fantastic as ever, and I made a mental note to thank the kitchen for including cerus fruit tarts. Those things were my greatest weakness when it came to events like this. Or really anyday.

Magda took the time to come over and chat for a while, doing her best to make me laugh in front of Clarisse. Delilah always found it funny when the pair of us were together at events, simply for the fact that our behaviours were so similar. I mean, it makes sense. They say you become like the people you spend the most time with, and she had been the person to literally forge my entire being ever since I was brought to court. It was the same way that Clarisse had been taught to mimic the ways of the monarch ever since she was chosen for her position. After all, even more than with the other ladies, no Queen would risk the dangers of childbirth- not when the fate of a country rested on their health and wellbeing. So, it was customary for her to adopt an heir and train her to best fulfil her duties. True, there were some who held the romantic notion that the practice reaffirmed the connection between ruler and ruled, but anybody with half a brain knew that it was a far more practical tradition.

Basically, we were each moulded to fill the role of our predecessors, and it most clearly showed in highly ceremonial settings. For Mags and I, it was evident in how we scanned the crowds at all times, fingers twitching at regular intervals towards the swords on our hips. By virtue of my role and her history, we were the only people other than the guards who were allowed to be armed at such an event.

Well, Enhani was wearing a sword as well, but judging by the ornate nature of the hilt compared to the length of the blade? I had the sense that it was a purely ceremonial piece. No way it would be correctly balanced for actual use.

It was growing close to midnight when the scuffle broke out.

On the dance floor a round of shouting had started off, sending the musicians stuttering into silence. It was apparently some inbuilt instinct for the other guests to form a ring around the disturbance, which Clarisse then proceeded to push her way through. Well, rather they parted in deference to her magnificent presence. And of course, I was right at her side.

Pretty inevitably, it was Alastair at the heart of the whole thing. At a glance, he was yelling to all and sundry although it was hard to make out exactly what he was saying. Lizzie was next to Sir Gavin, apparently having been dancing with him, although he was now half holding her back. Her face was flushed with fury as she screamed back at the ambassador. I got the sense that if Sir Gavin hadn't of had his hands full, then fists would have already been flying.

Enhani seemed to already be nursing a bleeding nose and was firmly out of whatever fight was about to break out. Light weight.

"What in the name of the Pantheon is going on here?" Clarisse's tone was cold, clipped, barely contained rage simmering below the surface.

Alastair strode forwards, only stopping when I stepped in front of the Queen to bar his way. Huffing, he threw his hands in the air, "I was only wishing to dance with your maid, and she snubbed me most rudely, then this oaf attempted to lay hands on me. My bodyguard was hurt in the scuffle. I demand recompense for such deplorable conduct!"

"Lizzie?"

"I was dancing with Sir Gavin when Alastair tried to cut in. I said no, repeatedly, and then he tried to grab me. Gavin was just trying to defend me, and the ambassador stumbled into Sir Enhani sending him to the floor. Alastair then began screaming at both of us, so I yelled back..."

The Queen nodded in understanding, taking a moment to place a reassuring hand on Lizzie's shoulder. Even I could see how she was shaking in fury. Delilah stepped forwards from the crowd to stand in solidarity with her friend, easing her and Sir Gavin away from the ambassador before turning to curtsey to the Queen. A gesture told her to offer up her testimony.

"Your Majesty, Alastair interrupted their dancing, making several comments about how he would like to take Liz back to his rooms. That he would show her what a real man could do to a girl like her."

"And what did she do in response?"

A slight cough which I had a suspicion was masking a laugh. "She fixed her tiara and asked him to repeat what he said. He once again told her that he would show her what a man like him was capable of. So... she told him to 'get down on his knees and prove it then'."

I was pretty sure that it was Magda that I could hear break out into hysterical cackling somewhere in the crowd. This was probably the best entertainment she had seen for a while. No doubt she was enjoying snacks with the show.

Clarisse seemed to be visibly holding back her temper. "I take it Lord Alastair was surprised?"

"Indeed Your Majesty. When he stated his disbelief at Lizzie's words, she told him that if he couldn't be respectful then neither could she. That seemed to be the end of it for a moment, but then Sir Gavin asked what she would have done if Alastair had gotten on his knees."

"And?"

Lizzie smirked a little at the Ambassador, "I would have told him, 'good boy'."

The man in question flushed scarlet to the roots of his hair and seemed to choke on his spit. Sir Gavin was looking rather flushed as well, if also awed and adoring of his dance partner. I made a mental note to congratulate Lizzie later.

Then again, this was two fights in as many days. She was more of a menace than anybody would give her credit for at first sight.

Clarisse tutted softly, drawing all attention back to her. She had the expression on her face which I knew all too well meant that she was inches away from raining down wrath and righteous fury on her target. Enhani actually whimpered a little, although that might have been from putting increased pressure on his nose. It waws still bleeding.

"Lord Alastair of Namet, you have tried our patience for the last time. You will leave this castle forthwith and return unto your own nation. You have three days to cross the border or else I shall remand you into the custody of my guards."

A ripple went through the crowd at the announcement, most seeming vindictively satisfied with what amounted to a banishment order. It appeared he hadn't managed to make any friends at court.

For a moment he sputtered in outrage, puffed up indignation sending his face from white to crimson in the space of three seconds. I wondered if he was going to simply drop dead on the dance floor. Alas not, instead he drew himself up to his full height with a vicious sneer across his features.

"I challenge you to a duel!" he pulled his glove off as he spoke and slapped it straight across… my face. I've said it before, balls such as this are a dance in and of themselves, you just have to step at the exact right moment. In this case directly in front of my Queen. I grinned at him, far too many teeth for it to be polite, as I very deliberately took the coronet from my head. A quick breath to the metal, a swift buff, and I smacked him full across the face with it.

Now there were two bloody nosed idiots on the floor.

"I accept."

I almost killed my charge as she tried not to choke herself from attempting not to cackle out loud. Lizzie was less subtle, but at least she was further back in the crowd by that point. Magda was howling fit to raise wolves. She would no doubt never let me hear the end of this.

CHAPTER EIGHT: SUNS OUT SWORDS OUT

We walked the corridors of the castle before the sun was truly risen. Clarisse was in her simplest dress, the one which she could get into with minimum fuss and only Sera to tie the kirtle. I had at least had the time to scurry back to my rooms and change before we set off for the duel. My standard uniform was much less of a pain to clean should the whole event go far worse than I anticipated. My main issue with this whole thing was that none of us had the chance to catch any sleep. Even with the challenge being issued, the party had continued until the stars began to fade. I could only hope that any yawning would not be taken offence at.

Delilah and Lizzie were going to meet us at the garden gate, so for a moment Clarisse and I were alone in the slowly breaking daylight. There was a stillness to the castle at this hour, at least on this level. The reality of castle life is that there is always someone awake and working, but in the aftermath of ball most were probably either tidying up the main hall or anticipating a slightly later start to the day.

At least in that moment, it seemed that we were the only people aware of the world. It was one of the few times that I let my guard down, just a little, just enough to soak in the silence.

Clarisse stopped me with a hand on my arm just before we could exit the keep. She was looking at me with uncharacteristic

seriousness. A brief hesitation, half a breath, "You know, for all that I am hard work, I do think of you as a friend." I blinked at her. "And I don't like the thought of one of my friends being in danger for my sake. So don't take any stupid risks, ok?" I couldn't really formulate a response. She quirked a small smile, "Although, if you can try not to humiliate him too badly..."
"No promises, Your Majesty."

And with that we were back to our normal stances. I tried not to let my confusion show on my face. Such a crack in her mask was not like her. Surely, she wasn't worried about this little tiff? I was pretty sure she didn't actually care so much for my safety. This was my job, after all. I could count on one hand the number of times that she had spoken to me so warmly. Literally the day before I had gotten hurt for real and there had been none of this concern. Maybe she was just overtired, leading her to be more emotional than she would normally allow. Or was thinking of the impact on her image if her bodyguard got beaten in an official duel by an ambassador.

I pushed it to the back of my mind as the maids joined us, having been collected by Sera, who took the chance to stick with the group. She caught my eye for a moment when the others weren't looking and held up a small cerus fruit tart, mouthing 'for breakfast after' and grinning as I clearly perked up. Now I really had a reason to get this whole thing over with.

The small party proceeded down towards the designated space for the duel. Should that be a comment on courtly life, that we even have such a place set up? It is a ring set up on the south lawn, marked out by carefully tended flower beds. They are meant to discourage people from crossing the line or trying to leg it if they realise that they aren't winning. Nothing ruder than trampling a flower bed, so some say it doubles the humiliation of such a cowardly act. I reckon nobles are just a bit weird.

Alastair was already there, still in his finery from the party, as was Sir Enhani. That was a shame. Those fabrics would be ruined by mud or blood. Although I hoped to avoid shedding too much of the latter. He sneered as we approached, puffing up like one of the chickens in a temper. "There is still time for your little lapdog to be spared, just apologise for the insult to my person."

Clarisse raised an eyebrow, standing tall amongst the roses, head high despite her choice to wear one of her heavier crowns. "Are you willing to apologise to Lizzie?"

"And if he were?" Enhani spoke, fulfilling his role as bodyguard and second to try and defuse the conflict before it came to violence. Somehow, he didn't seem to hold much hope for a peaceful resolution.

A benevolent smile. "Then I would be more inclined to let this matter drop, provided you returned at once to your kingdom with the understanding that you would not return."

"I don't know why you are acting so high and mighty. I am the wronged party here. You were inhospitable and disrespectful." He was almost frothing at the mouth in indignation. He actually seemed to believe what he was saying. His second looked half a breath away from either slapping him up the back of his head or just facepalming. I doubt this had been included as a possibility in his pre-mission training. Sometimes the hardest part of our job is protecting our charges from themselves.

The Queen's face dropped into barely veiled disgust. "Can you even hear yourself right now?" yeah, she was definitely too tired for civility. "One, you were the one who didn't listen when a woman told you 'no'. Two, you have shown no respect for the ruler of a nation. And three, you were the one who issued the challenge for a duel in the first place. Your aim was off and so you are fighting my bodyguard. Deal with it." The last was snapped out between clenched teeth.

For a moment all went still, those present freezing in the face of her wrath. She did have a bit of a reputation for her temper, which had occasionally caused more than a little bloodshed. Clarisse visibly took a breath, forcing herself back down to faintly bored and irritated by all of the drama.

She turned to me, blatantly dismissing Alastair and his man. "Now, can we get on with this? I know that dawn is the traditional time for these affairs, but I am getting damned hungry and could use some breakfast. As my guard it is your job to see to my welfare, so get this done swiftly so that I don't starve to death."

"Yes, Your Majesty."

I resisted the urge to roll my eyes at her haughty tone. But hey, she was the Queen after all, so if anybody had the right to have a snooty attitude it was her. That was an entitlement which literally came with the territory. I guess that is part of the reason why I would never make a good ruler. I just don't have that level of belief in my own righteousness. Doesn't mean to say that as a quality it isn't phenomenally aggravating at times. The day I have to see her act normal, or gods forbid humble, is the day that the world will come falling down around our ears.

Pushing those thoughts aside, I stepped forwards into the designated duelling ring. The roses trembled as I passed.

Alastair stepped into the area from the opposite side. It was interesting to see that his bodyguard, and acting second, looked rather less than enthusiastic about how the situation was unfolding. I wondered if he had been given orders before this visit to try and keep the king's brother out of trouble. If so, I felt for him on a professional level. My charge could be aggravating enough but at least she wasn't intentionally a git for the sake of it. Normally. At times...

The man was making a grand show of slashing his sword through the air, trying to make the blade whistle in the dawn light. The fact it wasn't working meant either he wasn't as fast as he wanted to appear, or didn't know his sword's make up well enough to realise it didn't have the necessary flexibility.

He eyed me up and down during his little warm up as I stood with folded hands in the centre of the circle. I just knew from his face that he was feeling overconfident by the fact that he had a good head in height over me. Then again, most people tend to be taller than me. Clarisse had once commented that I was travel sized for convenience. I argued it gave me an advantage since I operated just below the average person's eyeline.

Come to think of it, the height that his glove smack had been aimed at would have probably caught Clarisse on the chest rather than her face. I was just unfortunate enough to be the wrong height and so catch the damned thing right across my cheek. It was somewhat of a relief to realise that Alastair did in fact have some small measure of self-protective instincts. If he had hit the Queen in the face in such a way I would have cut off his hand, and then really made his ending hurt.

Those pleasant thoughts aside, I really had to try and focus on the fight I was currently in.

I know that Clarisse asked me not to embarrass him, and that would normally involve hamming up the duel a bit. You know, throwing in the occasional stumble, letting him get a few close hits. This twat though, he kept trying to clash our swords together. I mean... did he not understand that was not the point of such an exercise? With the exhibition he was trying to put on, we would end up with a pair of blunt blades in minutes, and I would be having to do maintenance work on it all night. Or put up with the smithy giving me the longest lecture of my life.

So, I ended up doing a bit of fancy footwork, drawing out the engagement, before getting fed up and just closing the distance.

I would like to say that it was a beautiful moment of controlled violence. Perhaps I should describe how the fabric of my split skirt swirled through the creeping dawn mist, metallic threads catching the glimmers of the rising sun. Would you like to hear how the blood pounded in my veins, adrenaline sour on my tongue? Or that from the corner of my eye, I could see the maids and the Queen watching with wide eyes and bated breath?

Yeah, that would sound much better. It would also be completely fake.

In truth, it was like I was back on the training field, running through another set of practice drills against one of the newer knights. I could see Lizzie and Delilah playing a coin toss game with Sera, whilst Clarisse kept yawning behind her hand. All I did was finally step in close, twist a little to the side, and my blade was resting on my opponent's throat.

At least he had the good sense to freeze, rather than try and escape. From his side of the ring, I could hear his bodyguard huff in exasperation. Alastair himself was panting, whites of his eyes flashing. Damn, either he was a great actor, or he had genuinely believed that this was some great duel. Had he never done this before? If so, he had certainly picked the wrong target to start with.

Clarisse clapped her hands sharply, making my opponent flinch slightly into my blade until a thin bead of blood slid down his neck. Hey, it may have been a basic brawl, but I of course keep my blades in top condition.

"I hereby declare my bodyguard, Nina, victorious. Honour has been restored. Alastair, you will withdraw from this field, and thence from my dominion." She shot him a poisonously sweet smile, "And I will of course be writing to your King with a full report of how you have conducted yourself within our borders."

At her motion, I stepped back and sheathed my sword. A bare nod of a bow later, and I returned to my customary place half a pace behind and to the left of my Queen. I did not turn to look back at him as we walked out of the arena. Clarisse was already focussed again on thoughts of breakfast, Delilah and Lizzie chattering about the timetable for the day.

Sera sidled up, pressed the tart into my hands with a small smile, and then darted off ahead of the group.

The whole thing had been hardly worth note in the grand scheme of things. That at least seemed the general consensus. I had the sense, deep in my gut, that it wouldn't turn out that way in the end.

CHAPTER NINE: SOME YOU LOSE

We were partway through another tedious hearing of court grievances when the messenger arrived. The poor kid looked almost ready to drop as he moved to the front of the audience queue, pushing past nobles who grumbled and only made way with prolonged, irritated, huffing. To be fair he had probably run as fast as possible from his masters.

All eyes were fixed on the letter clutched in his hand, tight enough that the paper was slightly crumpled in his fist.

Nothing short of dire news would be a reasonable excuse to come barging in unexpectedly like that. I could already see those present perking up like hounds who just caught the scent of game on the wind, despite all of their apparent annoyance. There were times when I wondered just what all these people did with their daily lives, as it seemed suggestions of scandal were their life blood. Or at least their only form of amusement.

Delilah gracefully intercepted the boy, taking the envelope to pass on to Clarisse and ushering the kid over to Serafina to be taken care of. The current plaintiff took the hint to back off for the time being. The Queen would no doubt make it up to them later, and the chance of being on the front line of gossip tended to be impossible for them to resist.

I watched with narrowed eyes as the contents of the letter were quickly scanned through, resulting in flared nostrils from Clarisse. If looks could kill, then I would currently be tasking Hanson with digging a grave. Such tasks would be beneath me of course. By at least six feet.

I took the chance to step closer, lowering my voice so we could talk without broadcasting to the rest of the room. Lizzie was already doing an admirable job of interacting with those closest to the throne so that they would be unable to eavesdrop.

"What does it say?"

She responded through gritted teeth. "It's from Magda, about the... incident at my re-swearing." For a moment I thought of the duel, then remembered what had gone on earlier in the day. In hindsight it really had been a hectic celebration. "The examination of the bolt suggests that it was in fact made in Namet. The crossbow however is an adapted design, something about the mechanism was based on their styles, but the manufacturing is undeniably from us."

Shit. Well, that was not good. If you wanted proof of international interference in our affairs, then this was practically served up on a silver platter. Even worse, as far as evidence against certain members of court went, this was pretty damning. The list of people recently caught dealing with Namet in a less than savoury way was remarkably short. Anar curse the bastard.

"What are you going to do next?"

"What do *you* think I should do?" I didn't bother to answer that. She wasn't really asking my opinion after all. If anything, it was a game she sometimes liked to play, almost as if she hoped I would say the wrong thing and she could prove herself smarter. I never understood why she felt the need to play such tricks. They served no purpose. So instead, I said nothing, waiting for her to answer her own question.

Mine was not to reason why. My lot was simply to stop people from killing her. If she insisted on making potential enemies with her choices, then I simply was more secure in my job.

That said, if Lord Arner was really the one behind all this, then I was personally furious with him. I had warned him. His nephew did not deserve the shit storm which was swiftly coming his way. With the obvious manner in which the news had been delivered, there would not be a lot of time for formulating a response. As soon as word got around that something had happened the guilty party was likely to cut and run.

My suspicions were confirmed as Clarisse once again read through the missive, muttering under her breath about what she was going to do to Lord Arner. And if I knew her at all she would want the outcome, one way or another, to be fairly public. Such treachery required an open response. People would begin whispering soon since news tended to spread faster than a wildfire. It would be vital that she direct the way that the story was told.

All that being said, it meant that I would have a dreadfully small window of opportunity here. Perhaps just long enough to do a quick perimeter check of the castle. Maybe even bump into that puppyish young man who dogged my steps on the regular, and his own persistent shadow. And if the result of that meeting was that certain people decided to take a quick visit to Magda, thence to a well-earned holiday, then it was on them.

It was a small treason. Should I be guilty for how naturally it came to me?

"Your Majesty, allow me to dispatch the guards to bring him to you."

"Yes." There was almost a furious glee to her tone, "Have them bring him before me so we can settle this once and for all. I gave him a chance and he has spat in my face. This must not stand."

I inclined my head in deference, turning to wave Hanson and Jeremy closer. It was purely by Inar's grace that they had both been on duty for the day. Possibly the universe did not have such a vicious vendetta against me after all. I told Jeremy that he was to take a couple of his most trusted men and bring Lord Arner in, receiving a salute in response before he hurried off about his duty.

I managed to unobtrusively snag Hanson before he could follow, fixing my eyes on his. "Now listen to me." He squirmed in my grip to no avail. Thankfully no one seemed to notice the small struggle. "You are to perform the task appointed to you by your Queen. To bring *Lord Arner* to the throne room." I made sure to stress the correct parts of the sentence. At last his eyes widened in apparent understanding. That was a relief. I was worried for a moment that I had trained him to be stupid. Or at least hit him in the head a few times too many. "And I would recommend that anybody else who could possibly be close by to the man should be advised to maybe visit another part of the castle for a while. I hear Duchess Magda is lonely and could use a companion."

If I am honest, I couldn't quite tell what the expression on his face really was. It was somewhere between confusion, fear, relief... I have never been the best at reading such emotions when they are directed at me. At the very least he scarpered off with an impressive turn of speed for all that he was weaving through the still sizable crowd.

Considering the extent of the castle, it was a credit to Jeremy's abilities how quickly he returned with the desired Lord. Upon their entrance the court dissolved into what they may have fondly hoped to be whispers. It was more like being amidst a flock of startled hens. The noise only got worse when Arner was thrown to the floor, landing prostrate before his monarch. A sharp word from the Queen had the nobles swiftly, if reluctantly, draining from the room.

Clarisse was pacing in front of the dais, footsteps echoing in the wake of her court's departure. Lord Arner was still in same position as before, not a muscle moved despite the overbearing presence of his sovereign's displeasure.

I turned my attention to scanning the room, making sure that her various nobles had in fact left, even though that I was almost certain they would be pressing their ears to the doors. From the corner of my eye, I could just see the slight ripple of wind on one of the hanging cloaks which gave away Mag's presence at the secret entrance to the room. It was a tiny slip way which almost nobody knew about. She used it shamelessly to get the inside track on all affairs of court. I only hoped that Hanson and Samda had reached her before she left her chambers, and been able to set things in place. Just in case.

Clarisse finally stopped partway through her steps, and I only realised then that she had been speaking the whole time. Perhaps she had been making clear her position? Outlining the limitations and expectations under which she was operating. Her station was such an eternally precarious one after all. And from all that we could tell, his crimes were somewhere on the scale between 'severe' and 'unforgivable'.

At last, she paused her endless trail, finally looking directly at her erstwhile councillor. I wondered if from her position she could see the same bald patch that insisted on catching my eye. Such notions were dispelled as she took a deeply steadying breath, looking him dead in the eye if only for a split second. I still reckon it counted.

"As such, the court has decreed that your actions are an act of highest treason." There was a steel to her words, a harsh tang to the way she spoke. She could have been made from clockwork herself as that mouse had been so long ago. Going through the motions as dictated by circumstance for the amusement of others watching.

Lord Arner managed to hold position, not moving a muscle aside from the faint flinch on the very hinge of his jaw. "It was… I won't say an honest one, but is was simply a mistake. A gamble for which the dice did not fall as I had hoped. Is that not the nature of business?"

I almost gaped at him. Was he really confessing to trying to assassinate the Queen? And saying it was for profit? I wanted to hiss at him to shut his mouth. It made no sense. There was no reason why he should so quickly take the blame. This was not like him. He was the sort of man who would try to weasel out of things, or at least buy himself enough time to gain some leverage. He was a vicious little slime, true, but one who had always had an end game in mind and that I could at least respect in its own right.

Once again Clarisse's eye contact broke. Was she confused as well? Did she suspect that there could be something else going on here?

For a moment, she attempted to fix her attention on the cloaks of the queens of ages passed. Perhaps she intended to feel a sense of power to be drawn from her ancestors. Alas, things so rarely worked out in such a way. Whatever she saw in those bolts of cloth with ages of myth, legend, and history embellished upon them, didn't seem to be enough. She chose instead to look out of one of the windows. "The evidence... cannot be overlooked. No one can prove how deeply your intentions ran... and so..."

Now Lord Arner finally moved, throwing himself face down upon the rough-hewn planks of the throne room. Legend stated that they were the very same boards upon which the first subjects had sworn fealty to the Crown. To this day they were the pieces stood upon at every coronation and re-swearing ceremony. To suggest that they were subtly replaced every now and then so that the floor didn't drop out from beneath the throne was to some people akin to the harshest blasphemy. It was the sort of idea which I didn't want to get into fights over for the simple aggravation of trying to argue logic to believers.

The gesture which Arner was making now was understandable by all to be heavily weighted with meaning and subordination. The final plea for clemency even if tradition held that it should never be on one's own behalf. That was the rule with such issues after all. To beg for your own life was beyond cowardice. And where was the honour in such a thing? Perhaps such a man really could have plotted to shoot his Queen in the back. But then again, why would he take such a risk?

Clarisse's gaze remained fixed on the horizon beyond my eyes.

He seemed to notice the chilling atmosphere, pressing his forehead hard enough into the wood that I feared any resulting bruises would in fact scar. "Please. We will leave court, and your gracious sight, forever. And be forgotten happily."

Is it bad that I only realised then exactly who he was pleading on behalf of? As I have said, I know his nephew. A sunshine boy of seventeen summers, with ink on his fingers and grease beneath his nails. A child of ingenious rodents and unerring eyes. We all knew that his name had been assigned to many layers of the paperwork, as discovered over the whole spy situation. Hanson had ranted at his friend for an hour about the importance of knowing what he was signing.

Despite the slight suspicion in the back of my mind, I refused to ask if anybody had compared relative signatures. Samda was known for his skill, and would no doubt be held to some measure of fault. There was no way that people would believe he wasn't involved.

The Queen took a deep breath through her nose, finally turning back to face the room if not her subject. "You may keep your life. That is all that I would be able to negotiate from the court and council, and that only if the full details are not made known." She meant from the nobles. Even if she had been inclined towards hesitation, it would have shown a dangerous precedent to any other ambitious courtiers. History was littered after all with the rusted crowns of those who thought it could never happen, that the gilding could last forever.

The way that it was worded made it abundantly clear that the argument had already been had. He simply had not been able to speak for himself. Would that have helped? To bring the council in and let him plead his case before them? Or would it simply have made everybody too awkward in his presence to let the debate continue long enough to wear people down towards mercy?

When he spoke again it was with a hoarse voice, as if he had used a lifetime's yells in one breath. "And my nephew?""
At least her eyes fixed on his face for once. "Red is on the ledger. And so, it must be paid in kind."

She didn't look my way, didn't see how my eyes were now the ones narrowing ever so slightly, for all that I kept the rest of my features blank.

"But..." the word was heavy with inference. Clarisse was watching him almost curiously to see what his reaction to the unspoken suggestion would be.

I hadn't truly appreciated just how pale a person could turn without having a length of iron shoved into an internal organ. It was a cruel mercy. The illusion that he had a choice over saving himself at the expense of Samda. I suppose it was one way to try and offer back a modicum of his honour, no matter how stained.

Her face achieved an aspect which I could remember, if only vaguely. It was an expression which my mind found hard to comprehend without wanting to blank out entirely, shut down, until there was only obedience left. It was the face of a monarch, an entity beyond such petty concerns as human allegiance. All was owed to her, all was due, and any who resisted were treasonous or plain stupid. At least, that was how it seemed to me.

When she spoke, it was in a voice rich enough to make banking nations weep, and hard enough that diamond trembled in its' presence. Or perhaps she simply sounded done with all of it. "From now on, your concerns are no care of mine, nor Lizzie, nor Delilah, nor any member of the royal household. I am sorry."

I couldn't bear to look at it anymore, to watch this parody of righteous rule which was the political reality of the woman whom I had sworn to protect. It wasn't the first time; it would by no means be the last. I had reached the grand old age of twenty-six by being pragmatic in a job which did not value such a skill set.

The small door covering Mags' spy point eased closed once again. She had always been able to walk silently, and I didn't bother wasting time to think about where she could have been headed.

Part of me wondered which choice he would make. Either way, his nephew would very soon be under fire. Whether from the guards hunting him down as a suitable tithe for his family's crimes, or from the remaining courtiers for whom he would be a reasonable scape goat for their own schemes. If a full investigation was publicly launched before this affair could be quietly settled and then presented as a finished incident, there would no doubt be a sudden rush of 'pin the scheme on the criminal'. There were always so many half baked ideas and unfinished plans floating around which could cause issues to individuals further down the line. It was remarkable how, when someone got caught, it quickly became evident that they had been the root of all evil for some time. The sole wrong doer amongst this court of saints. The only cat amongst the pigeons. And they would swear it with such earnest faces if it came down to a trial.

Whatever came to pass, Samda did not have long left before he would find himself in real danger. Would he stay? Try to salvage a little of his standing? Or would he run? If he chose that option, I could only wish him damned fast feet.

I shifted just enough out of my usual stance that the Queen's eyes darted to me of their own accord. I tilted my head towards the main doors, just beyond which the Court were no doubt growing restless. Clarisse had already afforded Arner more privacy than most would consider warranted. They were hungry for his fall. "They are waiting." My words were gravelly even to my own ears. I could not care.

Lord Arner grew still. Not for the first time, I wished that I could see inside his mind to know what he was thinking. It was something I had warned Clarisse against so many times- backing people into a corner. They were the ones who had nothing left to lose, the most unpredictable, the most likely that you would only realise had been stretched too far when they snapped back to leave a welt upon your skin.

The man looked upon his Queen, and after a moment of direct eye contact, he inclined his head in a truly elegant gesture of subservience. "Farewell. Your Majesty." His tone was one which would stay with me. It was so rare, after all, that I would hear a person speak with such certainty, such poise, the complete acceptance of the situation in which they found themselves.

Clarisse took a moment, seeming almost taken aback, before she nodded in apparent acceptance of what it was that he was really intending to say.

I would like to claim that I could understand where he was coming from. That his struggles had a meaning and value beyond this tale which I am telling so poorly.

But that would not be honest.

He was escorted from the throne room by Jeremy, through the whispering crowd just beyond the door. A night imprisoned in the east tower, and then an execution at dawn. Traditional. It took time to erect a scaffold, ensure that enough people would accept the invitation to attend. Just enough time for a man to make a decision.

All I can claim, is that I passed along the word for the Night Watch to keep an eye out. They made sure to clear the evidence of his final choice before Clarisse awoke the next morning. Debts are such an ugly thing, so unsightly to settle and unsettling to see. Red had been paid with red, alongside tiny flecks of white bone in interest, left on the cobblestones at the base of the tower.

The guards were less poetic in how they viewed the Lord's choice.

Nobility of sacrifice takes second place to the realities of cleaning up what mortal remains… remained?

His nephew vanished into the shadows before dawn, leaving

only a small collection of cogs in his rooms. For some strange reason, the search party had remarkably little luck in finding any trace of his path. And if Hanson seemed to have a far greater respect for Magda in the wake of everything, then it was simply due to his growing up. The events were in no way related.

CHAPTER TEN: WITH FRIENDS LIKE THESE

"Your Graces, thank you for attending this council. I am sure you are aware of the reason for our gathering."

"Indeed, Your Majesty." The tone was faintly strangled, for all that the head of the council was trying to project an air of calm control. The assorted lords and ladies seated around the ridiculously large table were doing an admirable job of managing not to meet each other's eyes. It was a rare skill which only those most well versed in politics could ever hope to master... Or anybody who had to serve the public on a busy evening, in which case it was a recognised art form.

"What is the latest word from Namet?" as if she didn't already know. The letter had finally arrived that morning, not a bad turnaround time to be honest between expelling the ambassador and hearing from his liege. Of course, Magda had received and already passed on word of its contents before the damn thing had even crossed the border. And yet we still had to sit through this whole song and dance, pretending as if Clarisse hadn't already decided what her course of action would be.

I could hazard a guess as to what the parchment had said. And I doubted it was contained to a single word. Probably more a chain of invective which would make any self-respecting priest blush. The sort of thing which Magda delighted on doing during confession, or at least so I heard. That woman had turned double meanings into a new sub category for bards to study in terrified awe.

The chancellor adjusted his collar with stiff fingers. Everyone was pointedly avoiding casting glances at the seat which stood empty. I would have preferred it to be removed, it was a tripping hazard just sitting there, but apparently Clarisse was keeping it a little longer as a not so subtle reminder regarding the fate of traitors. For all that the details were being intentionally kept vague, everyone knew that the late Lord Arner had intended harm to the Queen. The method didn't matter, nor did speculation on how close he got. If anything, the abundant theories, and the ever more ludicrous stories of the ways in which he was caught, served to keep people's minds off the destabilising situation from the wider political world.

Lady Cecelia cleared her throat, raising the letter and pretending to read the words which she had no doubt already memorised. "The King has expressed extreme displeasure at his brother's treatment. He says that the reaction was far too severe for the offence. In light of the recent… incidents… around the air ships and their impact on his cousin, there is a sense that we are intentionally provoking them."
"What rubbish."

Lizzie and Delilah were giving each other looks across the table, faces speaking subtly. They knew not to directly contradict their Queen in front of the nobles, but it was clear to anyone that there was something they wanted to say. I shifted my weight a little, just enough to get their attention and remind them of the audience.

Clarisse was still speaking as she cast her eye over the maps spread over the table. "He was the one to send an entirely unsuitable ambassador. If he had any intention of strengthening the bond between our countries, then he should have chosen more carefully."

Another awkward throat clearing. At this rate I was going to be expressing concern to the physicians that the entire council had caught some illness off each other. "That as it may be, Your

Majesty, the fact remains that in the eyes of the international community we are acting rather aggressively. At the very least we need to make it explicitly clear that we hold no ill will. Perhaps we could make a gesture of good faith?"

Lizzie tilted her head to one side, "Like accepting his new ambassador with a party or something?"

I felt my eyebrow twitching. Was she trying to be sarcastic? Or funny? Or had she genuinely not remembered that an ambassador at a party had gotten us into this mess in the first place?

Clarisse seemed to be trying to burn a hole in the table with her glare as she stared at the border lines so clearly marked out on the various parchments. "I think we need to make the first move in this instance. Instead of them coming to us, we should go to them."

Lady Cecilia hummed, "We send a representative? I thought we already had one there."

The chancellor nodded, folding his arms across his chest. "We do. Naturally what with Namet being our closest neighbour to the north. However, they have reported some difficulty since the original air ship business became common knowledge."

That made sense. Whenever espionage activity was discovered, the diplomatic envoys were the first suspects. Even if our representative hadn't been actively engaged, it was likely that had at least known that something was going on. After all, that is literally their job. It was possible that switching out our current ambassador for someone new could serve as the opportunity for a fresh start, especially if Clarisse decided to make an example of them. There was a certain level of disgrace attached to being recalled to court. On the other hand, it could either look like she had approved of the moves being made and was withdrawing an agent to safety, or even worse that she had been unaware of what her own operatives were up to.

It was a thorny issue. A truly delicate balance would be needed to resolve it.

Thankfully that did not fall under my remit. That was for diplomats with their specific education and political know how to come up with a solution which benefitted the country or at least saved face. I was only responsible for the Queen.

So naturally she decided to speak up with the idea, "How about I go?" I swear she does things like this just to mess with me. It isn't fair.

At least the other council members seemed about as enthusiastic as I felt. "A state visit? That would..."

She looked around the table, "Assure them of our continued dedication to strengthening the relationship between our countries. For all that there has been some recent unpleasantness between us, we have been friendly nations for generations. Not least because they rely on our timber exports to support their oh so precious air fleet development. And the coal to fuel them. They need us. And we don't need unnecessary conflict."

For all that she sounded convinced of her points, the others in the room seemed less than enthusiastic.

"Even so..." the chancellor was doing such acrobatic feats to still avoid looking Clarisse in the eye that I was scared he was going to sprain something.

She raised a hand, pre-emptively cutting off whatever arguments could have been forthcoming. "We will of course discuss this further, however for now I would like you to start coming up with a potential outline for the visit. Provided they are amenable, we will make sure that we have a pleasant tour and perhaps even update a couple of our treaties."

It was said with such assurance that there really wasn't much which the chancellor could say in response. The others around the table all looked as if they had been struck by the same, sudden stomach ache.

That's the trouble with those in ultimate power. They believe their own nonsense enough and everyone either gets sucked in along with them, or at least can't find a way to gainsay the plan without losing face of their own. This was a typical demonstration, the council simply inclining their heads in the face of her decisive order. "Wise as ever, Your Highness."

They bowed low as she stood from her chair at the head of the table. Delilah and Lizzie fell into step behind her, holding their tongues until we had withdrawn into her inner chamber. It was a lovely room, all wide windows which gave beautiful views over the fields beyond the castle walls. Even I could appreciate them as the location in regard to the layout of the keep made it impossible for anybody to take a pot shot through those same windows.

The maids settled themselves on their usual perches, as Clarisse all but threw herself onto a low sofa. I took up my customary position at the corner of the piece of furniture. It gave me clear lines of sight to every aspect of the room. It also put me within easy reach of the fruit bowl which sat on a side table. Popping a strawberry into my mouth, purely to check the fruit was safe to eat naturally, I waited for the fireworks.

Delilah was the first one to speak up, "Clarisse… this visit…"
"Oh don't tell me you think it is unwise as well?"
"I am just not sure that it is the right move at this time. Tensions are high at the moment. Surely we could think of another way to smooth things over?"
"What, write him a letter to say sorry that your brother is a dick and please don't hate us?"

Lizzie coughed into one hand delicately, "To be fair it was one of our Lords who started the whole issue."

Clarisse blatantly chose to ignore that fact. She was already at the point of jumping back to her feet to pace, hands waving to punctuate her points. "I will not have the world thinking that we are being petty. We need our alliance with Namet. That is a simple fact. And if I go in person, I can make sure that nothing else gets messed up. Surely you must see that this is the right move."

As much as I hated it, I could see the others looking at me to try and talk some sense into her. This was not going to go well. Then again, I am sworn to do my utmost to protect the Queen from harm. Let's call my input an attempt to neutralise a threat before it had a chance to fully materialise.

"Your Majesty... Clarisse... I don't agree." She whipped around to glare at me now. Perhaps that had been too blunt. "I think that your intention is good, and we definitely need to make some gesture of goodwill. Maybe agree to meet at a neutral location? We could offer to host a joint regatta on the lake for instance?" my imagination ran a bit dry there. Party planning was not my strong suit. However, I did remember something similar being done according to Magda when trade talks had stalled between the countries. The lake which crossed the borders was a shared location, and the events thrown there every spring and summer were a fantastic celebration of mutual cultures.

Lizzie at least seemed to be liking the suggestion, already eagerly nodding. "That would be a better option perhaps. It will be easier for each side to put on a display. I just worry that by going in person it will look as if you are apologizing for your actions. It could seem a little... desperate?"

Clarisse's eyes flared warningly at that. Her damned pride was always a thorny character trait to try and navigate. Liz was definitely treading a fine line. Delilah realised, speaking up as well, "I think they are right. Going in person might not be the best idea at the moment. We could do something on the lake instead, use it as an initial overture, and if thing go well, then we can then arrange a state visit."

I could all but watch the gears clicking through her brain like one of Samda's mice as she thought it through, apparently seeing the sense in what we were saying. I mean, it was a good point.

To go from a disagreement over an ambassador to a full state visit? It just didn't seem to track right. It could very easily set the wrong tone. The one thing to know with diplomatic issues was that fixing them was never a fast thing. It took time, with teams of people on each side deciding what was reasonable, and more importantly, how it would get reported on to their respective countries. The council would no doubt be driving themselves to distraction for the next few days to work out all of the details, but less so than trying to hash out a full official visit.

And who said that I never learnt anything? Listening in to so many years of such debates had apparently rubbed off on me more than I would normally be willing to admit. I took another swipe at the fruit bowl, securing a small handful of grapes, and popping one into my mouth as a reward.

A knock at the door interrupted the discussion. Serafina poked her head around the jamb, waiting until Clarisse waved her forwards to slip inside and close the door behind her so that the councillors wouldn't be able to overhear. From the brief glimpse I caught, it was clear that their poor scribes were already getting a fair bit of exercise in fetching reams of logistics reports.

Serafina curtsied low, "Your Highness." She held out a letter. It was still sealed, the crest on the wax clearly showing the mark of our ambassador in Namet. I raised an eyebrow. Talk about dramatic timing. I couldn't help but wonder how it had even been delivered without anyone giving forewarning. Perhaps Magda was slipping.

Clarisse waved at Delilah to take it, dismissing Serafina with a curt nod. I had always wondered what happened between those two. I still vaguely remembered how close they had been before the fire. But then, tragedy does change people.

Delilah opening the message brought me back to the present. She scanned it for a moment, before taking a breath and starting to read.

"Your Royal Highness, Queen Clarisse, Lady of the Gilded

Throne, High Priestess..."

"Skip all the openings."

"Right." She bit her lip, and I couldn't help but wonder if she was thinking of the same incident that I was.

A few months before, the maids had been bored whilst catching up with correspondence and begun making up exaggerated titles for each other. There may have been an excess of cider involved. When Lizzie had been declared 'Mistress of the Frog Catchers' the whole evening had quickly spiralled out of control. I still wasn't sure how many of them had been technically made official before they had all sobered up. It was enough that formal letters took significantly longer to draft these days and the scribes cursed their quills during treatise amendments.

"It is with regret that I must inform you of rising tension in the capital of Namet." Well that was no surprise. "The report which Alastair gave before the court upon his return was rather damning of your actions and character. The King is most disquieted by the apparent disrespect which has now been shown to two members of his family. He has made it clear that unless a significant overture is made, then the continued lenient trade between our countries is not necessarily untouchable..."

Clarisse held a hand to stop the recitation. She rubbed at her head with one hand. "So much for those hopes. I think my first instinct was right. This is going to require the personal touch. And from the sounds of it we need to move quickly. How soon do you think we can pull this together?"

She was already looking back towards the door which led to the council chamber. They were not going to like the accelerated timetable. At least before they could have presented the plan, a fault could have been found, the lake option re-offered as an apparent stroke of inspiration... all would have been appeased. I could see those hopes drying up into dust before my very eyes.

"Clarisse, take a second. Really think this through. I don't think that this is the right step to take at this time."

She tutted at me, "Look, all I need you to do is focus on the security side of things. I know this is going to be a bit of extra work for you but that is your job." It was said with a patronising smirk.

"I just..."

"Larry, you aren't thinking this all the way through." I couldn't help but wince a little internally at Lizzie's choice of words. The only time they were allowed to use her nick name was when things were decidedly calmer than the current situation. Delilah found herself moving forwards just a little, hands raised placatingly. "Whilst a state visit has its merits, there are surely other avenues to explore first-"

My head snapped to the side. The maids fell silent as the slight echo of skin on skin bounced around those glorious windows. From the new angle of my eyeline I could see the clouds starting to collect over the furthest fields. Perhaps it would rain soon.

My cheek stung ever so slightly. It was strange- despite the fact that the bolt wound from earlier was still healing, the impact of being slapped hurt more. It had been a while since the last time that had happened. The maids were ladies in their own right after all, both from powerful families who would no doubt take extra notice and offence should any harm befall their precious daughters. And a Queen had to vent her frustration somehow.

Lizzie looked at me with wide eyes, whilst Delilah had hers riveted on her seething Queen.

I loosened my jaw a little, running my tongue along the back of my teeth. No real harm done. No doubt the maids would lend a hand if a mark really started to show. They were both so expert at make up after all. If they could make themselves look like the Queen on a moment's notice, they could certainly hide the evidence of the woman's temper.

Just another hazard of the job.

I said nothing, simply setting my grapes back in the bowl and straightening up once again. Clarisse was not looking at me for all that her posture was rigid and unyielding. No doubt when she calmed down it would be all apologies and vague embarrassment for the loss of composure.

In the meantime, it seemed that we had a state visit to get planning. The council were going to love this...

CHAPTER ELEVEN: SOAR BECOMES SOUR WITH U

"Seriously?"

The hull of the airship reared high above us, clearly modelled after the grand galleons depicted on the cloaks of old. Considering the fact that the country was landlocked, aside from a small section of the Great Lake, naval power had never really been something to strive for. It was part of the reason why the airships had been such a key attraction for royal investment. It was a mode of transport that would open a completely new way of trade across many nations, by being able to travel so much faster than by overland caravan. Harder to tax for crossing over other country's airspace as well, seeing as how as of yet there was no solid deterrent for doing so.

Personally, I rather enjoy a good overland stretch. Perhaps it is simply a holdover from the culture of when I was a very young child, but the caravans which snake their way across the world are things of beautiful mystery. Hell, I had even enjoyed our ride out from the castle before dawn had truly broken. Somehow Hanson had even managed to drag himself out of bed in time to volunteer as a page and see to our horses before we set out.

Just as well, since it meant I could make a point of setting him homework. His eyes had gleamed when I handed over a new knife throwing set for him to drill with until I got back. We weren't going to be gone for too long, but it would be good to see how much he could improve whilst we were away. He had grinned far too happily for such an early hour.

We were a small group for this envoy, at least in part due to the short notice of the trip. I couldn't help but wonder if Clarisse had done it on purpose. She had rather less patience than normal for the council these days, most especially when they were weighing in on what she should or should not be doing. In fact, she had seemed almost elated to mount up at a time when any creature with an ounce of sense would still be firmly unconscious. There was an almost vicious flee on her face as the clatter of horse shoes on cobbles bounced around the courtyard when we set off. That sound would no doubt ensure everybody within the castle was startled awake. Queens are able to take pettiness to a whole new level.

All that said, I did enjoy the morning ride. That is the sort of expedition which I can happily take part in.

Air travel, however, I do not trust.

And I certainly did not think it a good idea to take an airship to our neighbouring country considering what one of the most recent conflicts between us had centred around. Clarisse could argue all she wanted that it was a purely practical decision; how it would make the visit so much faster, would be a point of common interest... honestly I stopped paying attention.

I knew what it was really about, as did Delilah and Lizzie. She wanted to show off what we could do. To make a statement that we were capable of standing toe to toe with them despite their supposed monopoly. It wasn't going to work. If the reports coming from Namet were anything to go by, their technology was so far beyond ours again already that we would only be showing how far we still had to go to even eat their dust. It was why Arner had chosen them to poach from in the first place.

And we were theoretically meant to be on a peace building mission. Now was not the time for making statements- other than a dignified apology.

Nevertheless, even I couldn't deny that the ship did look rather imposing as she sat in the middle of a field.

Since we were trying to keep this visit relatively on the down, low the council had elected not to let the party disembark from one of the official ports. Too high a risk was the argument, and to be fair there was some truth to that assessment. Ports of any kind were always a bloody nightmare for anybody in my line of work. With so many people coming and going at any one point, total control and maintaining a secure perimeter was a pipe dream. That, and the air ship ports were rather ramshackle affairs still, what with the industry only in its early phases at least in Tartyn. All in all not the best idea for funnelling a royal party through on short notice.

Now a random field? That I could do.

In the slowly wakening dawn, it didn't take overly long to load on the various pieces of luggage. The guards were helping, not wanting to have extra workers around, and I could hear Jeremy grumbling about how much could dresses possibly weigh? I smirked at him as I passed, making a point to take one of the bags from him, hoist it over my shoulder, and saunter up the gangplank. I could feel him glaring at my back.

Some of the decisions around this trip had certainly gotten a few raised eyebrows from myself and the maids, let alone the council. We were on a diplomatic mission to one of our allies, even if there had been some tensions between us for a few months. So why were there all the extra precautions? Normally it was hard enough to get her to agree to the usual escorts on a land-based journey, and even then there were plenty of rolled eyes involved. The fact that in the relatively brief planning session Clarisse had deferred to all of my security points got more than a couple of questioning looks.

All I could think was that something had her spooked. There was something that she knew that she wasn't sharing with the rest of us. And that pissed me off. It is my job to take care of her, to watch out for her, and I can't do that without all the relevant information. She likes doing this for some stupid reason, to push my limits and test my buttons and be deliberately unhelpful. She tells us that there are things which as Queen only she needs to know. I think she just likes the power of it.

It was true that we had received warnings about recent intelligence reports, stating that an unusual amount of soldiers had been spotted at the towns nearest to the lake. Which was in turn fairly close to our borders. The reporting agents weren't sure why. Their best guess was that some training exercise was planned over the lake, but it was still cause for concern. It had in fact been the tipping point for the council signing off on this whole venture: to get it from the horse's mouth so to speak.

Because one monarch would never lie to another's face only to stab them in the back later.

Still, according to tradition and a few highly irritating clauses in the constitution, a peace or at the very least non-aggression pact, could only be signed by the reigning Queen in order to be legal. And so, we are back to complicated.

That is of course aside from whatever nonsense had Clarisse's hackles raised. At least I could take some grim satisfaction in it all. Meanwhile, we had a ship to board.

From what I could understand of Hanson and Samda's frantic gabbling from the previous few months, the ship would be taken into the sky using the massive balloon of gases which dominated the overhead of the vessel. Looking on it as we drew closer, all I had thought was that such a feat went against several natural laws. The body of the ship itself was wooden, carved with many intricate flourishes along the railings and around the section which was no doubt the cabin areas. The balloon itself had even been painted to look like some sort of giant fish, for all that it was draped in nets to help secure it in place relative to the deck.

The secondary ship was much plainer, possibly some sort of

repurposed trader vessel which had been pressed into service for queen and country. Her canvas was the uniform yellowed white which you saw on any travelling vehicle be it on land, air, or sea. She would no doubt be sturdy, reliable, but not the lady of the sky which appearance of her counterpart boasted.

Both were decked out with a selection of sails around the main body, a larger one towards the stern and a smaller at the prow. I was more taken by the large, wing-like canvas stretches which were resting on the grass either side. No doubt in the air she would be manoeuvrable, able to glide through the thermals like a gull on the wing as she used those sails to catch every breeze. Whilst on the ground she looked rather more like a dead duck.

I could just see Clarisse eyeing up the pair of vessels and no doubt grumbling at the flight assignments. It was all part of the standard security plan for such journeys. Clarisse would be travelling on the secondary ship, which meant of course that Serafina and I would be joining her. Delilah and Lizzie would be travelling in style. That way there would be less time for anybody to pull anything to potentially cause harm to the royal party. It was by no means fool proof, but any extra bit of safety which I could impose on this ridiculous venture was welcome in my book.

Perhaps it is morbid, but by splitting up in this way we could increase our chances of survival in case something did go wrong. Also, with Delilah and Lizzie able to pass for Clarisse, it would be easy to divert attention to them when we docked at the other side. Whilst all eyes were on the supposed royal group, I could get Clarisse to a secure location and turned back into full monarch mode in time for the welcoming speeches.

Because that all sounds so easy when you say it in one go.

Frankly, take Clarisse out of context and pretty much anyone could be the Queen. At least in terms of how she looks. Not many outside of the court would be able to pick her out of a line up- they only have the portrait on coins to go from in the main, and many of those were struck under previous reigns. I still believe that part of the reason why only Queens are allowed to claim the throne is so that they don't have to remint coins.

And the likelihood of anybody recognising the ruse let along calling it out? Be honest- to stand before your peers and accuse the woman in a ball gown and crown of not being who she claimed to be? Takes a special sort of brave and stupid.

All of which worked in our favour on trips such as this. Even her elaborate hairstyles were all down to wigs, so we could literally switch Clarisse for Delilah between disembarking and walking into the throne room and nobody would see a hair out of place. Even if it did require a bit of quick costume management.

Thankfully there was very little time for grumbling considering the time pressures that we were under, meaning I had the perfect excuse to bundle Clarisse up the gangplank and into the Captain's cabin. Which he had naturally given up with a smile of gratitude for the inconvenience.

He seemed somewhat adorably proud about the fact that his ship would be transporting the Queen. I mean, I couldn't blame him at all- he would be more than handsomely paid, and it was the sort of story which would get him free drinks for years after. Seeing someone built like an ox almost swooning as the sovereign passed him by was a tad unnerving. If he did pass out from sheer happiness I wouldn't be surprised if he accidentally squashed Sera.

The lieutenant was less in raptures, seeming to be the one actually directing the others about pre take off procedures. It was my turn to repress a grin as he chivvied the guards along regarding how best to stow things for even weight distribution. From the look of it, Jeremy's patience was already ebbing.

The crews on these vessels were rather smaller than sea faring versions. It was part of why merchant guilds were all but drooling over the design improvements which were coming out every few months. Less workers meant less wages and so higher profits. Of course, that is what drives any concept of progress as we understand it. At least by always keeping aware of the bottom line they make sure to keep rising if only for their own pride.

Despite only having a few other people on board aside from ourselves, they still managed to have the ship launched in only a handful of minutes. It was hard to spot on first approach, but apparently the ships had been hovering just over the grass of the field rather than settling into the mud. All the captains had to do on each was to crank a handle, which released the securing lines, to send us slowly climbing into the skies.

I had heard that in Rhean, they had actually set up some sort of massive tower to act as the sky port. The idea was that ships could rest in slipways high enough up that when it was time to launch they could just sort of roll out into the sky. I wondered how long it had taken them to figure out the best way to get cargo up that high. Samda had babbled on and on about it once-talking winches and pulleys and platforms until I almost begged him to stop. It was a highly effective interrogation technique now I thought about it.

He would no doubt have had a running commentary going if he had been here to see this. I shook the thought away.

Some childish part of me really wanted to lean over the edge of the railing and wave at those we were leaving far below. To my right I could see the other ship rising, their ascent seeming slightly smoother than our own. I guess that was due to the larger nature of that vessel which could help steady it against any gusts of wind.

Delilah had no reservations about waving to us from her deck, even as Lizzie raced to the other side and heaved her breakfast over the railing. Until the day I die I will maintain that I did not feel the slightest bit queasy as the deck trembled beneath my feet. Not at all. Anyone who says otherwise is a dirty liar. And I only grew pale because it gets significantly colder the higher you rise.

They used to tell stories around the hearths I knew as a young child, about someone who dared to climb a mountain preferred by the goddess Anar, only to be burned up by the sun before they could reach the top. Clearly whoever had told it never went above a certain elevation.

I was particularly glad to pull out my winter travelling cloak and wrap it around my shoulders.

The captain and the helmsman were relatively unscathed by the harsh conditions. I guess they were used to it, each wearing only a lightly fleece lined leather coat. Then again, their faces did glint with what looked suspiciously like some sort of fat smeared across their exposed skin to negate the impact of the wind. Sensible. I didn't have a chance of convincing Clarisse to do the same. Some battels weren't even worth considering.

Serafina had almost instantly retreated below, muttering something about wanting to sit closer to the generators and engine heat to keep warm.

By our calculations, this little convoy would only take two days to reach Namet's second largest city, which had been agreed as the meeting point. At least it was on the shores of the Great Lake, meaning that there would be plenty of water-based amusements to act as a common ground for our respective monarchs and courts. It seemed there were more of my suggestions being used than anyone had expected.

Sometimes diplomacy was shooting your neighbours' waterfowl. And that was one of many reasons why I would never understand politics.

CHAPTER TWELVE: TELL YOUR SECRETS TO THE SKIES

It is very strange to watch the sun setting when you yourself are drifting through the air. The evening was beautifully clear, only a few whisps of cloud trailing nearby and giving the occasional burst of chilled mist to our skins as we passed through them. The lieutenant had positively beamed when he came up to take a shift at the helm and saw the conditions.

It was fascinating to watch how they steered the ship along the air currents. The main control wheel was actually made up of about five interconnecting systems which operated a whole other set of ropes and pulleys to guide the sails into position. I may have taken a host of mental notes as well as a couple of quick sketches whilst Clarisse settled into her cabin. Hanson would love it, and it would save me having to buy a souvenir or something. Not that I would in the first place of course.

From watching it so closely I had only gotten more impressed by how effortlessly they made it look as we rode the thermals. No doubt it required a high level of skill to be able to handle the variations, and I didn't want to even think about how difficult it would be to get caught in a storm or some such. Horror stories were told about such misfortune.

. Serafina wasn't around to talk with, having apparently come down airsick and so decided to try and sleep in her cabin until she didn't want to throw up anymore. With there being relatively little for me to do, I had been wiling away the time helping out with the preparations for dinner. The cook had been kind enough to let me put my knife skills to domestic use, and then been delighted with how finely slivered the onions were. There was something fantastically comforting about having the scent of herbs on my fingertips and know that they were all being used purely for flavour purposes for a change.

When the stew had been declared ready to both of our satisfaction, I ladled out a couple of portions. The cook made sure to pass me a couple of beakers of cider as well before I headed out of the galley, showing me how specially designed lids fixed to them and the bowls to keep the contents safe in case the deck shook, and I lost balance or something. It was pretty genius in truth. I wanted to get some for when we returned home.

With my cargo safely protected, I made my way over to the figure leaning against the railing like some tragic heroine from bardic tales. Clarisse had let her hair down fully, the wind sighing through it and lifting it from her shoulders to drift around her face. She had found the point on the airship where the wind was strongest it would seem, eyes closed to best enjoy the feeling of it on her skin.

I couldn't blame her really. It was the same look of blissful satisfaction she wore when we rode as fast as our horses could carry us. In that moment there were no cares on her face, the stress lines smoothed from her forehead. She looked like any other young woman.

Tapping her shoulder and ignoring how she flinched, I simply passed her one of the dinner portions and motioned her to come down and sit by the railing. That actually got me a nod of thanks for all that she was clearly disappointed to leave her newfound favourite spot. She dug in, apparently pleasantly surprised by how good it was. Her fingers curled tighter around the bowl to leech out the warmth.

I eagerly scarfed my own serving down, taking a measure of

pride in having helped to make something so enjoyable. For a few minutes neither of us spoke, and the satisfaction of a good meal began to be tinged with that faint awkwardness of a too long silence when there is something to still be talked about. Akin to being at the funeral of someone who had been not particularly well liked.

A heavy sigh, a gulp of the mulled cider, and I finally nudged her shoulder to get her to face me. "Alright, what has got you all twisted up?"

"I don't know what you are talking about." Her eyes skittered away from mine. I thought she had learnt how to lie for diplomatic reasons as a child. If this was how she tried to seem like all was well, then our chances for negotiations with Namet were not looking so great.

"Don't give me that. You have something else going on and you are refusing to tell me what it is. Which means you are being deliberately stupid. I know you." After so many years by her side it was impossible not to. That and it was my responsibility to. "I know every one of your tells and so every time something gets on your nerves or makes you want to laugh when it is inappropriate. And I know when you are scared. So, what gives?"

Clarisse leaned her head back until it was resting against the wood of the railings. Her eyes tracked to the side where the far more ornate airship was mirroring our course. If I squinted, I half imagined that I could see Delilah and Lizzie playing around on the deck. No doubt they were enjoying a bit of breathing room from their Queen. As well as a host of new targets for their amusement.

The woman in question sighed deeply, "It's silly."

I snorted. "Possibly. But you not telling me when it is literally my job to keep you safe? Silly is not the word I would use. And Mags lends me enough books that I have other options to list for you if you would like."

That at least got a quirked lip of amusement. It was one of

the running jokes of the court- Mags' great love of literature. The older nobles talk fondly of the previous Queen's fondness for such stories, and her insistence that the knights in training embroider scenes from them as needlepoint practice. A tradition meant to impart a useful life skill, teach patience, attention to detail, pride in one's own work, being used to best serve the interests of the queen. A tale as old as time.

"I got a letter."
"I see. Now it all makes sense." I nodded wisely, taking another gulp of my cider and doing my best not to choke from inhaling it by accident. "Such a clear and concise report of events. Would you take time out of your busy schedule to instruct the guards so that they can benefit from- "
"You are such an ass, did you know that?" she was actually angry at me for the jibe. Again, nothing new there. I seemed often to be a convenient target. At least if she got to the point of raising a hand then nobody else would witness it.

So I just smiled sweetly, "Yes."

For several breaths it was a stalemate, a standoff. She could snap, sure, slap me across the face and declare the matter done. But I still got the sense that she wanted to talk about it, to share what was on her mind. Even if she would never admit as such. One of us was going to have to be the adult here. There was no way that the Queen of the Realm would do it.

"You got a letter..."
"Urgh! Yes. I got a letter and that is all."
"The contents of which..."

She waved her hands around, almost upsetting the bowl where it rested empty at her side. "It was just a strange letter. It was... like somebody was writing me to say goodbye."
"Before you were going on a diplomatic trip?"
"Don't be like that! It was... I don't even know. Just the sense I got from the words: that it was a final goodbye; that the writer didn't expect me to come back."

It was her facial expression which stopped my next comment from being as biting as the others. There was a genuine upset there, a real issue gnawing at her mind. Whatever had been written was odd enough to make the lines around her mouth tighten, her shoulders slump heavily. I adopted a calmer tone, pulling myself back to professionalism.

"Do you have any idea who it might have been from?"
"No. Believe me, if I had, I would have started asking some pretty pointed questions." She gulped at her drink, steam curling from her lips as the heat contrasted to the growing chill of the air.
"And then told me so that I could investigate further."
"Sure."

The sun was finally dipping beneath the horizon now, sending long shadows streaking back across the ship. The temperature was definitely dropping. Hopefully the small braziers in the cabins would help stave off the worst of it once night truly fell. Although, I for one would be spending a bit of extra time outside despite the potential for ice on my eye lashes. The chance to see the stars from up here was not one that I was willing to miss.

Meanwhile, there were other issues to focus on.

"Can I see it?" it was possible that I could recognise the writing, or a particular turn of phrase used. It wouldn't be the first time. Last year someone had been sending secret admirer notes to Lizzie and she had enlisted my help to find out who. I will give you three guesses which member of the court they got traced back to. Point is a second pair of eyes could spot something new.

Clarisse was already shaking her head, all but mumbling into her cider, "I didn't bring it with me. Seemed like bad luck somehow."

A detective she was not.

As if sensing my disappointment, Clarisse abruptly shifted and clambered to her feet with an aborted groan. No doubt her legs had fallen asleep against the wooden planks of the deck. She downed the last of the mulled cider before passing her dishes to me.

"Deal with those. I am going to get some sleep."

It was as plain a dismissal as she could give. I rolled my eyes hard enough to worry about injuring myself. At her back. I still had to be in close quarters with her for another two days before the maids would be back and able to help diffuse the tension. No need to be idiotic and antagonise her deliberately.

I ducked into the galley just as Serafina made her way out, almost resulting in a clatter of dishes at the small collision. Nothing dropped, fortunately, and she just raised an eyebrow at whatever she saw on my face.

"Queenie giving you trouble?"

"Wouldn't be her if she didn't." I stacked the dishes by the small sink and made to clean them up only to be waved off by the cook. Hands raised in surrender and with a small laugh I chose discretion as the better part of valour. "How are you doing? Feeling better I take it?"

The girl laughed lightly and tucked her cloak a bit more tightly around her thin frame as we wandered back to the railings and watched the world below. "Much better after sleeping. I am finally getting used to it. And to be honest, dinner smelled so good I couldn't resist coming out for some. It is rather nice not having anything pressing to do. Just some light repair work that I have been putting off until a quiet moment. And the view has been something special."

I mirrored her smile, "that is true. This lady of the skies is doing an admirable job." I made sure to raise my voice on the last comment, watching from the corner of my eye as the lieutenant straightened his spine with renewed pride.

Sera was blowing air onto her hands, rubbing them to try and create more heat. She grinned ruefully at me, "I did want to stay out and see what the world looks like in the dark from up here, but I don't think I will be able to hold out for long."

I hummed, "yes, it is getting rather nippy. I wanted to see what the stars would be like from up here but even I can admit that my skin is getting somewhat chilled."
"A polite way of saying that you are freezing your arse off but are too stubborn to admit it."

I laughed a little, unable to deny the accusation. My attention was more drawn to where I could see the moon already rising far bigger and brighter than I had ever seen it before. There was a chill beauty to the sight, and I could have sworn that if I stretched just enough, I would be able to trail my fingertips over its face. The stars were not yet as bright, but no doubt they would soon join in the heavenly display.

Sera just shook her head a little at my apparent wonder, "you know, it is not often that I see you so excited by something." A hand clapped to my shoulder as she moved past me to head below where it would be warmer. "Don't stay out here too long. You need to get your sleep as well after all."

It was a fair point, and I inclined my head in acknowledgement of that. It didn't stop my gaze from turning right back to the skies. I just about saw her from the corner of my eye shaking her head at my folly as she took shelter from the elements. I could feel the lieutenant's eyes on my back for a while when I didn't make a move to retire, but I got the sense that he understood more than my travelling companions. After all, there must be a reason why he kept returning to the heights. Who's to say it wasn't for the sheer love of such moments.

I would eventually go below, and silently crawl into my bunk in Clarisse's cabin, to try and get enough sleep that I would be less inclined to regicide in the morning. But for that moment? Five more minutes.

CHAPTER THIRTEEN: THE UNLUCKY NUMBER

The first inkling that I had, the first tingle to my senses, the first warning on the winds and currents of the universe, that we were absolutely fucked was when the airship exploded. Sometimes the fates are subtle. Sometimes they blow a hole in your mode of transport whilst you are hundreds of feet above the ground.

The fact that I was thrown from my bunk rather than being torn to shreds at once by shrapnel was something to thank Inar for later. During the moment itself I was rather more concerned with doing internal inventory that I was still alive, and trying to wriggle out from underneath Clarisse. At least she had landed on top of me. If she had survived the initial explosion only to crack her head on a dresser and died, I would never hear the end of it from Mags.

Her bleariness I could put down to being so abruptly awakened. Judging by how loud she had been snoring, she had been sleeping deeply. I had just managed to get her on her feet and semi alert when Serafina began hammering on the door. Unlocking it, I got an armful of hysterically screaming maid. From what I could gather, something in the cargo hold had blown up and now the ship was losing altitude.

At the end of the passage where it opened out onto the deck, I could see the handful of crew members running around in barely restrained panic. The lieutenant's voice was bellowing orders and Sera gabbled something about the captain having been caught and killed in the blast.

The deck was shaking beneath my feet, a sickening tremor which seemed to echo right into my gut. There was a definite tilt now as well as the ship began to list sideways through the air. Grabbing Clarisse's hand, and the pack I always kept ready at the end of my bunk, I motioned for Sera to follow as I dragged the Queen out onto the deck. Staying in the cabin would do no good, especially if this got any worse.

Out in the open the night wind slammed into us with howling vengeance. I was immensely grateful that we had all apparently opted to sleep in our day clothes since nightwear would have had no chance of keeping us warm. At these altitudes the cold had a much greater bite, and I could see the Queen's nose already turning red.

Through the darkness I saw something else which made the pit drop out of my stomach. This high up the only lights for us to see by were the lanterns around the deck, the stars, the moon, and the corresponding lanterns on the lead ship in the convoy which were growing steadily closer as we continued to career sideways through the air.

"We're gonna crash into the other ship!"
"What?!"
"At the rate we are going we are going to hit them and take the whole lot down. You have to order the lieutenant to abandon ship and let it go before this ends in complete disaster!"

I could see how it was going to go. For all that the watch on the lead ship had probably noticed that something was wrong and were no doubt doing their best to start correcting their course, with the winds around us there would be very little room to manoeuvre. We could try to lose altitude, but with the ships having already drifted so close, there was not enough time for it to be a gentle decline. The rate of drop we needed to evade would in turn probably cause the ship to fall apart beneath us.

Clarisse was clearly drawing the same conclusion, and even as Serafina started yelling at us both again, she turned to the lieutenant to relay her command. I couldn't blame the man for looking rather relieved. I guess having been left in charge after his captain was abruptly killed, he had already been preparing for the worst-case scenario. Unfortunately, unless the Queen is incapacitated, the order to abandon ship cannot be given without her express permission. It was a protocol of travelling which I had always argued against. Luckily, she tended to listen to those who actually knew what they were doing, and the risks involved.

As the order was yelled out over the general creaking of strained wood and grunting of desperate crew members, I made sure to slip the straps of my pack more securely over my shoulders.

Thankfully there weren't many people on board, the entire point of having a baggage ship in the first place. There were three escape ships near the edge of the deck, tiny affairs with rapidly deployable mini balloons which were pretty much only able to drift gently downwards. One of them had clearly been a victim of the blast, half of its hull missing as if someone had taken a bite out of it. Thankfully the other two had been spaced apart enough to have avoided taking damage. Each could hold three people, and Serafina scuttled off to join the helmsman and cook whilst the lieutenant waved the Queen and I into his ship.

With nobody now trying to hold her steady, the ship suddenly lurched downwards. As the nose abruptly dropped there was a horrible screeching of overly stressed wood, the next gust sending a shockwave through the splintering decking. Which in turn fell apart beneath our escape ships.

Keeping his head, the lieutenant pulled the lever to deploy the balloons and I saw the cook on the other boat doing the same. Clarisse let out a small shriek as they took a moment to fill, our stomachs swooping up into our throats at the momentary drop, before we were caught and righted again.

Judging by the yelling coming through the air, the entire lead ship was now awake and had been watching everything unfold. A small cheer went up as they saw the gleam of the balloons in the moonlight, and the faint yell of orders suggested that they were planning to land near wherever we set down in order to pick us up. Protocol dictated that with such an accident, or potentially sabotage, we would take the fastest route back to the castle and investigate further rather than trying to continue on with the visit. Talk about extenuating circumstances. And so much for proving that our airship designs were on par with Namet.

For the time being, all we could do was drift slowly downwards and hope that we landed somewhere easy to be retrieved from.

Clarisse huddled a little deeper into her travel cloak, no doubt grateful for the thick lining. When she wasn't looking, the lieutenant offered me a swig of his hip flask as an extra guard against the cold. With a wry grin I took a sip, enjoying the burn in my throat. For all that alcohol doesn't affect me in terms of getting drunk, it was still a nice sensation.

I had never really appreciated just how quiet the night sky could be. As we coasted slowly down, even the wind whistled less. Or I simply got used to it as a background noise. None of us in the boat were particularly inclined to talk, probably all trying to come to terms with what had just happened.

It was a pretty surreal sensation to be honest, ever so slowly falling into the total darkness. I wondered if this was what it felt like to drown- sinking gently as your skin steadily grew numb, without any reference point as to how far left until the bottom. Possibly thinking similar thoughts, the lieutenant shifted a little in his seat to peer over the edge, trying to see whereabouts we were going to land. With how much we were being directed by the air currents as we descended, it was likely that we were being taken a fair way off course. I couldn't help but wonder which side of the border we would come down on.

Clarisse was shaking a little in her seat, and I was pretty sure that it wasn't due solely to the temperature. No shame in that. I gripped her hand, letting my heat leech into her fingers, and pretended not to see her smile of thanks.

After the chaos of those few minutes post-crash, all was eerily calm.

And then one of the balloons burst.

The noise seemed louder than the explosion had been, abruptly shattering the silence of the night far too close to my ears. For a second everything was slightly muted as I pressed a hand to my ear in pain. It came rushing back in a chorus of screams as I realised our gentle drop had all at once turned into a plummet.

The people in the other escape boat were yelling, for all that their voices rapidly disappeared as the distance widened between us. The wind was back with a vengeance, teeth tearing into exposed skin as it howled around us, making it hard to breath.

I barely heard the sharp twang of a cable giving way, and all at once we were hurtling down even faster as another balloon vanished into the surrounding void.

We had no idea how far we still had to go to the ground.

The boat was falling at a faster rate than us, being heavier, final remaining balloon notwithstanding. When that one inevitably burst, the wooden seats dropped out from underneath us entirely.

We had no idea what was below us.

I prayed for water to break our fall, or else the most solid of stone so that we wouldn't ever realise we had hit until we walked through the gates of eternity. The lieutenant screamed loud enough to crack his voice. I clutched Clarisse to me and covered as much of her body as possible with my own as we twisted through the air. Her nails dug into my arms.

Mags had told me once that she believed the only reason why she was still alive after all her years of service, was because one of the Pantheon gods found her too amusing to kill.

Perhaps it is a divine protection which automatically comes with the job.

Hitting the water was almost like the time I fell whilst scaling the castle walls. Except more painful. The sheer shock of it left me stunned for a good few seconds, and I am ashamed to say that I let go of Clarisse whilst my senses tried to pull themselves back together.

Cold.

Can't breath.

Ouch. Fuck.

I came back to myself before I could sink too far, resecuring my fingers in a vice like grip around Clarisse's wrist as I pulled us both back to the surface. Breaching the water, my first lungful of air burned sharper than acid. The resulting coughing fit sent me back down even as I tried to push the Queen up to keep her above the surface.

Coming up again I was able to shift us around until I had her limp body held securely once again, head kept out of the water as my fingers supported her chin to keep her airway open.

She was just unconscious.

With no lights to see by, I instead strained my ears to try desperately to find some clue as to which direction I should go. The cold was already leeching the energy from my muscles, it wouldn't be long before I seized up unless I could start moving and get us to shore. Carrying the extra weight was going to make this even harder.

She was just unconscious.

Part of me wanted to lose the pack which had somehow survived the crash, but if we... when we made it to shore the contents would be our key to survival. I tried to not to think of where the lieutenant could be. Maybe he had hit at a bad angle. Maybe he hadn't hit water at all. Maybe he was drifting only a couple of strokes away from me, but in the dark I couldn't see him. And even if I could, I was already hauling one body. I wouldn't be able to swim with two.

She was just unconscious.

My teeth had stopped chattering. I knew that if I could see my fingertips, they would already be turning alarmingly pale, nail beds creeping blue. Spitting out a mouthful of water, I began swimming to what was either the sound of small waves on a shore, or the desperate delusion of a frantic brain.

It is probably ridiculous, but the only thing I could think of was how pissed off I would be if we drowned, and I learnt in the afterlife that we had been only a tiny way from shore.

I don't know how long I swam for. There was only the cold, and the strain, and the spiteful determination forcing each stroke. It was so damned dark. I didn't know at what time the initial explosion had happened, no idea when dawn should be breaking.

The tips of my fingers were so numb, I didn't feel it at first when they scraped over pebbles. I came crawling out of the deep like some primordial monster, hauling Clarisse along as I scrabbled up the rocky beach. I collapsed when the weight finally became too much, and just hoped that my toes weren't still in the water. I couldn't feel enough to tell.

There were stones pressing into my cheek, almost bruising as I twitched with continuing coughs. How much of the water had I inhaled? How much had Clarisse? The thought danced away as fast as it had first crossed my mind. There was nothing I could do about what ifs and maybes.

Every bone in my body ached.

For all that I wanted to just lay there for a while, I knew that was a sure-fire way to die. Perhaps it was good to be so numb, purely on survival mode, because if I took a second to feel everything, or anything at all really, I probably would have curled up into a ball and fallen apart.

There was no time for such luxuries. My hands felt like they were burning in the relative warmth of the air compared to the water. I somehow managed to fumble the pack from my back and scramble around inside. I found the pouch with the candle and matches and breathed a prayer of thanks to whoever was watching out for us that the entire bag was waterproofed to fisherman level. The Queen's official cloak was kept in much the same way, seeing as how it would be vital for proving Clarisse's identity when we finally reached help. My own cloak was stowed in much the same way.

The flame catching was possibly the most beautiful thing I had ever seen in my life, half blinding me but providing a tiny island of gold.

In the light, Clarisse's face was startlingly pale, but I could at least confirm that she was still alive, chest rising and falling with steady breaths. No doubt knocked out from the force of the impact and then kept under by the cold. That was what I had to believe, because those were things that I could do something about.

Forcing my hands to keep moving despite the building cramps through my fingers, I dug out a blanket that was just about big enough for us both. A bit more shoving and I had removed both of our sodden cloaks, our wettest outer layers, until only our chemises remained. Keeping the rest on would only make us colder in the long run, preventing whatever little body heat we had from being shared. Grunting with the effort, I shifted Clarisse until she was on her side in case she needed to vomit as she came around, before I huddled in underneath with her to share whatever minimal warmth I still retained. I figured in these circumstances I could tell her to fuck off if she woke up and objected.

As much as I hated to do it, I had to blow out the candle to save it for whenever we might need it next. And with no idea where we had ended up, it was too dangerous to leave a beacon of our location shining out for all and sundry. I will not deny though that I flinched when the dark came rushing back in. The breath caught in my throat as I felt like we were falling all over again.

All I could do was lie there, trying to keep us both from freezing to death, and wait for dawn to help figure out where we were and what our next move should be

The exhaustion must have caught up with me enough to make me doze off though, as the next thing I knew I was blinking my eyes open to a sky tinged in welcoming blush. The Queen had twisted around in her sleep until she was half strangling me like a vine as she hugged me.

Nudging her awake was a welcome reprieve from her snoring so close to my ear. For a full minute she just looked vaguely confused, staring around the barren beach, our scattered damp clothes, and apparently not able to figure out why we weren't in a toasty cabin. I could pinpoint the exact moment that the events of the night caught up to her brain. At least she was relatively alright from what I could tell.

I at least had the decency to turn away and begin getting redressed, so as not to witness her having a minor break down and freak out over the entire situation. Fair dues to her for it not being a complete screaming fit. But then, I guess queenly training has got to stick in some ways. When she finally coughed, sniffled, and stood up, I turned back. She was clutching the blanket around her shoulders, slightly shivering in the breeze. Her hair was a tangled mess, face pale and streaked with dirt. At least we both had our shoes.

"Good morning, your majesty." At least my impression of her valet made her crack a slight smile, however tinged with barely constrained panic it may have been. I went back to my normal tone, "do you want the good news or the bad news?"

"Both."
"Well, the good news is that we are still alive."
She snorted, which turned into a full on sneeze.
"The bad news is, judging by the position of the sunrise and the shore we came to... we are on the wrong side of the border."

She hissed a filthy curse. I couldn't have agreed more.

CHAPTER FOURTEEN: DYING WOULD HAVE BEEN LESS EFFORT

When the sun had been risen for about an hour, and the heat had begun to seep into my frozen skin, I once again nudged Clarisse back to full wakefulness from where she had dozed off again. "Alright, Your Highness, time to get moving."

"Five more minutes."

I pulled her up by the arm, although I was nice enough to let her keep the blanket wrapped around her shoulders. "No Clarisse. Not five more minutes. We need to get moving."

Grumbling but accepting that I was right, would wonders never cease? She started to hobble around on the spot trying to get some circulation going before pulling the rest of her clothes back on. "Oof I am stiff as a rock."

I snorted, even as I rubbed my hands together as hard as I could to try and get my fingers to wiggling. "Yes, well, plummeting from the sky and then taking a dip in the lake and then sleeping on the ground all night is not exactly a recommended spa treatment."

I got a nasty look in return for that one, but compared to how she normally acted when being woken up it was fairly tame. She at least cheered up when I found that I had some dried apple slices deep in the recesses of my bag. True, they weren't exactly still dry, but they were still better than nothing. We munched as we marched, keeping the lake to our left whilst picking our way along the shoreline. As the sun steadily rose and the temperature followed, the mist began to burn away from our surroundings. It didn't really help much though; all I could see was rocky beach for miles in front and behind, with faint smudges of a forest on the horizon to my right and only endless water to my left.

"So, do you have any idea where we are?" Clarisse handed me back the blanket to fold away as she finally thawed out enough to not need it as a replacement for her damp cloak anymore.

"Some. Like I said before, I know that we came down on the wrong side of the border. Where the lake crosses into Tartyn territory is much narrower than this. Unfortunately, in the dark I just had to pick a direction and swim, so we ended up reaching the north west shore."

"What does that mean for our chances of getting home?"

"Well, navigating is going to be fairly easy: we pretty much just have to keep the lake on the left and we will eventually end up back home. I mean, that is the rough idea at least."

I could see her frowning beside me as she clearly tried to remember the maps of this area. She had never been the most visual learner, although she seemed to get what I was driving at. With the way the lake lay between our countries, it would serve as a handy guide for getting us back towards home. Even if we ended up having to cut further inland, it would act as a marker to reorient ourselves.

"Either way we need to get moving, hopefully reach a village or something and find some help. We'll just have to see what we come across as we go. We want to be heading southwest as much as possible to get back towards home, so let's keep walking down the shore this way until we hit onto some sign of life. At the very least we will eventually come across a trail which we can follow to civilisation."

It was as good a plan as we were going to have. With a shrug, she fell back into step with me. It was almost peaceful as we made our way along the shore. The quiet crunch of pebbles beneath our feet blended nicely with the hush of the waves lapping nearby. In the growing light the lake itself was beautiful, a deceptively inviting shade of turquoise which made you want to throw yourself in. No way I would be suckered into that anytime soon. My clothes were at least starting to properly dry out.

It was strange to think that this was the same lake that we swam in every summer. On our side of the border, we had a lovely summer palace on the far southern shore. Clarisse moved the court there every time the warm weather settled in, spending weeks dipping in the welcoming cool relief which it offered.

She broke into my musings with a heavy sigh. "What do you think happened last night?"
"On the ship?" I got a raised eyebrow in response. Right, what else would she be talking about? "Hmm, in my professional opinion something blew up."
"You are such an ass."
I raised my hands in surrender. "Alright, blunt version. Someone tried to kill you, Clarisse."
"It wasn't an accident?" her voice stayed steady.
"Considering that our escape ship was the one which failed in a way which is almost impossible to have happened by pure chance? Unless you made a deal with a demon and it has now come due, nobody has luck that bad."

My attempt at humour didn't get much of a reaction from her. I mentally shrugged as she crossed her arms over her chest. "Somebody tried to kill me."
"Somebody tried to kill all of us. Frankly I find it rather rude as my job is hard enough already. No way I am going to let you die from such an overly elaborate and yet ineffective scheme as this."

That at least got her to loosen up again just a bit, forcing a small huff of laughter from her. "You really need to work on your motivational speaking skills."

I waved one hand dismissively. "You are the leader of the nation. Fancy words and speeches are your domain. I am here to keep your behind in one piece."
"And a fine job you are doing."
"I like to think so."

There was a slight edge on the last of what she said. My hackles rose ever so slightly of their own accord, and I took a deep breath through my nose. She was scared, she was tired, she was hurting... and she had always been a bit of a bitch. She wasn't entirely wrong. True, I had saved her last night. I shouldn't have had to. I should have known what was going to happen, stopped it before it could get that close. Being human had no impact on that expectation. Zero tolerance for failure.

She cleared her throat, oh so graciously choosing to move on. "Do you have any theories on who exactly I should be wary of at the moment?"
"Well, this trip was not exactly a state secret. Plenty of people knew that you were going to be visiting Namet to smooth over relations after the whole incident with the King's brother."
"True."
I raised a finger to emphasise my point. "However, very few knew that we planned on taking the airship. We mostly put out the word that you had been planning to ride."

Clarisse actually looked taken aback at that. "Wait, what?"
"Yeah standard procedure. We even sent out a decoy party of riders just in case to help keep up the act." Magda had dispatched them with full fanfare whilst we boarded the airship.
"And yet they still knew to attack the airship."

Now it was my turn to sigh. "More- they knew to attack *your* airship. The one which was supposedly just for baggage. That was the one they targeted. Now, it is possible that it was meant to make the attack on you more questionable. The baggage ship tragically had an emergency and, in the confusion, it collided with the Queen's and took everybody down in a freak accident.

That would have been my preferred method."

"How often have you planned how to kill me?" she side eyed me as if trying to gauge my sincerity.

"Oh please- it is part of my job. I have to plan it so I can thwart it. Stay on track please. As I was saying, that is one possibility. However, the fact that the emergency ship failed in the way that it did... that tells me they knew exactly where you were going to be. I have no idea if the same thing happened to the other escape ship after ours failed, but it is highly likely that it went down as well. That is pretty dedicated and ruthless, and would have taken time to set up, which there wasn't all that much of. Which means..."

"There is a traitor at court."

There was something about the way she said it, as if her worst fears had been founded, as if somebody had begun caving away the ground to watch her dance on the aftershocks. There was genuinely confused sorrow as she spoke, "Who would betray me in such a way?"

I shrugged, "Hmm, that is the question. I mean, none of the spies we have at court currently would use tactics such as this."

"Wait, what?! You know of dissent in my court?"

I knew that my eyebrow was crawling up my face and was powerless to stop it. "Well... yeah?"

Ooh and now she was really seething. "There are currently foreign agents operating within the walls of my castle?"

"Naturally. I'm sorry, how is this a surprise?" there was no chance of me moderating my tone. Like, really? She had to know.

"And you know who they are."

"Of course. They have their uses, and we all respect each other's boundaries. Come on, there is no way you are this naïve." Hell, Mags had personally turned at least half of them. The rest were relying on the notion that they were still loyal, unwilling to acknowledge that the information they gained was carefully dolled out. I guess it is all about the pay at the end of the day.

I had stopped walking, looking at her incredulously. Who did she think she was fooling? Everybody knew how courts operated. For the sake of the gods, she had dispatched our agents to every ally and enemy on the books. This was basic, and why she was trying to pretend otherwise was frankly confusing. I wasn't some diplomat in front of whom she had to claim plausible deniability.

Clarisse finally deflated as she realised that the act was pointless and unnecessary. I swear, the woman makes no sense.

We began walking again. "Alright, so you don't think that it was one of them?"
"No. A better bet would have been your Uncle. I mean, he does hold the only semi-successful attempt to cause mass harm when he orchestrated that whole poisoning venture last year-" highly unpleasant for those invited to the blossom viewing tea party. Or at least, the ones out of favour who hadn't been warned and pre dosed with the antidote. He hadn't aimed to kill of course, just cause a fair bit of embarrassment to particularly pushy ladies who didn't get that *no* meant *no* and that being happily married to the one of the other councilmen should have made clear his preferences.

"That was him?!"
"Yes, but he was just acting out because he wanted to go home to his estates. Since you sent him away." After he got oh so publicly caught gambling with state money. At one of Magda's evening events. It was the least resisted arrest and banishment in memory, and I hear that he has been much happier ever since. According to rumours, he is soon to publish a guide to gardening and estate financial management. "Anyway, what I am trying to get at is that the incident last night is not in line with anybody's usual methods."

That was a given. There had been no indications of an attack of this size being planned. Nobody had been talking, more importantly nobody had been unusually quiet. Magda had received no indicators that things were this extreme. Which suggested that it might have been a plan in the works for far longer.

For some reason my mind went back to the fire which cost us Tabitha so long ago. There had been a similar lack of information around that incident. Even years later the ongoing investigation had never turned up anything useful. No one had anything to say about the incident which had almost cost the Queen her life, despite the initial appearance of a tragic accident. That in itself could be a form of signature.

"Could it have been Namet?"

Clarisse once again derailed my train of thought. "Huh?"

"I mean- what if it was a strike orchestrated by the Nametian king?"

"In return for the slight to his brother? That makes no sense." I shook my head, "There is no way that little diplomatic hiccup, which we were clearly seeking to smooth over, could work as a justification for an assassination attempt."

And that would be just as important if it was a nation-based attempt. If there was some greater plot for starting a war or some such, a strike of the kind which had been carried out would bring the other nations down on Namet's head. There were rules to diplomatic games, that much I knew from listening in on Clarisse's lessons.

On the other hand, I didn't have to bring up the fact that Namet was one of the fastest growing air powers at the moment. Apparently when airships had been invented, the King's cousin Lucille had jumped on the opportunity to create an air shipping business. She now ran one of the best ship manufacturers in the world alongside a highly lucrative trading empire. We had been taken down in a way which would have been very easy for them to execute. And with their growing influence, any retaliation from the other nations would be rather more cautious than we would perhaps appreciate.

It was a lot to think about, so many threads twisting together until it was as if one of the cats had gotten into my embroidery basket. Unpicking it all would take time. More than that, it would require contact. With the limited information which I had available my options for discovering the truth were rather truncated. All I would be able to do, was think it over and over and over again as I tried desperately to parse out the real from the supposition and fiction.

At least in that regard, the insane amount of walking which we had in our futures could provide the quiet backdrop to let me run through it all and reach a conclusion. Or perhaps I would just be left with sore feet and tangled thoughts.

CHAPTER FIFTEEN: NOTHING TO SEE HERE

As I had hoped, after following the shoreline throughout the morning, we had eventually seen signs of civilisation. A small marking post had been hammered into where the edges of the stones met the beginning of a field. When we headed over to investigate it had been the sweetest relief to find a path, worn and well-trodden, with what looked like some sort of village or hamlet in the distance. Clarisse had almost looked ready to cry at the realisation that we might be able to find some help, or at least decent food. Closing the distance was at a far faster clip than before.

It must be part of the nature of small village pubs that they are the meeting house for all of the inhabitants. True, there is always the place of worship, but if you want the proper hub for an area where you are guaranteed the best gossip then the pub is your place to start. The downside with such a small establishment is that strangers stick out like a sore thumb. If we were on a major travelling route, or in a larger town, then a pair of newcomers would get maybe a brief glance and a couple of questions. I had already briefed Clarisse that it would be best if she kept her mouth shut unless absolutely necessary. If anything, her accent would give away the fact that things weren't as they seemed. Nobody spoke with such rounded vowels unless they were rich as sin.

And if I were honest, I wasn't sure that I could trust her to treat people normally. She was a queen after all, and the habits of a lifetime could not be unlearnt in the space of a day.

As soon as we walked through the door, we had full attention on us. Thankfully there were only about three people present to gawk. I mean, I can't blame them. Not only had two strangers just disrupted the flow of life, but they were a pair of women who looked rather the worse for wear. That would be setting off alarm bells in any self-respecting landlord's head.

"Goodness me, are you alright?" the man who came bustling out from behind the bar was taller than Jeremy and broader than Sir Gavin. He reminded me inexorably of the biggest, fluffiest dog in the kennels. It was fair to say I took an instant liking to him.

"Afternoon." I gave him my best 'tired but positive' smile, nudging Clarisse to do the same. Mentally I swore that if she did anything to offend these people then I would throw her back into the lake myself.

The best hope of getting away with being somewhere that you shouldn't? Act like this happened every day. Be nonchalant, tell yourself that you have every right to be there, that you own the place, that you would never dream of being anywhere else. Fake it until you make it. People don't tend to question that level of confidence.

Without hesitation, I took a seat at one of the empty tables, putting my bag down and stretching my arms high overhead to shake out the kinks in my shoulders. Clarisse slid onto the chair next to me, and after a rough kick under the table removed her cloak to drape it over the back. The couple of other patrons gave us side eyed looks from their perches at the bar.

I shot the innkeeper my most winning smile as he followed us over and introduced himself as Johanson. "How much lunch can we get for..." I made a show of patting down my clothes, and letting out a little whoop of triumph when I felt the coins in my pocket. Pulling them out, I scattered a handful of copper pieces on the rough boards of the table. "Seven copper? Oh!" I rummaged once more, this time in my pack, "and some waxed thread?" another pat to my pockets, "and one vial of stomach soother. That stuff is straight from Inar's grace when you have eaten something bad."

He raised an eyebrow at my hopeful expression, eventually matching me grin for grin. "Hmm, well for that amount of treasure I reckon I can throw together a couple of plates of what we have going. Maybe even a couple of mugs of cider." He shot me a wink as he gathered up the thread, vial and five of the coins. He held up a hand to forestall any protest as he slid the other two back before heading back behind the bar. As he ducked through the door which probably led to the kitchen, I got a brief whiff of something which smelled heavenly.

A moment later and an actual dog came padding out into the tap room, heading straight for us to give a thorough sniff investigation. There was nothing fake about my smile this time as I held out a hand for him to get a good scenting. Apparently satisfied, he didn't seem to mind when I scratched his ears, rather all but melting into the floor and offering his belly. I have always liked dogs more than people as a general rule. Considering that I had spent the better part of the day walking with only Clarisse for company, this interaction was doing wonders for my sense of humour.

Clarisse seemed to be giving me a bit of a raised eyebrow at the performance she had just watched. Perhaps I was laying it on a bit thick, but people are generally more open to helping a damsel in distress when she seems sweet, cheeky, but helpless. Besides, it is always better to be nice right up until the moment when being nasty is necessary. Once you have showed your dark side people will never really believe or trust in even your most genuinely kind intentions. It was all the game. I tried to ignore how much my jaw was aching from so much smiling after a night of gritting my teeth against the cold.

At least Johanson hadn't seemed to notice anything off about my accent. A bit of variation was fairly normal in rural areas, with villages tending to develop their own version of a regional dialect. Hopefully any oddities would be chalked up to that rather than tipping them off that we weren't from near here.

When Johanson came back, I decided that I would put him forward for elevation to saintly status. Clarisse's eyes almost fell out of her head when he plonked down two enormous plates of food. I took one look at the pile of bacon, fresh bread, and slices of apple, and promptly declared my eternal, undying love, before diving in with gusto. And alright, perhaps I slipped a bit of bacon to my new best friend under the table.

I also internally vowed that when we got back to the castle, I would send out a search party to come back and get an agreement to buy his supply of cider because it was the best I had drunk in far too long. Although there was an estate which had the official warrant to supply the drinks for the castle, I would argue that this was far superior.

The Queen seemed to be enjoying her feast just as much, if not more, and I wondered if this was the hungriest she had ever been. A day's fast for religious purposes had nothing on near death experience and hours of exercise to whet the appetite. For a woman who once at a state dinner scolded a dignitary for putting his elbows on the table, she was all but tearing the meal apart with her bare hands. I was never going to let her live this down.

The innkeeper chuckled at our antics, leaning against the table as he sipped on his own mug. The curiosity on him was clear as day. I figured this would be his story of the week for all of his regulars when they came in at the end of the day.

"So, what are two young ladies such as yourselves doing on this stretch of the shore?"

Clarisse half choked on a piece of bacon. "Umm..."

I pounded her back hard enough to leave a bruise as I spoke

over her resulting wheezes. "We are good needlewomen, so our fathers are sending us to the city for better prospects." it was a reasonable story, a common enough situation I figured.

Even so, I didn't expect him to nod in instant acceptance and apparent understanding. "Ah, so you got called in as well?" I just hummed, already stuffing my face once again and using that as a reason not to give away the fact that I had no idea what he was talking about. The innkeeper shook his head a little, "Honestly, it's the trouble with having troops garrisoned in a trading town for too long."

Wait, troops? He didn't seem to notice my sudden intense interest, focusing instead on petting his dog.

"It is meant to be a place people mostly pass through; they aren't set up for housing so many for as long as they have." I made a vague noise of agreement to encourage him to continue. "They sent the word round here a few days ago for the same skills. We are sending our Martha along tomorrow morning." He actually looked a little proud at that, even if annoyed at losing someone apparently close to him for a while. "What with the traders due to pass through here, we figured that would be the best time so that she would be a bit safer."

I swallowed hard on a too large bit of apple, "At least the pay is supposed to be decent." It was a good guess. No way they would be sending whoever 'Martha' was without a fair reason, and he didn't look as if they had been intimidated.

"True." Another smile, which turned thoughtful as he looked Clarisse and I over. "You know, if you would like we can find some space for you in the caravan? It isn't the best idea for you to be walking these parts with only each other for protection. They say we are heading for dangerous times after all."

Clarisse looked somewhere between relieved and ecstatic, "Oh really?"

I booted her under the table once again. Hopefully two words wouldn't be enough to give her away. Regional accents were one thing, her courtly voice was something that could raise suspicion. I passed another piece of bacon to the dog. "That would be amazing! Thank you so much." A rueful chuckle, "I can't tell you how welcome the thought of some extra company would be."

"Hey!"

The innkeeper laughed again, shaking a chiding finger at me until I shrugged in approximation of an apology. "Well in that case, if you are willing to help out around here for the day, I can give you a space to bunk down. The caravan is due to arrive at daybreak, drop off some supplies for us and then continue on toward the border. You can link up with them then."

"Johanson, I think you are an angel sent by Inar herself."

He chuckled, flushing briefly, "keep that up and I will say that you are a travelling jester."

CHAPTER SIXTEEN: NOT QUITE A BEDTIME STORY

It will forever be one of my treasured memories that I got to spend an evening watching Clarisse try and perform basic useful tasks. The woman could negotiate treaties, direct armies, manipulate court intrigue, and was more than half decent with a sword. She apparently couldn't do household chores for shit. I had quickly resorted to assigning her darning duty whilst I fulfilled the various odd jobs around the place. At least it meant that the girl, Martha, was able to take advantage of her sudden day off to spend extra time with her family before her departure.

To be honest, overall it was one of the calmest days that I have had in years. Despite the fact that we were possibly in enemy territory, we were unknown nobodies. With it being mid-week we didn't even have to deal with too many curious patrons beyond sticking to our story of being sent to the city. Each had nodded in understanding and that was it. Were normal people just generally less curious about things which didn't directly impact their lives? It was a blessed relief.

Johanson also seemed more than happy with the outcome of our little arrangement, loudly praising the quality of Clarisse's needlework when he saw it. That at least helped to bolster our cover. Considering all our work he didn't even charge us for dinner, going so far as to wave me off when I tried to help with closing time. Instead, he had just told us to bunk down wherever we liked once he turned in.

I had made sure to settle us in a spot with a clear line of sight to the door, for all that we would be obscured by the various bits of furniture. People didn't tend to look down first when hunting for someone after all. From where I had angled my body, I could also just about see the door to the kitchen, and I had already taken the precaution of scattering a handful of gravel from the road behind the bar. I would hear anybody trying to approach that way. Naturally I would make sure to clean it up in the morning before the owner saw it and got annoyed. Or suspicious.

It had been a rather delightful surprise when only a few minutes later the dog once again came wandering over. I patted him a little as I got sorted, laughing when he apparently decided that he would be keeping us company and flopped against my legs. At least it would help keep me warm.

A bit of rummaging in my bag and I was pleased to find that I had even managed to keep my hairbrush with me. It was strangely comforting to be able to go through at least a small part of my normal nightly routine. Not to mention that what with everything we had been through in the last couple of days, my hair was beyond a mess. Working out the tangles and knots was more painful than I wanted to admit. And I just knew that once I had gotten it all out then it would fluff up like one of the castle cats. I raised an eyebrow as I realised that Clarisse was just staring at me. I didn't pause the motions of my brush. "What?"

She startled a little, turning faintly pink. "I just… I don't think in all the years that we have known each other I have ever really seen your nightly routine."

"Wait, seriously?" I raised an eyebrow. How could that be? But then… for all that I had to pay attention to every little thing she did, I was of no consequence to her in such a way. If it had crossed her mind at all, she had probably pictured something less calmly domestic.

"Do you always braid your hair before bed?"

My hands didn't pause in the well-practiced motions. "Well... yeah? I mean, unlike some people I could think of, I don't have attendants whose job it is every morning to make sure that my hair is in good condition."

"Hmmm, makes sense I suppose. What with it being so long."

"Yeah." And for some reason my mouth kept moving, words still falling out. "You know, hair is kind of a big deal to my people. We only cut it when a person dies. Symbolic. Turns out your army cuts the hair of their prisoners- practical, lice related reasons."

Another silence. This one slightly more... I wouldn't say awkward. That would imply that she had some measure of guilt over what had happened, and we both knew that wasn't true. No, it was more that sense of when you revisit something which you know that you will never agree on but also don't bother to argue about.

I secured the end of the plait keeping it snaked over my shoulder. I remembered how awful the stubble had felt underneath my fingertips even after so many years. For the first few weeks, whenever I had caught sight of my reflection, I thought that I must have died and been sent to Tartyn for punishment. Thankfully it had grown out to the same thick lengths that I remembered. Now, when I saw myself out the corner of my eye, I would sometimes think that it was another woman who I once knew following along in my footsteps. But that was ridiculous. I couldn't even really remember how my mother had looked.

Curling myself in my cloak, I made sure that the pack was by my side in easy grabbing reach if it should prove necessary. One of my knives was in my hand, a reassuring weight against my palm. Sleeping with one had been the norm for so long that I didn't worry about cutting myself by accident anymore. In fact, I had been told that it was scary how little I moved when asleep. Small mercies, I guess.

The dog huffed at me a little for disturbing him, before settling back as a comfortable weight along my side.

Clarisse clearly took her que from my organising, scrunching her own cloak around to try and get comfortable. I had at least been able to give her the blanket to fold up under herself as an extra layer of protection against the stone floor. Although, after a night spent sleeping on the ground, things were definitely looking up. I could even still feel the warmth from the banked fire radiating through the stones.

Hopefully she wouldn't be snoring again. Because that would just be more than I could handle.

She did shift around, huffing and sighing as she tried to find a position which didn't make her limbs hurt. It was a shame that the inn didn't have any rooms to let, but I guess that travellers weren't the sort to come through this way unless they were visiting family or some such. Or in the case of the expected caravan, they had their own places to sleep along with them.

As if following my train of thought, Clarisse huffed once again, turning her head to face me for all that I kept my gaze stubbornly on the ceiling. "Are you sure that this caravan is the right move?" I hummed a little, "We don't have the resources to by a horse, and there are no airports near this area." Not that either of us would be willing to consider that any time soon. "Our only other option is to walk. That would take us significantly longer to get back to Tartyn."

She snorted, "True. My feet are bloody painful already. But... can it really be trusted?"
"It gives us a better chance than if we tried to get through on our own. From what we have heard, there is much more going on here than we thought. It sounds to me as if this section of the world has become rather crowded, and mostly by people who are likely to carry weapons."

I shifted a little as the aches of the day started to make themselves known, flexing the toes of one foot and then the other to ease out the impending muscle cramps. "Even if it weren't, there is safety in numbers. Two women travelling alone across unknown terrain is not a good idea." Now I did turn to look at her, "remember, you are just one of many now. There is no status to prevent someone from trying something on. Things happen to women on the road every gods damned day. I just want to get you back in one piece. A caravan has a reputation to defend of being a relatively safe way to move between places, as well as meaning that we will be able to blend in easier if we happen to come across any other travellers."

She couldn't seem to find any argument to make against that. In truth, I don't think she was against the idea of linking up with a caravan, but it was simply part of her nature to second guess whatever I suggested. Some habits die hard. Instead of trying to answer, she readjusted her blanket for the hundredth time, wiggling so that she would be less likely to roll into a chair leg or something in the middle of the night.

We were as safe as we could be at that moment. Clarisse's continued grumbling aside. It was just about possible to make out her endless litany of complaints about how she, "was the leader of a great nation damnit. Why am I reduced to sleeping on a tavern floor..."

It was hard not to scoff. She didn't rule much of a 'great nation', at least not when you put it into wider perspective. In fact, she was queen of a fairly small piece of land, which just so happened to be rich in timber and coal. The country, like its rulers, also seemed to have a habit of punching above its weight on international matters. Like one of those small lap dogs who believes itself to be a full-blooded hunting hound. Or a horse. And others are just a bit too polite or incredulous to remind it otherwise. Considering they managed to take over my homeland it is rather embarrassing.

I ignored her, instead running over potential outcomes for the morning. All in all, there was no denying that we had gotten lucky with the bar owner expecting a caravan to come through this way. It was a fantastic bit of providence and would do wonders for our mathematical likelihood of surviving to the border. Perhaps the gods really did favour their monarch.

It was imperative that we got back home as soon as possible. If what we had heard being talked about earlier was any indication, with troops being shifted and readied, things were already spiralling out of control. It was so fast. I couldn't help but be either disappointed or suspicious. I have said it before, but politics has never really been my thing. I didn't have the patience for it. If you wanted to hurt someone then you should just sort out the problem, at least in my opinion. But then, I hadn't been born into the world of schemes and dreams like the others.

Even so, I couldn't help but think that it shouldn't all be able to fall apart so quickly. Right? The government of a whole nation shouldn't be so delicate as for a single attack to end generations of relative peace. It was beyond frustrating to not know what information had made its way back to Tartyn, what version of events was reported and believed. Hell, the news probably hadn't even really been verified yet simply considering the distances needing to be covered. And moves were already being made in possible response. That simply didn't happen in politics.

Not unless there was somebody else behind it all, pushing buttons, shifting pieces, specifically waiting for the signal to strike.

I hoped that was the case. That this was an orchestrated set of steps put into motion. Partly because I wanted to have a modicum of job security. Partly so that I would be able to know which threat I should prioritise for my charge's defence.

Whatever. There was nothing I could do about it then and there. All I could do was get Clarisse home. And for that I would need to get some rest. I was never a deep sleeper, and I didn't doubt that the hundred and one sounds of a new place would keep me right at the surface. Either way, any rest was good rest.

A deep breath, eyes closed, mentally running through the

muscles in my body and forcing them to relax.

Clarisse began to snore.

CHAPTER SEVENTEEN: NOW THIS IS TRAVELLING IN STYLE

The breaking of the dawn was led in with the faint ringing of bells. As the weak light stole through the gap under the inn door, I nudged Clarisse with one foot. She grunted, snorting awake with a truly impressive nest of hair. I barely smothered a laugh as I gathered up our small pile of things to stow back in the pack. Shaking out my cloak, I offered up a prayer to whatever deities may have been listening in that I would soon find a change of clothes. For all that I am trained to ignore discomfort, that doesn't mean that I can't appreciate the joys of personal hygiene.

We stumbled out into the morning, Clarisse yawning wide enough that if we had been in court, it would probably have started some sort of crisis. I waved a small good morning to the innkeeper, not wanting to intrude any further as he fussed over the girl he was sending with the group.

It shouldn't have been as much of a surprise as it was when the caravan finally got close enough for me to see them clearly. The bells alone should have warned me. In my defence, the eternally tinkling melody was one which I hadn't heard for far too many years.

Seven wagons came rolling down the village road, each one decked out in the brightest colours possible. Swirls and patterns were painted across the canvasses, and for all that I hadn't seen the symbols since I was barely bigger than a grasshopper,

I was still able to make out the familial crests woven in with the messages of what wares they carried. To an outsider they would have just looked decorative, a traveller's fancy doodled on a bored night. I saw Clarisse's eyes skim over them with little attention paid.

One of the women who was sat on the driving bench of the second wagon caught me looking. Her eyes raked me up and down for a moment, before a small smile broke over her face. She nodded to me. I flushed even as I returned the acknowledgement.

The couple in the lead caravan were busy with the innkeeper, clasping each other's arms and half bowing in greeting. A few snapped words and the younger travellers made quick work of unloading an assortment of barrels and bags. No doubt the supplies for the inn, preserved meats, fruits, spices, whatever was needed and could travel well.

Martha was ushered over to one of the wagons, pulled up into the welcoming arms of the driver who quickly got her settled with their own family.

Taking advantage of the distraction, I sidled up to one of the horses. They were a special breed of the nomadic tribes, about half donkey and far less imposing than the noble chargers you would see at a tournament. They were also far more precocious. Thankfully the one closest to me seemed happy to be petted. I had forgotten just how wonderfully soft their noses could be.

As the people flowed around us, I took a moment just to breathe in the remembered musk which had once underpinned my idea of home.

After a heartbeat of hesitation, I gave a final pat to the horse's neck and stepped forwards. Clarisse almost tripped over my heels as she followed. The innkeeper gave me an encouraging smile as he drew the head driver over, finishing whatever he had been saying regarding inventory with, "And these young ladies were hoping to hitch a lift as well."

I actually had to tilt my head back a little to look the leader in the eye. She was a good foot taller than me, although most people tended to be it was true. Ah the joys of your formative years being spent with a touch too little food. Dark eyes ran over me and, widening as I deliberately tilted my chin further so as to expose my throat fully. It was an old form of greeting, one I remembered a woman who might have been my grandmother teaching me.

A wide smile broke over the leader's face, "Sand sister!" she stepped forwards, bracing a hand on each shoulder and tilting her forehead forwards. I mirrored the action until we met in a gentle press. As excited chatter went up from the caravan, gossip flying back quickly, I saw Clarisse staring with slightly open mouth between me and the leader.

It was almost amusing, watching as she put together the similarities between us.

"Sand sister." I echoed the greeting, the words leaving a bittersweet tang as they rolled off of my tongue in a language I hadn't spoken in far too long. If there was one time I had truly loved Mags, it was then. She had been the one to help me hold fast to my culture in whatever ways I could, and that had included helping me find those who shared my mother tongue.

I motioned Clarisse forward, "this is my charge. I am seeking to return her to her home." It was all the explanation I would need to offer. Amongst my people, curiosity over the affairs of another was frowned upon. We had patience to wait until others were willing to share.

"A worthy goal. One we shall be happy to assist with. You may call me Amara, and shall ride in my wagon." I appreciated her decisiveness.

"Most gracious. She is Clarisse, I am named Ninacra, or Nina for short."

A brief hand clasp, and then we were being helped up into the wagon, settling into the veritable nest of pillows and blankets which kept the wooden slats comfortable no matter how many miles you were due to rattle over. Taking a moment before anyone else joined us, Clarisse hissed at me for a translation of what had been said.

I raised an eyebrow at her. "You don't speak Santari?"

"No. Obviously. What were you saying?"

"Wait," I was doing my best not to stare, keeping my voice to a veritable hiss, "you conquered my people, claimed our land as yours which included the inhabitants. You are technically their ruler. And you don't speak the language? You speak so many!"

She huffed a little at me as if I were deliberately missing the point. "Yes. I speak the languages of my allies and rivals as a sign of respect. These people are neither. As you say, we conquered them, and so they should now speak my language. Besides," she seemed genuinely unaware of how I was staring at her, "you can always translate for me."

There was a moment of awkward silence. I couldn't find words, in any tongue, to quite explain to her how that had made me feel. It would have been less painful or shocking if she had simply slapped me. My complete inability to respond seemed to at least make her vaguely uncomfortable.

Clarisse was doing her best not to appear overly stiff as others climbed in alongside us. A low whoop went up from Amara, being echoed back along the caravan. The wagons started forwards, and I stuck my head out the back flap to wave a thankful farewell to the innkeeper. Johanson nodded back, then focussed all of his attention on waving furiously at the wagon holding Martha as it peeled off after the others.

He faded from view faster than I would have thought as the group moved away from the village and into the surrounding fields. We cut across the open land for a while, skimming the edges of the intermittent woodlands, before our path began to merge with a more well-travelled trail. Eventually it gave way to a far wider road, beaten down to compact dirt. The wheels of the wagons fell into well-worn ruts. I could almost image that the horses were stepping directly into footprints which they had left before.

The road which we were following was angling away somewhat from the lake where Clarisse and I had crash landed so abruptly not that long ago, although its course was remarkably straight and true. I figured it must have been a route used by the military- they tended to make things as easy as possible for their troops no matter which country you found yourself in.

Whilst nomads were more than happy to roam over hill and dale as the wind and Inar's grace took them, general wisdom dictated that it was best to respect when certain countries demanded that you stick to their paths. However tempting it was to try and explain the fact that borders and trespassing laws were highly unnatural and a purely social construct intending to make taxation easier, the average patrol did not care to weigh in on a debate.

As the caravan trundled along, I couldn't help but pick up the signs all along the route which whispered that a sizable force had passed this way before. And recently.

That's the thing when moving large numbers of people- it is literally impossible not to leave evidence along the way. From the blatant signs of broken gear or leftover food discarded to the side of the road and not yet picked up by others, to the subtleties of the level of wear on the road. Clearly someone had moved a large company through the area.

Clarisse was snoring like a hog from inside the wagon. I could hear her even through the thick canvas. Funnily enough, the other passengers had all decided to walk for a while or join their friends in different parts of the caravan.

I was ambling along at the side of the column, enjoying the feeling of the sun on my face even though I kept an eye on the people moving around me. It was an unavoidable instinct. True, I was technically back amongst my people, but I was still working. I still had a mission. That hadn't stopped me eagerly accepting the change of clothes when they had been offered.

My own had been through hell and back, and whilst they had been designed for travelling, the events of the last few days had probably been outside of the tailor's scope of imagination. When we made it back, had I tried to give the outfit to the laundry, they would have strung me up by the thumbs for use as target practice.

Definitely wiser to recognise a lost cause.

The hem of my new coat ended at my ankles, moving with every step, and managing to not get tangled in my legs. It was the traditional dress of my people, split tails so that it would be easy to ride if necessary. The jewel blue tone fastened across my chest at the level of my ribs, leaving the rest of me covered by a breathable shirt which had been graciously donated by one of Amara's sons.

I had been embarrassed when it was first given to me. Not for the gesture- such generosity was the foundation of nomadic society, the giving to all with the understanding that when your time of need came the same would be returned unto you. No, a flush was forced to my face when I realised that my fingers could not quite remember how to tie the clothing correctly to keep it fastened.

The grandmother of Amara's wagon had just smiled sweetly at me, a too deep understanding in her eyes. Her wrinkled hands had guided my movements until we wove the ribbons together to keep the clothes secured. She patted my cheek, then turned to scold one of the little ones who was trying to crawl over the edge of the wagon bed.

At least the split skirt was a fashion which Clarisse's nation had adopted soon after they had annexed my country. They had apparently found the 'exotic style' a key inspiration for fashion over the last few decades. The one I wore now was far lighter than any fabric I had put on for far too long. I relished the slight jingle of the coins which were sewn along the seams. Similar coins adorned the veils which some of the travellers were wearing to help keep the dust from their faces, glittering with every spec of sunlight.

It wasn't even really the guidance which got something sharp stuck in my throat like a swallowed blade. The clothes were lovely, that is true. But what truly got to me was when the grandmother had given me the coat. She had handed me a purple one at first, a beautiful piece with careful embellishments of flowers along the hem. It was lovely. And made of the wrong fabric. I don't know why, but there are some things which when I touch them make my spine try to crawl up out of my body. This was one of them.

My fingers had recoiled of their own volition before I could make myself accept the gift. She laid her hands on mine to stop me before I could try to draw it onto my arms, taking it from me with only a smile and handing me something far softer in a rich blue. I felt the heat climbing up my neck. I was being childish. Something as small as a texture shouldn't make me want to snap at someone trying to help me. Just as her acceptance shouldn't make me want to cry.

The woman had just smiled gently at my confusion, moving to help me get into the garment. "I wish to provide comfort. You understand? If what I am doing does not do such then it is on me to correct, not for you to endure. Otherwise, I am not doing what I said I would." She tilted my chin up with one weathered finger until my head was once again raised proudly. "You should not cause yourself pain from not wishing to cause offence. If such a thing as a personal preference on a coat could cause me upset, then I need to see more of the world to gain perspective. How small a life could I have led for such a thing to hurt me?"

I had snorted at that, leaning my cheek for just a moment into her calloused palm. She patted me on the head and told me to go and play with the other youngsters. All at once I felt five years old as I jumped off the back of the moving wagon with a fancy twist, revelling for a second in the impressed whoops of those around me.

Axels creaked over rougher patches of the road, punctuated by the occasional whinnying bray of the horses. All around me people were talking, laughing, sharing gossip and jokes as they flowed between the wagons and the surrounding woods and grassland. It was the way nomads operated, constantly gathering and living off the land.

Every now and again we would come across a pocket of people-working their field or waiting on us to pass by within close distance to their homes. The wagons didn't fully stop, even as people moved amongst us to trade with the various families. The shoppers would then melt back to their own lives, as the caravan continued on.

This had been the only way of life I had known, once upon a time. At least until my mother had decided to settle into one of the city hubs which tended to attract those of my people who didn't have a column's support to continue roaming. It was that decision, and that she hadn't lived long after the brief war broke her heart, which had put me right into the hunting path of the Queen's Guard. But then, my mother had been travelling spirit roads for long enough by that point, I doubted she would have remembered to watch over me anyway.

It felt... strange to be back. For the first time that I could really remember, I was surrounded by people with the same darker tint to their skin, the same penchant for bright colours. My ears were all but swivelling on my head as I tried to listen to as much as possible, soaking up the voices speaking in my own language.

From somewhere near the back a person was strumming on an instrument, voice lifting above the others in a melody which the rest would occasionally roar out words to. It was maddening. I could have sworn that I recognised the song. It was almost there, an itch in my brain. I forced myself to let it go. I could always relearn it on this journey.

A sharp whistle and I almost missed the ceras fruit which was thrown at my head by one of the kids on the fourth wagon. There was no fighting the grin which stole over my face. The fruit had always been my weakness, and I inhaled the deliciously sharp scent as I pierced the purple skin with a nail. I was pretty sure the shade of my skirt had been thanks to the dye which could be made from the peel.

My first brush with death was thanks to the fruit. When I was three, I had choked on one of the seeds. My mother had smacked my back hard enough that it left a handprint for a week. When I finally coughed it loose, and stopped crying, I promptly scoffed the rest of the flesh. My mother planted the seed in the patch of dirt outside our house. I wonder if it ever grew to bear fruit.

CHAPTER EIGHTEEN: RELIEVING ONE HEADACHE IF NOT THE OTHER

There was a tranquil sort of joy that night as we sat around the campfire. Clarisse was asleep in the caravan behind me, her heavy snuffling a reassuring undertone to the subdued hubbub of people just existing in contentment. I was pretty sure that the caravan members were in awe of how much she could sleep. But then, I suppose she had been rather busier than normal lately. The night was a far cry from the usual tumult of court. There were no echoes here, any whispers were solely for the person into whose ear you intended.

I breathed deep of the woodsmoke, the remaining tang of herbs and meat from dinner, the musk of the animals where they settled to sleep by their traces. Tilting my head back, I saw the stars in a way that I hadn't for so many years. I had been taught to navigate by them, using positioning and mathematics to decipher coordinates. I couldn't remember any of it then, just the stories which had once filled my evenings on my mother's lap. There were heroes and monsters up there.

Across the campsite I watched with a half-smile as a small braiding train got set up amongst some of the youngsters, low laughter teasing through the air. Amara's grandmother helped guide the movements of the youngest, teaching her how to avoid pulling on her brother's locks.

Every muscle in my body froze up as hands were placed on my head. How had I not realised that someone was approaching? The breath caught in my throat, every instinct screaming at me to clench my fingers tight around the hilt of my knife and drive it straight through the eye of whoever was daring to try and take me on. I could grab Clarisse and be away before the rest of the camp even knew-

All thought processes screeched to a halt as gentle fingers smoothed their way down my scalp.

For a moment I stayed in a painful half alert state. Tension was thrumming through every nerve, a voice in the back of my head shrieking that I should throw off the touch. Hands couldn't be trusted, no matter how sweetly they may begin. That was a lesson I had learnt very quickly, one which had been reinforced enough. I knew better.

The fingers teased oh so softly against the crown of my skull.

Is there shame in admitting how thoroughly I melted?

The person behind me let out a low chuckle, no mocking in the tone but rather pure pleasure at my apparent surrender. She eased her hands more firmly against my head, pressing the tips of her fingers through my hair, drawing them back and around. Again. And again. Now sweeping down around my ears, now smoothing back up through my head, now applying just a slight bit of extra pressure to my temples.

It was sheer bliss.

It got even better when she pulled out a brush.

I had tried to explain it back at the tavern, just a little, to Clarisse about the importance of hair to my people. Our hair is our life. The length shows your years, the quality shows how you value yourself. But more than that- it shows if you have other people to care for you. Brushing one's hair is more than a solo chore. It is a familial moment, a bonding time, a mutual care to build trust.

To have somebody else take the time and attention to brush your hair until all tangles have gone, to then braid it into an intricate style which you could never achieve on your own... it is a symbol to anybody you meet as well as a reminder to yourself of the fact that you have somebody at your back.

I don't know how long she spent on easing the tangles and snarls from my hair. I fell into that blissful state where things just don't seem to exist in the same way. Nothing matters, except the sheer enjoyment of being taken care of. It was as if someone had poured warm water directly into my veins, leaving the rest of me delightfully floaty.

Only when I saw the clip which she was going to use to secure whatever design she had made did I wake up a bit more. Clearly sensing my interest, she handed it to me first, letting me run my fingers all over the piece. It was ingenious. At a glance it was certainly beautiful- cunningly designed so that when all the pieces had been threaded into place it would look like a butterfly resting on a flower. My discerning fingers, used to searching for more in everything, could also feel the almost invisible latches and hooks inbuilt to each section. I flicked one of them open with the teasing edge of a nail, a slightly feral tint to my smile as I saw the small blade which popped into being. Another twitch and it was once again hidden.

As a hair piece it was a work of art. As a tool it was pure genius.

"Hmm, fascinating item, is it not? A boy who travelled with us for a while as you do now, gifted it to our people in thanks." Amara's voice was melodic, soft.
"Did he indeed?" my tongue felt heavy in my mouth, words slightly slower as I still didn't feel completely back in my body. She took it in stride.

"Yes. I suspect he came from the same area where you and your charge are intending to strike for. Fascinating child. Apparently, he had met a sand sister before. Told us how a 'desert dweller' at his home court had once showed him how to best hide things in plain sight. That she had taught him and his best friend the importance of having the right tools for a job. Imagine that."

"Hmm, well education can take many forms."

The last piece slid into place. "That is very true."

My muscles were nowhere near ready to begin cooperating. I had no idea when I had last felt this relaxed. It was so foolish- we were in the middle of unknown territory, surrounded by strangers. My charge, the Queen, was sleeping underneath the wagon at my back. It was my duty to stay awake and on guard, to see her safely through when we were in hostile areas.

At that moment in time, I couldn't have cared less. Whatever I had grown up knowing, being taught, all faded into the background. Because I did know these people. They were my people. They understood parts of me which I had done my best not to notice for so long, and didn't judge me for the choice to forget that which was too painful to keep. And that was core of my people's existence- we survive. We always survive. We help each other to do so, and when we find someone who can't hold on any longer we cradle them close and let them rest for a time. Our creed teaches that one day someone could do the same for us. And even if they don't, if they leave us to shrivel and fade to dust under the sun, then Inar will embrace us with the ultimate sanctuary.

For years I had been living with those who operated on extremely different ways of thinking. We had different values of kindness, of duty. For once I wasn't having to run the conversion chart in the background of my interactions.

The life which I led... it was not what I was born for. But a sword can still take pride in being a sword, even if it remembers the simple purity of the earth which birthed its core and would forever form its heart. In truth, it must find solace in its function, less it purposefully blunt its own edge. Or worse, start to crave the blood of its wielder.

Once again my eyes tracked up to the unending skies above us.

Embers from the campfires spiralled up in an eager imitation of their eternal brothers. Those hands were back, smoothing down my shoulders now, easing tension from muscles which had been braced since that knight had charged me down on his horse when I hadn't been fast enough on too small feet.

There was a vibration in my throat as I hummed along to whatever someone was singing in the darkness, a lullaby to their child perhaps. I let my eyes flicker closed, feeling as I was lowered slowly down, a cushion slipped beneath my head.

For one night at least, I could come home.

CHAPTER NINETEEN: THE ART OF SNEAKING

I was woken by someone's hand fastening itself over my mouth. They almost died before I was fully conscious. Luckily for us both they jumped back just fast enough to dodge the blade which came slashing out from the cushion I had snuggled into.

It took a moment in the dark of pre-dawn for me to realise that I recognised the assailant. Amara. She had her hands raised on each side, spread wide to show that she was no threat. There was no judgement in her gaze for the near evisceration. Fair enough, she would have known the risk before engaging. Otherwise, she never would have lived so long as the leader of a caravan.

The fire was burned low in the middle of the camp, various groups scattered in the grass or huddled together. There were still soft snores of the elderly who slept in the wagons drifting as the only sound to the scene. Even the birds weren't warming up their voices yet. It was early enough to still be late.

"You must waken your companion. Danger is close." Her voice was low so as not to disturb the others sprawled around the campsite.

"What's happened?" I didn't wait for an answer, already gathering together our things and kicking Clarisse until she snorted awake like a startled hog. The cloak I threw at her face smothered any complaints she may have tried to voice.

Amara's face was serious as she helped me shrug into my pack straps. "Mikail was scouting ahead. He reported that there is a checkpoint about seven leagues ahead of us. Many soldiers. Looking for somebody."

"Inar's tits."

A half smile despite the tension in her shoulders. "Exactly. You must leave us. Now. Before the others wake and know anything lest they be asked."

She meant the children of course. And their parents. It was better that they could answer truthfully that they had travellers with them who vanished into the night. I knew that if Martha hadn't been with them then they would have simply denied everything. The tavern girl was an unknown quantity who could not be relied upon to follow the story.

Clarisse at least seemed to have figured out that something was going on, managing not to grumble as she pulled her boots on. It seemed there were still some miracles left in the world after all. She even refrained from hissing for a translation. It might have been the most trust she had really ever shown me.

"Which way would you recommend we go?"

"You head for the border, yes? Go southwest. You will reach woods, cross through. Then keep heading for the south. When you get to the border, look for our way markings and cross in the wild lands. I think you should know your way home once on the right side of the line."

"Of course."

She stepped close, placing one hand on my shoulder in an unspoken question. I closed the distance myself, pulling her into a fierce hug. It was returned with equal strength.

"May you walk in day's shadows and star's warmth." The words were whispered in my ear.

"May streams guide your feet and wind cool your brow." I don't think I had exchanged the traditional parting words since I left the temple for the last time as a child. I had never had the chance when I was taken my home, for all that I had muttered the phrases to myself over and over in lieu of any prayer that I could try to remember.

Amara clasped a hand to the back of my neck, giving a small squeeze, before finally letting me go and standing back. She inclined her head to Clarisse, switching back to Tartyian. "I wish you well."

"And you." There was at least some ingrained courtesy in the Queen despite the beyond early hour.

We picked our way carefully from amongst the sleepers, walking quietly out of the boundary of the camp and striking out across the grasslands. I sent a prayer to Inar that neither of us stepped into a rabbit hole or something. At least the moon was still pretty full and cast its cold light on our pathway.

Neither of us spoke, the only punctuation of our passage being the plumes of breath on the air which themselves swiftly vanished. At least the exercise kept us relatively warm.

The silence held until we finally stepped into the shelter of the trees and Clarisse promptly tripped over a root. I caught her before she could hit the ground, but there was still an impressive stream of curses from the Queen. It was quiet though, hushed, possibly less from wanting to stay beneath notice and more that was simply the volume demanded by the still sleeping world.

It was like when you walk into a library, and you know that you are supposed to be quiet. Even if there are no people or signs to tell you so, yet still your instincts tell you that a hushed approach is the better option. No sense in raising your voice and so hell along with it.

The walk was almost peaceful after that initial stumble. As the sun rose, we could see better and feel the warmth on our skins through the lattice of the tree branches. At some point I passed Clarisse a pack of dried fruit for her to munch on as we moved. For all that she grumbled about wanting a hot breakfast, she didn't waste the breath of suggesting that we stop.

We were getting close now, so close to the border and the promised safety. All we had to do was cross and we could get help at the nearest village on Tartyn's side. Maybe we would even get extremely lucky and stumble on to some noble's country estate which would speed things up significantly.

I couldn't help but think about the check point found by Amara's scouts. There was no reason for it to be there. It wasn't a normal toll point, otherwise the caravan would have already known about and expected it. Which meant it had to have been dispatched there deliberately to check travellers heading towards the border.

That didn't make much sense considering that they were supposedly encouraging people with trade skills towards the nearby towns for the hastily garrisoned troops. Not unless someone thought that there was a survivor of the crash. This, naturally, raised several issues.

Primarily, from what we had seen and heard; nobody knew about the air crash in the first place. I figured the ship must have crashed into the lake in the dark, seeing as how no one had been raving about it falling from the sky and squashing an unfortunate family member. There had been no mention, no rumours, no gossip. The events of that night were kept on strict lockdown. Except, it seemed that someone knew what had happened, and even had the chance to figure out that there could have been survivors.

Perhaps they had an operative nearby who had watched the whole thing, or enough resources to dredge the wreckage and realise that there were not enough bodies. Maybe they had forced the other ship to land, and got the witnesses to admit that safety craft had been deployed. Maybe they had kept them prisoner... That was an option I chose not to think overly closely about. I had to focus on the mission at hand, first and foremost.

Whatever the reasoning may have been, the fact remained that I had to assume someone was looking for us. Someone with influence enough to set up checkpoints on major roads on the off chance that their hunch was correct. There was more to this entire mess than either Clarisse or I had thought before. We were clearly in more danger than initially guessed. Considering how screwed I had already believed us to be? The fact that it was more was in many ways impressive.

In truth, none of it made a damn lick of sense. And between being bloody knackered from all the hardships of the last few days, along with being on constant high alert, I didn't have the necessary brain power left to really think it all through.

On the flip side, having every sense jacked up to highest alert meant that I sensed the moment that things took another turn for the worse. At this rate I wouldn't have been surprised if somebody told me that we were in fact on the spiral down to hell.

Back to the point. As the sun had risen over the woods, the wildlife of the area had in turn come to life. The birds had voiced their songs, deer had kept a wary eye on our progress, a fox darted across our path.

The one thing which did not belong was the unmistakable whinny of a horse as we approached the thinning edge of the trees.

We both froze, dropping low behind the nearest cover of underbrush.

Seconds later a mounted patrol went ambling by along the edge of the woods. They hadn't noticed a thing. We didn't exhale until they were passing around the next thicket.

I motioned for Clarisse to stay low, ever so slowly unfolding until I could look out across the terrain. This section of woods were coming to an end, there was some sort of open meadow, and then another patch of trees. They would provide us more cover. If we could sneak in without being spotted, then we would have a real shot of getting to the end of this cursed journey with only stories of close shaves to share when we returned home.

It is probably fair to say I jinxed us with the mere thought.

We were halfway across the meadow when the shouts went up just at the horizon. It seems that two women stick out in a meadow in the middle of nowhere. Clarisse broke out into cursing again as the unmistakable sound of the hue and cry going up echoed across the still young morning. I told her to save her breath and use it to her advantage.

Apparently, we would be in a race after all.

CHAPTER TWENTY: PERHAPS IT WAS ALWAYS GOING TO GO THIS WAY

Clarisse was panting as we took a moment to rest behind a small outcropping of rock. Darting back into the woods had meant that our pursuers had lost sight of us, but the rougher terrain was having a toll on her majesty's stamina. I couldn't really blame her. I was exhausted to. The meal from the night before felt like a lifetime ago.

I chose to stay quiet, instead passing her the canteen from my pack and trying not to glare as she downed half the water in one long swallow. Not just because I was thirsty- she was likely to cramp out if she kept that up. When she was done, I took a sip, holding it on my tongue and swirling it around my cheeks for a moment so as the better hydrate my mouth. An old trick.

My charge ran one hand through her hair. It was remarkably similar these days to a bird's nest. "But why are they trying to kill me at all?"

I couldn't help but snort a bit as I returned the water to its space. "Frankly, due to your rank personality…"

"I think you meant to say: 'rank and personality'."

"Sure." I kept my eyes on the surrounding forest.

She flicked a piece of bark to hit my cheek. "Hang on, what's wrong with my personality?"

"Now is seriously not the time."
"We are going to talk about this later."

I clamped a hand over her mouth. Her brief struggle and outraged shriek died down at whatever she had seen on my face. And then she heard it too. The unmistakable jingle of tack, the murmurs of soldiers. Considering how trees could deaden sound, they were already damned close. I freed her mouth, grabbing her wrist instead and pulling her through the thicket as quietly as we could manage. We didn't have a lot of time.

Our current patch of woods was on the crest of a ridge, and as the trees thinned, I was able to point out the trail which we had been shadowing from a distance. For all that ideally we would have used the caravan trails instead, this would be the fastest option given our current crisis. More exposed, but far more direct. It would lead to the border; it was our way home. I could almost believe that the smudge on the horizon was the trade checkpoint on Tartyn's side that we had been aiming for all this time. The one which marked safety, where there would be a garrison, where we could get help.

Or at least where she could.

Casting a quick look over my shoulder, I released my grip on her arm, half pushing her down the slope. "Go! Now! And that's an order!"
She actually bristled, whether at my tone or the implications as she realised that she was about to have to go on alone I don't know. "I'm your Queen don't you tell me-"
"We don't have time for this bullshit. For once in your life listen to me because I know what I am doing. Go!"

They were drawing closer; I just knew it. We wouldn't make it if we stayed together. For all that I complained about her I knew that she had at least some common sense. I had to trust that if I bought her the time that she needed then she would be able to make it. They were looking for a noble woman after all. She definitely did not fit that description these days. At first sight they might hesitate.

And I would go riding home on a unicorn. A quick bit of manoeuvring and I pulled her cloak from my pack for the first time since the crash. It was still in its protecting covering as I pressed it into her hands. With wide eyes she clutched it close, realising exactly how serious I was.

Uncertain, she hesitated on the decline, holding onto a sapling for support as she looked back at me.

"You are going to fucking run and you are going to make it home. You are going to tell everybody what happened and what we have learnt." I took a step closer, grasped her tight by the shoulder and forced her to look straight into my eyes. "You are going to end this budding war before it can begin and keep our people and home safe. You are going to be the Queen you were always born to be." I could hear the yells getting closer, the ground shaking with the hoof beats of the patrol as they finally spotted our trail. "And when I get home, because by all the gods I will get home, you will be there to open the gates wide for me."

She swallowed hard, then nodded. I shoved her away, taking a moment to watch as she dodged between the trees, picking up speed as she went. The border wasn't far. She would make it. I would buy her that time. She had her cloak, and it was unmistakable to any of our people. Clarisse was going to get there.

So long as I did my part.

I cinched the straps of my pack tighter one more time and darted through the thicket on a tangent from where she had taken off. The hue and cry went up behind me almost at once as I crashed my way through the woods. Their blood was up, and I was blazing a trail with all the subtlety of a hurricane.

Losing them for a second as I skidded around a fallen tree, I took the moment's reprieve to slip under a small outcropping of rock. There was a space underneath, and I huddled in like an animal in its burrow. Head down, I held tight, waiting. Waiting. Waiting.

There!

My teeth were vibrating out of my skull as the riders went charging over the head of my hiding place. Mentally I counted them off, squeezing my hands into fists. Part of me wanted to reach into my pack and retrieve my larger dagger, but I was pretty sure that I would need two free hands for what I had planned.

The last one passed over my refuge.

I erupted from the hollow.

Shouts exploded from the group as I launched myself at the last rider. He was taken completely aback, slamming backwards from his saddle in a flail of limbs as my heel met his face. It wasn't quite enough, experience letting him start to right himself. At least until I drove my fist into his face at point blank range. The angle was pretty bad, what with me trying to get a grip on his mount, but I still felt the sharp crack through my hand as his nose exploded into a shower of blood.

He went tumbling, his foot catching on the stirrup for a moment before a harsh dip in the land sent his foot snapping the wrong way and luckily out of the loop. Whatever god he believed him would hopefully stop him getting trampled by his own companions as they wheeled around in a spray of dirt.

The horse panicked for a moment, bucking wildly until I managed to wiggle into the saddle properly. There, much more even playing ground. I bared my teeth at the rest of the group briefly before making the horse turn around and begin to race away as I shrieked over my shoulder, "Bring it on you bastards!"

The patrol only stayed milling about for a moment as they tried to force their mounts around and track me at the same time. Making sure I had the reins in a secure grip, I dug my heels into the flank of my new stead, unable to repress a whoop as it shot off into the woods.

I have always loved to gallop. It was dangerous, reckless, nearly suicidal to do so now, in an unfamiliar wood on an unknown animal. I didn't care.

We came bursting from the treeline onto an open field, the slight downward slope lending extra speed to my horse as I let it take its head. The other riders broke cover, picking up their speed to try and match mine.

A spray of water as we dashed through a stream. I held on for dear life as my horse acted on instinct to send us sailing over a low farmer's wall. For a moment I was flying. For a moment I was back in the fields of my home. For a moment I was just running for the sake of it. For a moment I was once again plummeting from the heavens.

An arrow went whistling through the air to the left of my ear. Damn. Firing from the saddle, at speed, took some serious skill. Another clipped the seam of my coat, leaving a thin tear to the fabric.

I prayed to whatever gods were listening that they didn't strike my horse. I would feel incredibly guilty for the poor animal if they did. It was only by Inar's grace that the creature hadn't been injured yet.

Their archer sent up a whistling arrow. Damnit. That meant there were more of them around.

For a span of heartbeats, I had actually entertained the idea of losing them, then doubling back to the road which would lead me home. How fantastic that would have looked, to sweep the Queen off of her feet and let us ride for the border. Alas, despite what the bards would have you believe, such luck does not come often to mere mortals.

Another brief span of trees, my horse nimbly weaving its way between the trunks even if we did end up losing a bit of speed. Another clearing. And then I saw them.

From the valley there was another party of riders coming,

having clearly heard the signal from their soldiers. I almost balked at the size of the encampment around the edge of what seemed to already be a fairly large town. I remembered having seen the place once on the maps at the castle. It was the site of the largest trade centre for our respective countries, lying as it did so close to the border. They seemed to have decided that it could serve well as an army basecamp.

There was only one reason why such a force could be so close to our borders. I really couldn't catch a break.

My mount was slowing a bit now, no doubt nearing the end of its energy reserves. The men behind me were following suit, confident to ease the chase now that they could see the hunters closing in on me from both sides.

A sudden turn, yanking harshly on my horse's bit with a quick apology for the treatment. I was nearly thrown as we changed angle. I have always been pretty direct. I had to buy time.

We charged the oncoming party.

Have you ever played chicken? I did as a very young child, long before I was taken for training. I remembered when they had come for me, how I had stood in the middle of the road as I was charged, diving out of the way at the very last second in order to take off running whilst the guard was trying to process if he had just trampled a child. In the end of course, I hadn't been able to outrun them even with my tricks.

This time I didn't try.

Instead, I turned my mount to charge straight at the leader of the oncoming riders. Passing the reins to my left hand, I let one of my small knives slip into my right.

My horse had more sense than me, swerving at the very last second before we could fully collide. The animals clipped each other, both lurching at the sudden impact however glancing at such speed. I had been counting on it, feet already slipped free of the stirrups.

In an echo of my earlier tactic, I used the sudden direction switch for its momentum to launch myself from the saddle, tackling the leader out of his own seat. We hit the dirt. Hard. He was below me. He didn't get up. I did.

The impact alone would have been enough to wind him, probably break a bone or two. The thin length of steel which punctured through his eye assured me that he wouldn't be a problem for me any longer. More blood beneath my nails, but at least the blade didn't break when I yanked it free.

Our two horses were trampling around in terrified confusion, forcing the other riders to slow so as not to hurt their animals or themselves. With the momentum lost they had to dismount. So many people think that a person on the ground will always lose to the one on the horse. Not true. Given a second's hesitation I could have even tried to slip through the chaos and away. Unfortunately for me, these men were apparently trained cavalry.

In that case, it would be far better to strike first. I was the more mobile one in this battle after all, and if there was one thing which I knew how to use to my advantage, it was sheer recklessness.

Is it worth describing the fight blow by blow? Not really in my opinion. A fight is a fight is a fight. They are all different, and if you are fighting with intent, then they are all desperate. My job was simply to make it last. The longer they were engaged with me, the longer it would take for them to remember that they had been sent out after two people. I had to buy her time.

And that meant forcing myself to grapple soldiers from their saddles. It meant striking out with a blade in each hand and a vicious slash of a smile on my face. It was taking a blow to the face and responding with every ounce of coiled power left in my muscles. Breathing in copper heavy air, panting, and wondering if the slight whistling was from the busted nose or whether there was a new gap in my teeth.

In the court which had been my home for so long, I had always had a bit of a reputation for being feral. Partly from the role which I fulfilled at my queen's side, partly a stigma attached to my heritage. Desert rat is such an unimaginative epithet to tag someone with and yet always inevitably returns. But now? Now it was a label I lived up to in a way which would have made Magda both proud and exasperated.

I did pretty well against the original group who had been hunting me. Their reinforcements were another story. But then, it had never been my aim to win the fight. Every blow traded, every slice, every dodge, was another space of breaths which Clarisse could be using to run for the border. And if this was to be the way that I went out, then I would give them a story worthy of being dedicated to Anar herself as Inar welcomed me home.

For the record, I did my duty. And I did it well.

CHAPTER TWENTY-ONE: ASK ME NO QUESTIONS I'LL TELL YOU NO LIES

I was panting from exertion by the time that they managed to get me secured to the chair. I mean, yeah, I had let them take me in the first place. I had fought until I knew that I couldn't do so anymore, and then let the wolves descend. They were too exuberant on their own violent satisfaction to realise that I had effectively surrendered.

Sly hits after your prisoner has been secured are generally frowned upon within the context of the knight's code. For regular soldiers it is often a good way to pass some time and vent frustration.

That was my job after all, to buy time in whatever way that I could. Time for Clarisse to escape and get back and maybe, just maybe, find a way out of this shit show before war could break out in full and consume everything in its wake.

The guards were glaring at me from their positions in the corners of the room. At least two of them had scratches across their faces, and I vindictively hoped that they got infected or something. My nails were dirty enough. The one whose hands had wandered rather more than professionally necessary was periodically spitting blood from the gap where a tooth had once been. His nose would probably never point the right way again either. It was an idea I took vicious pride in.

His more aggressive friend was starkly missing. I idly wondered if whatever medics they had would be able to save what was left of his hands. Retribution had been worth the loss of my blades.

It was almost a relief when the cell door finally swung open. At least there was no squeal of rusty hinges. For one, that would have been far too much of a cliché, and the noise would have given me a splitting headache which would always put me in a foul mood.

The man who stepped into the room was definitely someone from higher up the food chain. If there was one thing I loved about military uniforms, it was the tendency to make those in higher positions stand out in some way. My little assassin's soul was laughing at the elaborate insignia which rested over his heart. That would serve as a perfect targeting point should the need ever arise.

One of his subordinates slipped in behind him, the movement drawing my attention. I tilted my head a little, squinting at the man in the relatively low light. I knew him from somewhere. No doubt about it. His was a face I had come across, and not too long ago. It would probably be easier to place him if one of my eyes hadn't almost swelled shut.

It was a nice distraction from the heavies who followed him in and grasped my arm. There was not a word spoken as one of them mashed my hand flat against the arm rest of the chair, almost cracking the bones as he forced the fingers straight. It occurred to me once again just how filthy my hands had become. I was actually mildly embarrassed.

The other stepped in and without a single flourish used pliers to rip the nail of my middle finger straight away from the bed.

For a heart stopping moment, I could only stare as he held the evidence of what he had just done. He let the piece of flesh drop to the ground. And that was when the pain of it finally slammed into me like a horse at full tilt. I let out a sound like a kettle just boiled, a hissing screech erupting between my teeth before I could choke it back down.

Damn.

Fuck.

The ranking officer took a moment to look me up and down, perfectly sculpted brow not raising an iota at the general state of me. I panted through clenched teeth, willing the pain to take a back step before I showed more weakness. Instead, I focussed on something else entirely. The hems of my split skirt were several inches deep in mud. There were to rips in my coat. My boots had practically changed colour. If I tried to approach home at this point, they would sling me into the moat on principle. Jeremy would help throw me. Hanson would laugh without meaning to.

The apparent interrogator dragged a chair in from the corridor, swinging it around to straddle the seat as he watched me. He even managed not to catch the edge of his sabre's sheath on the wood. I wondered how long he had practised the move in the mirror.

I tilted my head a little to the side, watching him with my less swollen eye. "Sir Evil Intentions I presume. I would shake your hand if you would be so kind as to loosen these ropes a little?" I forced the words out, letting my tongue run away to distract my brain from the point of fire at my fingertip. "Not usually what I would go for after all, my tastes run less constrictive in general." I waggled my eyebrows in a parody of flirtatiousness.

He raised his chin in apparent disgust at my words, for all that it was belied by the glint of intrigue in his eye as he looked me over like a particularly interesting experiment. "So, are you really going to die here today? For her? You are going to sit there and claim to be that noble?" he was all but placing a hand to his chest in dramatic shock.

I hummed a little, the burning in my hand banking down as I

forced myself to solely pay attention to the conversation. "Ha! Me? I'm not noble at all. Kind of the point really. I was the commoner kid who didn't run fast enough when the guards came hunting." A lopsided shrug, "At least they managed to train me so that wouldn't happen again. That's my job now. To die for her. Or any of them really, but they placed special emphasis on her life over the rest of us."

Words, words, more words. I had always had a tendency to babble.

"So, what, you believe that you are worthless?" he sounded genuinely shocked, almost caring, a concerned uncle perhaps who just realised that his niece was teetering on an edge. The subordinate in the corner, who as of yet had said nothing, looked truly disheartened by my attitude. Gods above I knew him from somewhere...

My smile actually hurt, far too wide with too many teeth as it stretched the bruises on my cheek before I just let it fall. I held his gaze with wry amusement and the same sense of surety which had followed me all my life. "No. I am just worth less than them."

Hands on my wrist. Metal on index finger. I closed my ears to the sound it made as the nail was torn off with no ounce of hesitation. At least this time I had known what was coming, could send my mind somewhere else entirely for a handful of heartbeats. I had always been good at that. Almost as if I had a secret power to send myself outside my body when everything became a bit too much. Mags said it wasn't the healthiest coping mechanism. I argued it had always worked for me.

The silence was loud in its own way. A deep breath, feeling every part of my lungs inflate. Steady exhale, opening my eyes again once the last of the air had left my body.

"Now listen here, you son of a bitch."
He made a show of examining his pristine hands, "I will have you know that my mother is a truly virtuous woman."

"Oh, so sorry. Listen here you son of a son of a bitch..."

Whatever I might have said was cut off by a backhand which cracked my head to the side. At least now there was grime on him. Only fair really.

I could almost see the man running calculations behind his eyes. It was an old game after all. People always want something, and his job was to get it from me on demand. Mine was to not let him. So simple really. Much easier than the time Lizzie tried to teach me chequers.

The familiar guard, who on reflection had been less than caring for his presumptuous colleague earlier, spoke up. "I think she's serious. Sir." The honorific was tacked on, almost forgotten. I couldn't help but wonder who he could be. No way a career soldier would have such a form of address as anything less than instinct.

I snorted, putting on my most playful smirk and leaning back as far as my bonds would allow me. "Ooh kinky. Glad to know that you have a bit of something else going on in your life. Damn, does this make me part of your scene?"

The subordinate actually flushed a little at that. Damn, I might have been close. Hang on... I felt my eyes widen enough to almost fall out of my head. "By Inar you were the one on Alastair's protection detail. You hooked up with one of the knights!" the words all but fell out of my mouth before I could really think about them. The man flushed a truly impressive shade of scarlet right to the roots of his hair.

His boss at least did not appreciate the brief trip down memory lane. He slammed one hand down on the back of the chair in a move which was probably meant to be more intimidating. The relative lack of sound did him dirty on that one. "Enough. You will die here, eventually. But not before we have extracted every ounce of information from you possible. There is a war on after all. The general rules of civility have been somewhat suspended you see." A faux sorrowful expression on his face, the exaggerated shake of his head. He waved at my hands with an airy gesture as if to emphasise the point. "Being a woman will not protect you."

No shit, jackass.

I rolled my eyes hard enough that I worried I would sprain something. "Oh please, that has never been the case. There is a reason the elite guards are female. We face so much more bullshit than everyone else from the very day that we draw breath. You underestimate us. I mean, seriously, I go through excruciating pain every single month, and am an expert at getting blood out of clothing. Like, that is a useful skillset for my profession." It was an allusion to a topic which never failed to make men vaguely uncomfortable. He was no exception. I chalked the win up in my own mind. "Now, can we please get on with this?"

"So eager to die?" he sounded almost wondering.
I shrugged as best I could, "Eh, a good friend of mine tells me that growing old isn't all it's cracked up to be. She will be so jealous when she gets the news. Send her my severed head or something would you? So that she knows I died smiling."

The guard who had spoken up before was looking at me with vaguely dawning horror. Did he remember me from before? When last we met, and I was annoyed if fond of the people who surrounded me. Decked out in silks, and despite the steel ever present on my hip, had he just seen another courtly bloom? Perhaps his dalliance with the knight had left a rose tint to his memories of the court.

I could see his counterpart from the other side of the doorway staring with terrified awe. It was rather nice for my ego really. Especially when I winked, only to have him stumble half a step back. Perhaps I was dancing rather too close to the line of insanity, but it had been a hell of a week and there is only so much a person can take before finding an alternative to sensible reality.

Mr interrogator, and the fact that he hadn't introduced himself at the start was really starting to irritate me, that is simple decency, rubbed one hand to his head. "How the fuck did we end up catching the batshit crazy one?"
"Uh, sir? She more or less gave herself up." The talkative guard half shrugged.
"Didn't she take down seven guards before we could grab her?"
"Well, yes, but she managed to only kill three of them. The others were just wounded."
I chimed in once again, "Yep- only lightly maimed."

It was true. My best tactic at the time. If I had continued fighting at my top capacity, they would have probably simply gone for a killing blow rather than trying to capture me. I needed to buy Clarisse time, and that required doing the unexpected. They were so intent on getting me secured, it had taken them a good few minutes extra to remember to send people after my charge. At the same time, by intentionally not killing all of them, they were more likely to leave me in one piece. Damaged, sure, but I would be less likely to have to fend off other guards bent on revenge for their fallen brethren. When in the enemy's stronghold you have to use every edge that you can find.

"You have got to be kidding me." It was said under his breath, but considering we were at such close quarters I could plainly hear. At least he seemed to finally get the memo that he was dealing with a pro. He stood, turning his chair around and sitting like a normal person. Finally. The straddle thing might work normally to make people think that he really had no cares in the world, but the vein jumping in his temple had been giving him away.

Once settled again, he crossed his arms. "Fine, such a meaningful sacrifice."
My nose wrinkled of its own accord. "Not really. See, I already got what I was after, and anything else is just a bonus." I leaned my head the other way, letting the edge of my teeth highlight my smile. "I am not locked in a room with you, rather you are locked in a room with me."

"What?" he didn't seem to get it.

"Well, you were so relieved that I surrendered it wasn't the most thorough search procedure I have ever gone through. So, you know, pick a god and pray."

The noise which followed was a good a psalm as any I could conduct for Anar's glory.

CHAPTER TWENTY-TWO: NOTHING COULD SURPRISE ME AT THIS POINT

I could feel the blood running down the side of my face, one side of my lip slowly swelling already. I tried to keep my head down as I moved through the streets. It wouldn't be long before someone realised that the screaming from the cell had stopped. In a dungeon silence would always draw attention.

I hadn't been lying about not having been frisked down particularly thoroughly when I had been taken. But then, even if they had, I doubt that they would have found the blade I had hidden at my wrist. One of the oldest tricks of my trade really. It is easy hide a razor sharp, if deceptively small piece of metal under a fake piece of skin. The flap had been sown to my real flesh for long enough that I sometimes forgot it was there. A last resort. Gruesome sure when I tugged the stitches out in a hurry, but any port in a storm.

Using the ruse of cradling my damaged hand to my chest it had been but the work of a moment to arm myself. Between one blink and the next the main officer had been choking on his own blood even as I launched myself at the next nearest guard. My plier happy acquaintance would no doubt find it hard to grip his tool of choice in the future.

With all of them down, I had enough time to frisk their pockets for the key to the cell. My first bit of luck in quite a while had been the lack of extra guards posted in the corridor. I suppose they had been a bit overly arrogant after all. One could only hope that in the future they used this series of events as an important case study for their next generation of torture enthusiasts. Professional pride and development is important for any industry.

Those concerns of interrogation school curriculums aside, it was time to focus on moving my ass before the powers that be came to ask for a progress report or something.

As if summoned by the thought, the hue and cry went up behind me. For a moment I half hoped that I would blend into the crowds which thronged the streets of the city. Even though the place had become a stopover for the military, there were enough civilians swarming around that I had a half-baked plan of fading into the masses.

Then again I was liberally caked in blood and dust, which was becoming a particularly unappealing form of mud. People had been giving me wary looks ever since I reached street level, even if nobody had said anything outright. It seemed that city folk were the same whatever country you were in- firm believers in not getting involved in other people's dramas.

So when a small squad of soldiers comes clattering onto your road and starts actively hunting for someone? Then they seemed to all but vanish into the surrounding buildings. Which was not in line with my plan of hiding in the crowd.

Naturally I got spotted. I could feel the moment their eyes locked onto me even before the call went up. "Stop her!"

I ran. My feet hammered on the stones, sending harsh jolts through my already battered joints. Why couldn't this be happening on a lovely soft field? I was getting too old for this nonsense already. No wonder Mags sometimes moved so slowly when it was about to rain. Possible premature aging of my body aside, I pulled enough of my flagging reserves together to put on another burst of speed.

Skidding around a corner, I almost tripped over my own feet as I saw another group of guards burst from the street ahead of me.

I wasn't going to make it. It's such a strange sensation, to feel that complete certainty wash over you. They say desperation is the mother of invention. Adrenaline for sure gives your brain an extra burst to problem solve on the fly. In my current condition there was no way that I would be able to go through them. Options... options...

I spotted an open doorway just up ahead, darting inside before a hand could close on my shoulder. All but flying up the stairs, my lungs were heaving from exertion. I was pretty sure that I could hear my ribs creaking under the strain, even over the thunder of my heartbeat. All but gasping my heart up my throat, I burst out onto one of the flat roofs of the city. Slamming the door shut behind me bought me another few seconds, but I could already hear their thundering footsteps closing in behind.

I ran again, to the only place I had left to go.

It's amazing how quickly a ledge can appear in front of you.

The door behind me broke down and guards came pouring out onto the roof. Someone yelled. Someone screamed.

I leapt.

For a half breath I was weightless, soaring, wind blasting into my face for barely a blink. I stretched every muscle to the very limit.

With desperate hands, I reached out for the ledge of the next building. My body slammed into the rough brick, knocking the air from my lungs in a pained wheeze. My fingertips dug into the lip of the balcony I had managed to hook onto. If the interrogators hadn't already ripped my nails away, they would surely have been torn off by the stones. As it was, I knew I had to be leaving red streaks everywhere.

My own blood was working against me. The small grip I had was going, unable to hold as I began to slip.

It was a long way to the ground. This was going to really fucking hurt and if this was how I died then I don't know-

Something wrapped around my wrist. I was being pulled up. Over the railing. My feet landed on solid ground.

There was a woman in front of me, eyes wide as she gaped right at me, stare not even breaking to look at the hollering guards on the rooftop opposite. Her nails were digging into my wrist, right where it was still bleeding from releasing my hidden weapon. I couldn't really feel it. My entire attention was focussed on her.

I knew that face. I hadn't seen it in eight years. Hell, she was literally meant to be dead. I knew she was dead. And at that moment I could have been hallucinating. I could even possibly have died myself. Maybe the last few minutes had all been some weird fever dream of my failing brain in the last moments before my soul fled this plane. Perhaps all this time I had been falling from the airship.

But despite the heavy mat of scarring, I would know her anywhere. The sound which crawled out of my throat was the shredded echo of a sob. There was no thought in my head as I desperately wrapped my arms around her. I was so far beyond done. Tears streamed down my face, no doubt cutting rivers through the dust and blood.

Her arms slowly curled around me in return until she was holding me as tight as I was grasping to her. "It's okay," Tabitha said, "you're safe now."

CHAPTER TWENTY-THREE: I WAS WRONG

I think it is safe to say that over the course of the next… I don't even know if I am honest… things kind of caught up with me with a vengeance. There is a blur across my memories for a time, punctuated by short bursts of awareness.

Someone gave me a bowl of water and I washed the blood and grime from my face with jerking, unconscious movements. I could have sworn that I felt the weight rising out of my skin. The towel was embarrassingly dirty when it was taken away. A cup of water was pressed into my hand. I forced myself to drink slowly. No point in being sick and losing even more moisture in the long run. Sliced cerus fruit appeared. The juice stung the split in my lip. It was worse when it danced across my fingertips. The taste was marred by an overhanging layer of copper.

I resisted the urge to spit it clear. The floor was too shiny for that.

In fact, the whole place was remarkably up market. All polished stone and plush rugs. Somehow, I was sitting on a low sofa which held my body more gently than any lover could have tried.

Tabitha lounged across from me. I found myself staring at her as she gave orders. Orders which were obeyed. By her servants, by the guards who had apparently picked up my trail and burst in only to be shooed away with barely restrained condescension.

No denying, it's rather embarrassing when your unexpected and hopefully heartfelt reunion with somebody is interrupted by people literally breaking down the door. Whilst I am flattered that they thought I still had enough energy left in me to attack anybody, their attempt to drag me out of my saviour's arms only resulted in my very inelegant slide to the floor.

Somebody was yelling about their Lady's safety, someone else was screaming about extending their protection... it was a whole mess. In a brief moment of clarity I almost thought that I saw Sir Enhani once again. That was proof enough that I was in some sort of waking nightmare. There were hands on my shoulders, another pair on my waist, and then a stray elbow caught me under the jaw which had me checking out for a little while.

I'm pretty sure that there was more screaming from all sides. And then someone lifted me onto the nearest piece of furniture with reluctant care. Silence. Beautifully soothing on my racing brain. Did someone pass a cool hand across my brow? They might have done. I knew that I was shaking like a leaf in a gale. The funny thing about when the adrenaline all dies down is just how hard it hits your system. I trembled, I shook, I tried to remind myself that it was a natural response to everything I had been through. I hated myself and my weakness anyway.

And peace reigned.

I could taste only ashes and copper.

At last, I blinked back into my body. My brain protested the return to full awareness. There were far too many damage reports coming in from every inch of my mortal frame. It provided a strange level of clarity. At least I was pretty sure I wasn't actually dead. No, death didn't hurt like this. I chose to believe that, because the thought of the end just being a continuation of what I lived through meant it was no longer a viable option of escape.

But if I wasn't dead, then neither was *she*. True, this could all be some sort of fever dream. Maybe I snapped under torture, and my mind had constructed this as a way to not exist without the finality. Then again, I was pretty sure that I didn't have this much imagination. Also, if it was all in my mind, then I was certain that I would have made the fruit taste right.

The other woman in the room seemed to sense the shift in the atmosphere, the awareness bleeding back. Maybe it was the same instincts which told you when someone was watching, or when a predator stepped too close to your hiding place. The same sense which had kept me alive even as I had been buying time for Clarisse to escape. Some experiences are universal after all.

"Tabitha?" I hadn't meant for it to be a question. If the guards had been there, I knew it would have been a statement, a declaration, a point to anchor to and pretend that I had been simply lying low the whole time. But it didn't come out that way. The name was spoken softly, almost not making it past the swelling which was taking over one side of my face in a faint mimicry of her own markings. I was under no allusions that this put us anywhere close to an even footing. Hell, I didn't know if I would ever feel steady again.

Still, I had been trained to fight even on shifting ground.

"Nina." Ah, so she had all the confidence. Unfair to hoard it like that. "Do you mind if I move closer?" I just blinked for a moment at the absurdity of the question. Why was she asking? If I had gleaned anything even whilst my brain was effectively numbed, it was that she clearly had some standing in this place. She had command, was in control, could do whatever she damn well pleased.

She waited for my answer.

I resisted the urge to lick the juice from my smarting hands. The pressure of my tongue would no doubt make it all worse. Instead, I made a gesture to invite her over. Even that small motion made the bones in my wrist creak like old trees in a gale. I knew I could hear it, feel the grinding of every muscle through the movement. Had she?

Tabitha walked with innate grace. It was as if she expected the musicians to strike up at any minute, to make her gossamer on a breeze. She settled next to me on the sofa, staying just outside of arm reach. It was hard to tell whose comfort that was for.

"You... you are Tabitha, right?" I mean, it would be just my luck. To somehow barrel into a random stranger's bedroom and act like I knew them. Maybe she was just a bystander who felt sorry for the apparently crazy bitch who came falling form the skies. Some princess who had never left the confines of the palace, had no idea about the cruelties of the outside world, and so only knew how to react with undue kindness.

Her laugh was a harsh thing. No silver bells there. The image of fae royalty slowly deflated from the puncture. I couldn't tell if the sound was due to her derision or the physical damage which would no doubt mar her vocal chords.

"That is a... difficult thing to answer."

Oh, Inar's tits! I really had accosted a stranger. This was beyond bloody awkward. I was half convinced that embarrassment could be a cause of death. One part of me even wished that it was in order to give me a quick exit strategy. Was it possible for this situation to get any weirder? Any worse?

The woman took a deep breath, fixing her eyes to mine. "I... I am actually Clarisse."

So apparently it could.

My first thought was that this was all some elaborate plot by the interrogation squad to make me spill my guts. My second thought was that was the fucking stupidest idea in history and that I was mildly ashamed of myself for even coming up with it.

Next option: she was batshit crazy and I just had the absolute worst luck when trying to crawl out of hell. That concept held more weight. My life experiences up to that point were strongly in support of such an interpretation. Right, so I had ended up in the grips of someone clearly influential but also a few apples short of a bushel. I could work with that, earn her trust and then slip away...

There was something in her eyes which made the most absurd, unreliable, dreadfully childish, mortifying that it still existed after all that I had been through, part of my soul hiss at the rest of my reason.

The only outward sign of this internal whirlwind which I allowed, was the way that I froze for exactly seven heartbeats, before deliberately folding my arms across my chest. I hope I kept my face smooth. Or at least that any signs of imminent shut down, break down, general refusal to continue, were placed solely at the feet of my assorted physical traumas. That was something which could be forgiven after all. Split skin and spilt blood and splintered bones were a hurt that could be quantified and compared and so responded to with definitive answers in terms of pain scales and treatment plans. That sort of agony was far more acceptable to the rest of the world.

"Prove it."

She seemed taken aback for a moment. What had she expected? Complete, instantaneous acceptance? Unrelenting, equally swift denial? I was trained better than that.

"You love cerus fruit."

It was a weak ploy and we both knew it. Purple and crimson still dripped from my fingertips. "Please. Everybody knows that about me."

She hummed in acknowledgement. "You told me once that when you were a child, you wanted to be a temple dancer." A brief flicker of a smile even given the situation, "you used to try and practice in the road by your house."

"Nope. Other people know that." Because I do in fact have friends, thank you very much. It was the sort of thing which people tended to ask when you had known them for a while. The classic, 'was bodyguarding what you were always called to do?' Funnily enough it was only ever nobles who asked that. My other friends understood without being told the level of inevitability which accompanies a life of service to another.

She narrowed her eyes, the motion pulling on the scar tissue which ran so completely down one side of her face. "Just before the fire you were ill. You almost died." She held up a hand to gain say my upcoming comments. "I read to you before I was taken away to the summer palace." Leaning closer now, one hand hovering briefly over the cushions as if wanting to reach out and bridge the gap. "I read you a story about dragonflies at an oasis. I wasn't supposed to have a copy of it. The tale had come from your people. You had told me before that it was the last thing your mother had shared with you. On that day you thought I was her."

It is strange how misty a room can grow in the heat of the day. The silence was weighted, waiting. I could have picked it up from the floor and swung it as a weapon.

Now my voice was the harsh one, splintered words forcing their way out of my throat and no doubt leaving scratches in their wake. "Not enough." It wasn't. Someone could have overheard. Been listening in at the crack of the door. That was the way of things in the castle after all. An eavesdropper could have heard it all, saved the scene for a rainy day, gotten a pay day with some cheap information.

It was possible.

Now I was the one closing the distance. I could see the slight tremble in the woman's muscles as her fight or flight instincts warred behind her eyes. Bared teeth, the urge to growl rumbling in my chest but I didn't give in to it. Now was not the time.

"There is only one thing which you could tell that I would believe." And it was true. There was only one memory, one instance, one ripple in the time space idea that Arner's nephew had once tried to explain to me, which would make me give any benefit to these doubts.

She was watching me expectantly, an eager veneer crawling over her face at the thought that I would even be willing to consider buying what she was peddling. How would that change when I told her the terms of such consideration?

"When we first met." Her glee dropped faster than any sabotaged airship could ever hope to emulate. "What was the first thing that you said when you saw me?"

Now it was her turn to be silent, unsure, unwilling to dig deeper into the memory. Had she thought it would be something that I would never bring up? True, it was last resort for a reason. And if she could answer me then it would have served its purpose. I would never say that it had been 'worth it'. I have more self-respect these days. And more anger.

They say that forgiveness and letting go is the truest sign of healing. I disagree. I worked so hard for my rage. To value myself enough to feel anger at the way that I had been treated. That to me is recovery in and of itself. At least one facet.

"What did you say?"

For all that I have forgotten many things in my life, from important dates to the names of people I see every day, this is one instance where I could never quite erase it from my brain. Even repeated hits to head had never quite managed to shake it loose. I could still feel the harsh rope biting into the skin of my wrists. The stones of the cell floor had been cold; my bones had pressed sharply into them.

It had been a pocket dimension carved from darkness and despair into which I had been thrown with a handful of other sand sisters. We were too young to really understand it. Can you ever be old enough? To comprehend what it means to have your world fall down around your ears and for someone to pull you kicking and screaming from the rubble which you so desperately want to hide beneath until an official burial is the next logical step?

They had talked around us, although never to us directly, about how we would serve a purpose, how we would be made useful. Part of me had understood, that same desperate part which clung to reality no matter how badly I wanted to retreat from such ideas. There had been talk of a war, things which my mother had tried to explain when word began reaching us of men in armour marching through the towns and countryside.

I had known that I was a prisoner. That much had made sense.

It was also clear that they had chosen a few of us. Hunted down deliberately. They wanted us to do something. To become something.

And then she had been there. On the other side of the crude bars a woman had appeared. Dressed in light combat leathers, there was still no mistaking the quality of the clothes on her back or the steel at her hip. Her hair had been painstakingly braided, curled and pinned into something impressively high on top of her head. There had been a circlet of gold across her brow.

And a girl in her shadow.

The girl had seemed only a year of two older than the rest of us. She held herself with a high chin for all that her eyes flickered across us. I remembered how I used to eye up apples at the market.

The woman had told her to choose.

Eyes like the colour of an oasis' central lake drifted across the huddled limbs and trembling flanks before her. They fixed on mine for half a breath before sliding on. The girl had huffed, clearly irritated at being asked to perform in front of such an unworthy audience. The woman adorned with gold had raised a harsh eyebrow at her charge, forcing her to look again.

The same result.

I could feel my lips moving in the real world, the current time, forming words in a language which my younger self would not have understood even if I had gone back in time to stand in my own defence.

"What was it? What was the first thing you said about me?"

A face half melted leaned back now, putting a faint distance between us once more. She at least didn't avert her eyes. We had grown up too much it seemed, to feel shame for actions taken so long ago.

"I said... what use could any of these things ever serve?"

When I had been a child the blatant dismissal of my personhood had been a horse kick to the chest. But then, as children, Clarisse hadn't met my eyes. We were older now. It was all but a memory. How she had left, still not having chosen, the Queen at that time following with barely restrained impatience for her ward.

The next day the slavers had numbered us and drawn names out of a hat. And so, I had been sent to the castle.

I very deliberately never speculate about what happened to the others.

Now, years later, those same words actually served this time to define a portion of my fate.

Because nobody else had ever known that.

There was no way that Tabitha could have ever heard of it. Clarisse had never spoken of it after the fact. Even when we properly met, me then introduced as her bodyguard in training, there had been no recognition that we had ever previously crossed paths.

And this woman had known. She had known. She had known. Which meant...

Part of me wanted to laugh. Loud. Long. Until my ribs sank into my lungs, and it all came bubbling back up my throat in impatient red and impassioned heaves.

What use indeed?

CHAPTER TWENTY-FOUR: WOULD IT BE UNPROFFESIONAL TO START SCREAMING?

There had been possibly the most awkward silence of my life between us for long enough that I could hear the guards shifting at their posts outside the door. I found myself resisting the urge to squint at the woman opposite me, looking past the heavy scaring to try and find something familiar. Was her nose the same shape? Were her eyes the right shade of green? Her hair seemed a little darker. But then that could just be my imagination trying to provide some clarity to what I had been told.

"So, you are actually Clarisse?"
"Yes."
"As in the Queen?"
"Yes."
"Not Tabitha."
"No."
"And she set the fire to try and kill you, stole your identity whilst you were unconscious and has since been living as you?"
"That's right."

I took a moment to process this, mindlessly nodding. A deep breath, "So… you are actually Clarisse?"
She smacked a hand to her forehead. "Nina, I swear by whichever

gods you prefer that if you say that one more time, I am going to throw something."

It was a fair reaction. We had been on something of a conversational merry go round without an apparent exit. It's not my fault that the concept was a bit much to try and wrap my head around. If what she was saying was true, then my understanding of my life and the world had taken a steep nosedive into 'beyond fucked up' territory. That sort of journey takes a bit of time to come to terms with.

I all but bit my tongue to ask one more time.

Have you ever been beaten? Or at the very least had to travel a fair distance in a short time? Nobody can ever really warn you for how much it hurts. Your muscles ache and burn every time you try and sit more comfortably, each twinge a warning bell that they are not happy with the abuse you put them through. There was a constant flare going off at the tops of my legs from the pressure of going downhill at speed, whilst my shoulders were making it abundantly clear that they did not appreciate having to hold the pack for as long as I had. Every joint felt overextended, almost swelling up now I was at rest.

No matter how much training you put yourself through, or how common pain is as a part of your life, hurt is hurt and will not be denied. All I really wanted was to be home, in the castle, curled up in my own bed. That was it.

Instead, I was trying to ignore the demands of my body, whilst the woman in front of me explained how everything that I thought I knew was a lie. More than that- she was telling me that the person I had done this to myself on behalf of was in no way worthy of such a sacrifice.

Unfortunately for the delicate balance of my psyche, as that initial piece of information finally took root, a new picture began to take shape from the other available input. The outlines were drawn by the recent diplomatic mishaps, the details filled in with assassination plots and unsettling rumours, the shading completed by the literal army that I had stumbled across a stone's throw from the border.

"You're planning on taking it back. Aren't you? Making a move and reclaiming your throne."

"You always were a good strategist." She actually nodded in approval at me, "Yes. Yes, that is exactly what I intend." There was a grim satisfaction on her face as she spoke, a hard smile pulling at the scars splashed across the left side of her face.

I huffed, slouching further back in my seat, and crossing my arms. It pulled at some of my fresh bruises, so I let them loosen again. "Why now?" it was a valid question in my book. Why hadn't she said any of this before? Directly after the attack, if she was to be believed about what had happened, she would have had a better chance of gathering support. It still would have been a hard sell, for sure, but in those earlier days perhaps someone would have noticed the change. And not just assigned it to the shock. To the impact of narrowly escaping death and losing a dear companion in the process.

"The stars were not in the right position before." A stale joke. We let it sit where it landed. "No, I'm just kidding of course. Quite simply for about a year I was still mostly incapacitated. It took another to figure out what truly mattered. Since then, I have focused entirely on this one goal. And now? All I can say is that I am now ready."

I mean… when she put it like that, I could understand it a bit better. I am not the best witness for what went on around that time as I had been so desperately ill that I couldn't remember at least half of those few months.

Another thought. "How did you get the resources for all this? You *are* being backed by the King of Namet, right?" I mean, unless it was a criminal set of coincidences and circumstances which saw her just so happening to be sharing space with a sizable force of Nametian soldiers. Even the deities of the Pantheon weren't that lazy. (If they had been, then there would be far less for priests to drone on about). So, she had some serious backing. How had she gone from nearly dead and exiled to this?

Tabitha... no, not Tabitha. But I couldn't very well call her Clarisse. That would just get my own brain in to a twist trying to keep track of which one I was thinking about. The woman who would remain nameless for a moment was quirking a smile at whatever thought was in her mind. "Well, brothers-in-law do tend to be somewhat doting."

The distraction of trying mentally to reconcile the best way of refering to her was responsible for that statement taking a few extra seconds to process. I stared at her and hoped that no flies went into my mouth. "Wait, what?"

A laugh, the picture of slightly embarrassed happiness. I got the sense that it was an expression she had spent time perfecting in a mirror. "Oh yes- I got married."

At least now my brain was working a bit better. "To the King's cousin, I presume? The extremely rich one?"

"That's her. Lucille. A simply charming lady with the most fascinating mind. She's currently visiting one of our laboratories to the west to test out a new propulsion technology which a recent recruit is pioneering."

"I see."

My words were softer. I did see. More than I necessarily wanted to. I remembered the dossier on the King of Namet's cousin. Frankly everyone knew at least a little about her after the initial Arner situation. She was the genius mastermind behind the flourishing of the airship sector. It had been but an impractical pipe dream to have air power so readily available only four years ago. And then someone had noticed what a gem was hiding in their court and taken a gamble.

I got the feeling that I now knew whose discerning eye that had been.

The investments into her research had more than paid off,

resulting in the kingdom being able to swiftly corner and control a market which on its own produced the capital of a small nation. And yet from all reports, the brain behind the designs and continuous improvements was less of an extrovert than your average religious hermit.

There had been rumours of another partner being involved, one with the shrewd business acumen and strategic brain to take the concepts and market them to the world. It seemed that I had finally found the person who fit that role. That had to have been Tabitha-Not-Tabitha's doing. And the collective had most certainly reaped the rewards.

One thing immediately slotted into place with regards to this entire mess. It made a sickening sort of sense at long last over what had happened with the airship explosion which had landed me in this whole damned mess. It was clear that Her-No-Longer-Highness was largely driven by thoughts of revenge. Call me an empath. I could pick up a hint from a room. Or an amassed military force sat on the border who had been actively hunting me and my charge across a foreign countryside. The clues were subtle but there.

Her wife was the person who knew most about aircraft in possibly the entire world. And unless they never spoke, it was likely that Tabrissse had picked up more than a few points of interest over the machine's possibilities. What I am trying to say, is that like a bolt of lightning the certainty that this was the person who had orchestrated the crash hit me between the eyes. Maybe she gave instructions to an agent, or even sent one of her researchers to sabotage the engine. Whatever mechanism, she was the mastermind.

Somehow it didn't really change the way that I looked at her. Not in any way that mattered at least. To be honest it was just another strike of craziness in the latest round. At the same time, it was the first thing which had started to make a lick of sense. At least now I had some context for everything that had been going on. Apparently, it had been bubbling for far longer than any of us had realised. I had considered a diplomatic dispute, a trade disagreement, a power grab or monarchic machinations. This whole situation? Not something I would have seen coming. Magda would no doubt claim that she had considered the possibility.

When all this was over, I would spend some quality time reading fiction and listening to bards so as to widen my imagination.

I realised that I had been sitting slightly cross eyed as my thoughts ran almost faster than I could catch. It was a lot to process. And looming just on the horizon of my awareness was the question of what the hell was I to do next? Now I had all of this information, I was sitting having tea with the person who had directly told me of their intentions to kill the Queen. Sort of. Considering the fact that the Queen was not the Queen...

Had I been one of the bad guy's lackeys this whole time and just not realised it?!

But to circle back around to the main issue here- what was my next move?

There was a sense of sinking right in the centre of my chest, bleeding into my stomach. My skin all at once felt too tight across my bones and I flexed my hands as if hoping that the motion would split my knuckles open and relieve the pressure in my limbs. The food didn't taste right, and I could still hear the guard shuffling at his post and the fabric of my skirt was stiff and filthy against my legs and...

A hand secured itself over my own, squeezing hard enough that my entire being focused on that one point of contact. I wanted to scream at her to get off. I wanted to clutch back and not let go until I crawled back into my body properly.

I settled for sitting still and breathing deeply through my nose, out through my mouth, seeing how my lungs would be inflating and relaxing in my mind's eye.

When I could finally bring myself to look directly at her again, there was a deeper form of knowing in her face than I had ever seen from someone outside of Magda. No confusion. No condemnation. Just recognition.

I stubbornly refused to acknowledge the slight heat in my cheeks. Frankly it would be impossible to see anyway through all the bruising.

"I know this is a lot. And I want you to know that I don't expect anything from you here and now." Her voice was strong, rich, tinged with a different accent than what I was used to hearing. No doubt her years abroad, and her wife, had an impact on her. "I am going to arrange for you to have a bath. There is a lovely natural hot spring in this building. I actually think it's why it became the headquarters for the region. You can have a soak; get cleaned up."

Her eyes were scanning over my face, flicking down the rest of my body and very clearly cataloguing the evidence of what I had been through recently. "I can have medical supplies provided as I know you will probably be more comfortable treating your own wounds." A finger under my chin forcing me to look back at her directly again. I hadn't even realised that my gaze had wandered away. Everything was vaguely blurry anyway. "But if there is something more important which you can't treat properly, you have to tell me so that I can get a physician to take a closer look. Understood?"

I blinked. She must have taken that as agreement. People are always free to interpret my expressions in whatever way best suits them.

"Have a bath. Have some more food. Have some sleep. That is all I require of you at the moment. I will have someone bring you some spare clothes." A slight clearing of her throat, "I'm afraid it will probably be an army uniform, simply because we have those so readily at hand in every size..."

"I would like to keep my coat." My tongue felt thick in my mouth, but I am pretty sure the words made their way out. I didn't care about being in the wrong uniform. Clean clothes were a beautiful notion. But I had grown rather attached to the coat which my sand sister had gifted me. I idly wondered if my pack would find its way back to me during all this apparent care. If the contents had all been returned after the inevitable search. They had certainly taken it with them when they finally brought me in.

"Of course. I shall have it laundered and returned. Are you ready to go? I will escort you myself..."

My muscles finally remembered a bit of how to function, jerking my head into a belated nod. The motion made my brain feel as if it were sloshing to the front of my head and back again.

Standing to follow her lead towards the door nearly brought tears to my eyes. I had locked up from being in the same position for too long whilst wounded. It wouldn't surprise me if she could hear the creaking snaps of each of my joints. The thought of a hot bath was sounding more and more like the greatest gift in the universe.

I took one more moment to scan the room as we left. A habit born from the job. Even though I was no longer on the job as such...

All I could see of note were the red scuff marks on the windowsill from where I had scrabbled so desperately. At that time the only thing I had to worry about was whether I would lose my grip and make a mess on the street below.

I wondered if it had been immensely good or bad luck that this was the balcony I had launched myself over.

I wondered what this hospitality was going to cost me since nothing in the world came free.

I wondered how long it would take for someone to clean the streaks from the stones.

CHAPTER TWENTY-FIVE: I NEED A FIVE MINUTE BREAK FROM REALITY

It was almost a delightful surprise that I didn't hear Tabitha as she stepped out onto the balcony where I had taken refuge. If I had wanted any proof that my senses were finally on the wind down, comfortably blunted for the first time that I could remember, it was that I only knew she was there when she tripped over an empty bottle. To be fair she probably hadn't thought to check the floor for such things.

"Oh gods, have you been drinking?" the tone was half disappointed and yet also amused.

I tilted my head back to try and see the stars, only to tilt sideways until I had to grip the railing harder. "Yes."

"Are you drunk?"

"It would seem so." The empty spaces where my nails had once been cracked open to weep on the roughened stones.

I grinned at her the same way as when I had learnt my first cross stitch. Or when I had landed my first thrown dagger on target. I raised the half full bottle in my hand, surviving cousin to the one Tabitha had tripped on, in a parody of a salute before downing the rest in one smooth breath. It would seem that many of the skills I had honed over the years could be repurposed.

"For fuck's sake." She stormed over, yanking the bottle away and tossing it over her shoulder. I barely registered the shattering glass, and simply retrieved a new one from my coat pocket. "You are literally trained to be immune to poisons. How could this even happen? What in the hell did you drink?"

"Where there's a will there's a way." I tried to stifle a hiccup. "In my defence, I did ask the barkeeper what was in my drink, and he told me to ask my gods when I met them. I figured that was a fair answer and so got a double. By the way I charged it to the treasury."

That landlord had been far less polite than the one that had helped me out right after the crash. Johanson. He had been a delight. This guy was apparently called 'grunt' or possibly 'angry muttering'. He didn't have a dog. Then again, I got the sense that he had been dealing with bored soldiers for quite a while which would put anyone's patience to the test. On balance I couldn't really blame him for the irritated reaction when I had slipped through the door and onto a barstool. I was wearing the military uniform after all, even if the coat would have certainly been against regulation.

The bath originally ordered for me had been sheer ecstasy. Just having warm water and proper soap had made my senses dial it down a notch, for all that I was vaguely embarrassed by how murky it became. Every muscle in my legs finally relaxed just enough that I could find it in myself to move less stiffly. Even so, I had to keep my hands out of the water. One touch of it to my exposed nail beds had me choking on a howl of sheer agony. Once I could bring myself to climb out, a more concentrated stretching routing nearly made me cry, but it did at least serve to get me able to move again.

That was followed by a veritable feast of bread and meats, my consumption of which put rabid wolves to shame. Having finally given in to the demands of my body, and once my various hurts were stitched, salved, and wrapped, I had all but passed out in the bed. It had actually been my clothes being brought back which had woken me up.

The guard had nearly pissed himself when on opening the door to put the uniform and coat on the table, he had to stagger back from my instinctive lurch upwards knife in hand. From what I could gather of his yelling he was mostly furious that I had somehow gotten hold of a weapon. So, it seemed that I was under a certain level of restrictions. It made sense.

For anybody curious, it was one of the butterfly hairpins which had somehow survived all of the nonsense.

He confiscated the blade, with my permission, and told me to call if I needed anything.

I had agreed, got dressed, and figured out how to get my hair brushed and braided out of the way using my remaining pin. I then spent five full minutes enjoying the fact that I was clean and dressed in fresh, new clothes.

For the record, it is amazing what a difference food and sleep make to the body. Things were generally at an aching level rather than the imminent system failure which I had been operating at since leaving the caravan. As such, it had taken remarkably little effort to crawl out of my window.

It seemed that I had been housed on one of the top levels of their headquarters. Possibly to stop me doing something stupid like trying to climb down the side of the building. I was a professional. I would not do something so ridiculous and dangerous. No, instead I went up until I was properly on the roof. There is always an access ladder or something of the kind down from the roof. This one thankfully dropped me into a fairly empty courtyard.

The impact had juddered through my entire being like streaks of lightning radiating from my ankles. I was sharply reminded that I had been going through relative hell for a fair stretch of time, and that sort of damage took more than a brief, deep sleep to heal from. For possibly the millionth time, I figured that I was probably getting too old for this. All the more reason for me to find a distraction from my own fragile mortality. Namely: a drink.

The few people who did spot me focused solely on the uniform and let me past. As ever, the key is to walk with confidence. Act like you own the place and most people tend to believe that you do. I marched myself straight out of the parade ground and into the nearest bar. Quite a lot of shots later... I may have just caved and downed a bottle. It had tasted somehow of overly ripe strawberries and young nettles. A strange mix, I could understand why I seemed to be the only person keen to down more of it.

I got another few for the road and staggered my way back into headquarters. There were less people around given the time of night, but they were far more open with staring as I weaved my way back towards my room.

The guard had gaped as I came around the last corner. Maybe he thought that I'd been sleeping the whole time? I tilted the open bottle in cheers to him as I crashed through the door, promptly slamming it in his face before he could get his wits together to follow me or ask any questions. After that I had taken refuge on the balcony and kept at it with the drinking.

It seemed the spoil sport had gone to report my absence to whoever was in charge of keeping me contained.

And then I finally remembered that Tabitha had asked me a question. No, Clarisse... Tabitha... this was annoying when examined through the bottom of a glass. I think I was saying that out loud, at least some of it, as she finally just exhaled hard through her nose and told me to call her Tabitha. That was the name she had been going by for all this time, why complicate things further now?

My shrug was far looser than my usual motions, all my limbs feeling half detached from gravity. I almost wanted to twirl around in a solo dance of waving arms and staggering feet, simply because I was curious to see how more movement would feel.

So I did.

I couldn't remember the last time I laughed like that as I twirled briefly in the small space of the balcony. The sound of it rose high and lonely into the night until I found myself once again clutching the railing with one hand and the bottle neck with the other. Definitely giddier.

Tabitha came to stand behind me, sighing a little as she looked me up and down. Her lips twitched in response to my own hilarity. She rested a hand on my shoulder in solidarity, and possibly so I didn't pitch over into the darkness below.

"So how do you feel?"

"Well... my head is kind of spinning... my balance feels like the time they were teaching me how to walk on a high wire..." I started humming, swaying to the melody at the edge of my mind. I remembered I had heard it once, years ago, when a new bard came for the Coronation Ball. The party had lasted for a whole week, and I had to be stone cold sober throughout the whole thing. Now I could finally join the party.

I found myself leaning further over the balcony rail, not just for the extra support, but to get a better view at the buildings sprawling out below amongst the pock marked stones. The city, what little I had seen of it, was really rather lovely in its own way. As was often the nature with such trading towns, there had been enough money in the area for people to indulge their artistic tastes when it came to their infrastructure. The barracks had seemed more like some ducal palace than necessary housing for soldiers.

Part of me wondered what sort of a life those soldiers had. It had been a fair while since Namet had last properly gone to war, the few standard border skirmishes aside of course. No matter how much training troops went through, there was no substitute for really seeing a battlefield in all its glory. And from what I could tell, these men were more used to having an element of luxury in their daily lives. Then again, no need to judge them when I hadn't yet seen them in action. All that mattered for the moment was that the city looked rather pretty in the night where it spread below my window as a handful of golden fireflies drifted past on a light wind.

The breeze tugged at the ends of my hair and licked at the hems of my clothes which were still the wrong uniform. I figured it would be best not to request my old clothes back. The heresy of a hemline after all.

With some effort I brought my attention back to the woman at my side. "You know, it is a lot more fun to choose to take the poison yourself. Rather than having to because it is my job, or because you are too small when they hold you down..." my sentence trailed off as my mind wandered off again for a moment. I couldn't quite tell what the expression on Tabitha's face was, and not just because my vision was deciding to blur just a little at the edges. The lights had never looked so soft before.

"Come on, let's get you to bed."
"Urgh, you are no fun. Not anymore."
"Well, a lot has happened since we were girls. But no matter, for now we are just going to let you sleep this off and then-"
"I know." Gravity was back with a vengeance, pushing on the back of my head and bowing my neck. I couldn't see the lights anymore, just the stone beneath my fingertips. "In the morning you want me to ride with you and help you bring war to the gates of Tartyn."

A harsh breath sucked in through her teeth, "No. That's not..."
"Tabitha. It is what it is, and what it always has been." I took a deep breath through my nose, blowing it out through my mouth and urging myself to come back to reality. "You want me to get your forces into the castle, so you can find Clarisse and kill her for the throne." Why else would she bother with taking care of

me, keeping me around at all? It had to be because I would be useful to her. That was all I had to offer in any real sense.

"No!" there was fire in her eyes, both of soul and of memory, "Whilst I will be taking that bitch down, and yes enjoying it after so long a wait..." she hesitated, visibly forcing back that visceral rage, "I won't ask you to be a part of that."

"Come on. I am not a child anymore." I don't think I had been for so long.

She looked away from me, head tilting back for a moment to look not at the stars but the banners flapping in the night breeze. The glint of their embroidery was just about visible in the lights from below. She took a deep breath, releasing it along with a fair amount of tension from her shoulders. When she turned her eyes back to me, they were a mirror of my own tired gaze.

"How do you choose not to feel it?"

"What?" I was genuinely confused, choosing rather to tilt the last dregs from the bottle into my mouth than try and think of what she could be asking. I could choose ignorance one time more.

She raised her hands in a vague gesture between us which may have meant to encompass the entirety of our respective lives. "You know, all the things you have done, and seen, how does none of it affect you?"

I resisted the urge to snort. Instead, I took a moment to let the liquor settle and burn in my gut. To feel its scorch. My next words were clearer. "I guess... I never had the luxury to feel it. I couldn't. There was always something more important than whether or not I wanted to scream or cry. So long as I could keep my hands steady- that was what mattered most."

"So, what?" she sounded desperate, a woman begging for water in a desert.

"So... I tamp it all down, and sit on it tight, and let it burn me so that nobody else gets caught in it because that is not my right to inflict." My knuckles were tight around the neck of the bottle. I wanted to send it sailing away into the night to shatter and take as many people with it as possible. To claim its pound of flesh, its tithe of blood, because that was the only right way for something to exit this world. Until all would smell of strawberries and nettles and copper.

Tabitha spoke after a beat of silence. "I could never figure out how to do that. How to let go of it."

"Oh, I never said that I let go. Don't make that mistake."

"Hmm... I guess that is a skill I never learnt." Now she was the one lifting her eyes heavenward. "No. My rage, my pain? That was something far too powerful for me to ignore."

I hated the implication. The arrogance of assuming she knew exactly what I kept locked away down deep enough in my soul that I could only feel the faintest tremors of its claws. But she had always been born to be a queen. It was quite simply her nature. And besides, she could afford such luxuries as feeling.

She stood beside me now, looking out over the place which had been her haven and home for so long. The place which would now be sending troops to fuel her fight. Namet would no doubt have its own Jeremy, and Hanson, and Sir Gavin, each with their own friends and families and lives. All of which they would be placing in the hands of someone they trusted to lead them to righteous victory. Or at least a hefty payday. I wondered if she regretted asking them for aid, if she knew the men who would be sent to fight in her name.

Somehow, I doubted it. This was a monarch on a mission. She had believed in her own divine purpose and Inar help anyone who got in her way. Or worse- tried to make her doubt her own cause. People had been destroyed for far less.

"I know you. Your loyalty has always been your strongest quality." I noted she didn't say best. "So, I won't ask for you to help me in that regard. This isn't a game. People are going to be hurt, to die, and that is the reality of command and reign. That is not your burden to bear. All I was going to ask, is that you protect me."

I mulled it over for a minute. Maybe longer. "You do realise that you are always going to end up just sitting down and talking." My words were sharper than they had been for this whole talk. My blatant refusal to let myself slur on such a topic. Tabitha didn't twitch so much as a muscle as I continued. "The only question is how many bodies will the negotiation table be resting on at the end?"

Another bout of humming, something which I had once caught Hanson singing to one of the fussier servant children. A babe, only just old enough to understand when crying would get their heart's desire and when it would just make other people angry. Such a precious age. For some reason the melody had always seemed eerily close to one which had been sung in the temples of my youth, and which I had imagined dancing to in days when I still believed that art could exist for its' own sake and that the goddess could direct our paths with only her own whims.

From the corner of my eye, I watched as Tabitha shifted her weight from foot to foot. "Have you ever tried Talan berries?" it must have seemed apropos of nothing, but she could have been carved from the stones of the balcony. "They can make water become beautifully sweet when steeped in it. Tastes worthy of the Pantheon." A bark of laughter which wasn't all that amused even to my own ears. "It can send you to them as well."

A moment of watching her reactions was all the confirmation that I needed. The holy water poisoning had been her doing as well. She really must be determined if the very heart spring of her homeland was a viable target, a resource to be used towards her own ends. It was something that I could understand, even respect. That level of practicality was a quality not often found amongst nobility.

It also confirmed beyond a doubt my long-held suspicion that she had an agent at court. Someone was her puppet. Her hand to reach out and control aspects of the court. I filed the thought away for future examination with a clearer head. All at once I remembered Lord Arner, crouched against the floorboards and taking the fall for a plot which I had never believed to be his own. And where was Samda now?

I fixed my eyes on the heavens once again. "So what? You invade, take the capital by storm, kill the Queen, and claim the throne? I am guessing that you have at least been intercepting and altering the Tartyn ambassador's correspondence to disguise your movements. All the better for a lightning strike attack of shock and awe." I raised a toast to the plan, knocking it back and trying to tell if it still burned as satisfactorily. The fact that the bottle was empty suggested not. "If somebody told me that tale, I would accuse them of being boring. And then of course, if events did unfold in that way, the country will naturally be annexed by Namet."

A hand on my shoulder, willing me to listen to the genuine passion in her voice. It seemed all so far away, as if I was viewing the scene on some stage in a far-off village who could only afford travelling players. "No! We will still be a sovereign nation... just with a special relationship." The glint of the stone in her wedding ring in the lamplight caught my attention like an errant moth to an unguarded flame.

"Oh of course, completely different." Was I swaying again? Possibly. Whatever my body was doing whilst I was not paying full attention, it felt right. Like soothing a deep ache in my muscles, or the itch under my skin. Moving in such a way, just because it was comforting, had always been something to be told off for. At that moment I couldn't find it in myself to care. I figured I owed myself a few moments of blissful relief from propriety.

When I spoke again it was in a soft rasp. "And if it doesn't work that way?" I couldn't bring myself to turn from the beautifully glitter strewn heavens. "You get stuck in a stalemate, or a protracted siege. How long will your wife's family support such a campaign when you will only be losing them money and reputation? You really have backed yourself into a corner here."

I threw my head back, laughing at the skies, high and unbridled. At the same time, I felt every muscle bracing itself in anticipation of how sharp a blow I would receive. Alcohol-soaked system or not, the words I had spoken were barely a half step away from outright treason. Even as I said them, it felt like finally letting a mouthful of rotten food fall from my mouth. One which I had been holding onto long enough to sample every nuance of disgusting flavour. The relief was immeasurable. Well worth any punishment which could fall upon my shoulders for such a speech.

She turned fully towards me now, gripping my arms until I looked her in the eye. "You swore an oath to me. Right at the start. To me. To protect, to serve,"
"To support and defend."
"With faithful allegiance." Her eyes bored into mine, even as the lights cast her scars into far starker contrast with her natural skin tone. "Does that still hold?"

I was so gods damned tired.

The first time I had spoken those words I had been repeating back sounds made by a stranger in a foreign land. They had no meaning other than that to pronounce them correctly could result in a ration of food. Or being allowed to sleep. Over time I learnt the language of my new world, the rules, the nuances. The words didn't change no matter which level of society I was implanted into. I had repeated them so much that they had once again become sounds. Although at least now I knew what they were supposed to mean.

The tune had trailed its way out of my head once again although it didn't leave any silence in its wake. Turning my gaze down at long last, I was almost surprised to see that the barracks had largely fallen quiet. A city never truly sleeps of course, but this one seemed to have for the most part given in to the pull of the night.

"My oaths stand unbroken... and shall remain such."
An arm around my shoulders, almost a hug, but she was using the hold to steer me away from my balcony spot. We were inside. Right. I would need to get some sleep. It was going to be a long day tomorrow. She was still speaking. "I never doubted you."

She had also not answered one of my questions or allusions. Hadn't refuted even one accusation.

I thought of watchful guards and strange tasting tea and the fact that she hadn't taken her weapon off once whilst we had been alone. There was an attempt at a smile on my face, but any wavering could be blamed on the numbing effect of alcohol on my indulgence. "I know."

Perhaps she wanted to say something. Maybe impart one last persuasive plea or pearl of wisdom. Whatever words she may have been trying to form, apparently died in her throat before they could draw breath. Instead, Tabitha headed out of the room, leaving me to wander back out to my balcony.

There was nothing left in the bottle, no last comforting dreg to finish the conversation with. I watched my hand almost of its own volition, reached out over the railing, and simply let it go. There was a second of silence, and the tinkling crash of it hitting the cobbles below. How careless. So dangerous. Someone could have been badly injured by such an attitude. Nobody yelled from the street, no hue and cry were raised. I wondered who would be made to sweep up the shards in the morning.

CHAPTER TWENTY-SIX: HOW DO YOU STOP YOUR CLOAK FROM FRAYING?

It felt like a lifetime had passed since I had last taken my cloak from my pack. It was almost a minor miracle that it had made it all this way. How many days had really passed since we boarded the airship? My fingers traced the well-known lines of stitching, following the various swirls and edges of each pattern part. My whole life story, fit on one piece of fabric. Hours upon hours of work.

"Your cloak looks like it has seen better days." I had heard Tabitha duck into the tent, expected her to visit me on the eve of our crossing the border.

I knew exactly what she was talking about. There were more than a few patches on mine where the stitching was less than perfect. One of the many hazards of the job. Pretty much they showed when an interrupted attempt on the Queen's life had left me paying the price. So often during recovery my hands would shake too much for my stitches to be even. For all that this did somewhat damage the appearance of the overall design, I chose to see it as a form of honour. Each bit was a sign of when I had done my job well.

I raised an eyebrow as I looked at her own cloak which had been smoothed over her shoulders by her maid. "Same for you."

The servant shot me an offended look from where she was still fussing around her mistress, but Tabitha just waved a hand in dismissal. The girl bowed out of the room, and without prompting I took her place in fastening the pin with her crest into place. The top of the fabric was left as a strip of white, stark against the scars on her neck. The following few yards were a chaotic selection of irregular stiches, clear snags, tangles, and knots visible. After that the patterns became clearer, recognisable, events picked out with skill and confidence.

She met my eyes in the reflection of the mirror. "It was my shroud, you know. Tabitha... well Clarisse I suppose... she wanted me dead. One of the ministers who was still loyal to me, who knew what had happened, told her I had succumbed to my wounds. And she sent me a shroud. I guess I just put it to good use."

Such a traditional gift to the dearly departed, the oldest form of respect. The idea was that their spirit could start a new story on the other side, using their shroud as the start of their next chapter. I couldn't fault her for the way that she had stuck to the spirit of the custom in the truest way.

Tabitha turned to face me fully, placing her hands on my shoulders and mimicking the way that I had fixed her cloak in place. She eased her hands down the fabric, resting briefly on the flawed areas. "I would never want you to be hurt in such ways again. I know it is unavoidable to a degree, the reality of your life and service. But I will do all in my power to build a world where it isn't necessary."

Her voice was earnest, the words supposedly heartfelt. I could recognise the work of a good speech writer. I suppose I was a good way to practice before she had to motivate her troops. They had a long walk ahead of them after all.

The sound of her voice was like a centipede crawling up my back. I didn't pull away from her for all that my spine stiffened rather than relaxing into her hands.

"You know, nobles talk a lot more than people realise. Especially when they are drunk. Or believe that you are drunk." I deliberately didn't look at her, instead turning to fix my sword to my belt. Some ceremonies are just too ingrained, I guess. At least I had already stashed all of my smaller blades in their usual spots. Nobody was meant to know about all of those ones. Professional pride you see. That was the only type I indulged in.

My voice was intentionally light, knowing, sharing a well-known and oft repeated story between simple women. "I never would have put you down for liking poison as a weapon. Talan blossom is agonising by the way. It burns your throat on the way down, your blood as it processes through your body, and your throat lining on its way back up."

She was still behind me, hands frozen from where she was securing her own weapon.

"Sure they taste delicious, but the way that they make you convulse uncontrollably is not pleasant." I finally turned to face her again, raising one eyebrow. "There were no doubt others, and I always had my suspicions about that set up with the throne room trap. I had wondered why someone would go to the trouble of making sure not to risk harming one of the historical cloaks. It got me instead you know, managed to slice a nice piece off my flank. It healed."

A swift pat down to make sure that no obvious bumps showed on my body. She still hadn't said a word.

"It was... gratifying to have my suspicions about foreign backing confirmed though. There had been a bit of disagreement over the nature of the threat which we faced." I offered her a small smile. "You said it yourself- with my training for immunity to poisons, did you really think I could get wasted? It was good booze. But I was more interested in what you would say. So, tell me again, what sort of world are you trying to build?"

Tabitha took a breath, visibly straightening her spine. "Does this mean... is this your way of saying that you can't be there with

me? If you are worried about the morals of my actions..."
"Oh please. You know me better than that. Or at least you did once. I don't care if you do right things for the wrong reasons, wrong for the right, or any combination thereof. Good or bad is not for me to judge. I'm just there."

At last she cracked, rueful hysteric embarrassment taking over. She laughed and I laughed, and she laughed and I laughed, and she laughed and I realised I had forgotten how to cry.

I headed for the door, "It is my job, always has been, to protect my charge. From all threats. It's pretty simple really. All I ask? Don't lie to me."

These days I am too tired to enjoy illusions. They just give me a headache.

She watched me for a moment, searching for something in my face. "I'm going to go and address my troops. I am going to explain the mission to them, thank them for their service, assure them that I will do all I can to bring them home again." Stepping now to the door, she opened it and looked back at the last second even as her attendants fussed at her about being late. "I hope you can find it in yourself to stand by me. To at least consider me worthy of your protection. To believe that I am still the Queen that you once pledged to."

There was nothing else to say. Tabitha left. And I stood alone in the room.

In the mirror on the wall, I could see the story of my cloak spread out across my body. The uniform was barely visible beneath. I had my coat from the stowed and ready to change into. It would be far easier to move in after all. You only wore cloaks in serious moments, when you were declaring to the world exactly who you were, what you had gone through, what you had deemed important enough to immortalise forever in thread and pricked fingers.

At that moment it seemed such a small story. The marred parts had always been on someone else's behalf. Because that was what I knew. That was who I was. That was what I had been made into and lived for longer than any other form of life.

When I put it that way... there was only one place that I could really go.

The doors seemed to open in slow motion, the heavy wood falling open beneath my hands as I strode into the room. The soldiers were arrayed before me, spears at perfect rest and glinting in the light of the torches. I walked between their ranks, not looking at their faces. To me they had none. They were soldiers, made to serve. At least that was what I told myself. That man on the end did not look like Jeremy. The one three ranks behind was nothing similar to Sir Gavin. No sir. No way. Not at all.

The aspiring queen was at the front of the ranks, on the dais which served as her viewing platform. I sprang from the floor to her side without a sound of effort.

I didn't bow. I met her eyes, not letting anything cross my face. She smiled at me in welcome. My expression did not change as I moved to stand at her side. We overlooked the gathered army, the forces who were preparing to mark on Clarisse's castle.

I knew a choice was coming. I would have to make it. For now, I stood, and waited.

CHAPTER TWENTY-SEVEN: CROSSING LINES IN MORE WAYS THAN ONE

The smoke which drifted across the plains was strangely sweet as it tickled my nose. The cloud had settled like a pall over the ever-advancing column of soldiers, shedding ashes and dusting their uniforms in grey.

We had ridden up a small rise to try and get a better view of the lay of the land. I had almost swallowed my tongue when we had been joined by Sir Enhani- it seemed he had scored a position as being part of Tabitha's guard detail. I wasn't sure what that said about how highly the King prioritised her safety. The man was at least a tad more respectful, perhaps sobered by the reality of being in an actively dangerous situation rather than a diplomatic punch up. Perspective can change a person after all. I could only hope that it would make him less of an ass to deal with for however long this all lasted.

"Your highness, we have been receiving reports from our scouts that the opposition is continuing to pull out of this region."
"No doubt falling back to protect the capital."
"That would be the most likely option. Afterall, there aren't that many strategic points in this country which could work as a stronghold."

It was an unfortunate truth, and one which was the point of

focus for many a battle planning session. What Tartyn lacked in defendable structures, it more than made up for in large fields and plains which would be suitable for mass charges and cavalry bravery. However, given the relative sizes of the armies involved, that would not be the best tactic. Considering that about half of the army was probably still in Rhean, Clarisse probably only had enough troops under her command to either fight a pitched battle outright, immediately, or defend the castle. She couldn't do both.

It didn't even matter if they had been sent for as soon as the invasion happened. It was a simple, logistical reality: that much manpower and equipment could not move quickly. Possibly the cavalry would be leading, travelling ahead of the rest of the forces to get back home and defend, but even then, they would take longer to reach us than we would need to reach the castle. Tabitha at least deserved credit for perfect timing.

If Clarisse did choose the former option, it would be a desperate gamble that she could hold out for long enough that reinforcements could arrive. Even if their beloved Pantheon blessed them with success, it was likely that Namet could just send another battalion or two to pick off the remainder before they had the chance to really regroup. Frankly, the King had the treasure to do so.

It was a sad irony that a lot of that payment had come from trade with this very country. Ah the joys of friends going to war.

Anyway, the point was that Clarisse's best bet would be to draw Tabitha's forces to the castle so as to best protect the resources which she did have until another factor could shift the balance. All of which was a very long way of saying that due to the harsh realities of war, the countryside was being pretty much abandoned to the invaders. They probably reasoned that so long as the capital held, the country was still theirs.

One of Tabitha's aides was hurriedly sketching out all that he could see, for a moment reminding me of how Lizzie would scribble down whatever events happened to later be translated to thread and cloth. The aspiring queen herself was watching with calculating eyes the rate at which her troops marched, a thousand calculations taking place in that ever sharp brain.

I could see how her wife had to have been so attracted to that keen intelligence.

From our vantage point, all I could stare at was the dancing flames as they greedily ate the trees of the orchard to the east.

The place had once produced the finest cider, a delicacy enjoyed at court and exported to our allies. I remembered how Tabitha, Clarisse, both if I am honest, had been so excited each time the new year's crop was brought in. Now she stared with hard eyes as the ancient trees crumbled down.

When we had visited the orchard that spring. The apple blossoms had fallen like snow. The owner had gifted each of us one of the flowers preserved in a special type of resin, as thanks for the continued patronage of their family legacy. She had even given one to me. Arner's nephew had fixed a small hook to it so that I could use a ribbon to tie it into my hair.

I thought of warmed cider sipped between clouds. I remembered how much better Johanson's produce had tasted. I wondered if the family had made it out of the farmstead. If they had enough warning, enough survival instinct, to run before the soldiers had arrived under orders. Or had they stayed? Pride and an inability to comprehend what was happening forcing them to try and holdout.

There was a second line cutting its way across the landscape, far thinner, less organised, trickling its way ahead of the advance. I knew what I was watching. It was the civilians pulling out, leaving their homes before they could be overrun by the invading force. They would probably be heading for the woods, seeking refuge in the ancient forests to the west which in peace time were the lifeblood of the lumber trade.

Such an innocuous thought- which trades were popular in which region. I had always thought that the nation was one which had punched above its weight, fuelled and backed by the abundant natural resources. And that was all I could think of as I traced in my mind how families were running from peril. That was my mental point of clarity, of context. Perhaps I had been more tuned in to council meetings than I had ever thought. Or maybe my brain was just that desperate for one small detail which had nothing to do with what was happening in front of me.

Whatever. None of it mattered in the long run. Or the short, for that matter.

The villages which we moved through were empty, possessions taken by any capable hands, those small tools regrettably left behind had been ensured to be of no use.

I had watched with a hollow chest as a soldier had taken a celebratory bite of a fruit from an abandoned kitchen table, only to howl in pain as he found a shard of glass embedded within. Humans have always been so creative in their vengeance, a vicious pettiness ever waiting to break free. The solider had looked far too young as he wept over his ruined mouth.

Not everybody had been able to run of course. Some had been too proud, too stubborn. I had heard reports that there were prisoners of war being taken- those who had chosen to take up arms against the invaders who came marching into their home. It turned out that if you hear the word 'casualty' enough it loses its meaning to a certain extent.

The queen-to-be was good at keeping in thoughts fixed on her end goal. She seemed ever mindful of the fact that she needed a land to rule when all of this was done. There was no point to operating on a completely scorched earth policy, not if she intended to have any hope of holding the throne when she took it. And she was more than certain that would happen. There was a sort of manic hunger in her eyes every time one of her aides brought forward their maps showing how far their forces had already advanced.

I couldn't help but wonder how much of this land she remembered. Was it with fondness? Was it with pain? This had been her birth right after all, the land which she had been brought into as a screaming babe and now intended to claw back as a howling woman.

There hadn't been any major skirmishes yet. I could give Tabitha that much credit. She had done well to disguise her movements in the run up to this invasion, and when it had reached the point of ignition she had moved swiftly. No doubt the real army was being rallied somewhere else, likely having pulled back to a better defensive position. There wasn't much around these parts which could act as a strong point to engage an enemy.

How far would this go before we met proper resistance? Until then, the soldiers proved their mettle against teenagers with their grandfather's swords, boys with broom handles and delusions of bardic glory. I found myself praying to Inar that any who could, would run, and those who stayed would find Her grace and protection. I wanted to call upon Anar, to sing praise to my goddess of wrath and vengeance and ruin... but I did not know who to call Her for. And She was not one to invoke lightly.

Others had been simply unable to leave ahead of the advance. Tabitha had made it extremely clear that there was to be no violence against the people we came across. She made a point to visit any civilians the army encountered, to reassure them personally wherever possible that she bore them no ill will.

The last one had spat in her face.

Soon after the embers had begun gleefully dancing amongst the dry grass of the orchard.

As if able to hear my thoughts, Tabitha flicked her eyes to the side to try and meet my own. I found myself unable to look away from the flaming trees. "They will understand." She sounded so sure of herself, no doubts in her own righteousness. "When the war is over, and they realise what a lie they had lived under for so long. They will see why we had to do all of this. Why it was necessary. Painful, true, but don't physicians have to take drastic measures to save patients?" she moved back to her horse, hoisting herself up into the saddle with practiced ease. The smile on her face was hard as she looked down at me. "They will understand."

I stayed on the spot as the rest of the little group began to move away, back down to where the main column continued to snake its way through the fields. Perhaps she was right, perhaps the people would understand. Would find a grim sense of acceptance for everything that was happening.

I couldn't help but think that understanding did not automatically mean forgiveness.

CHAPTER TWENTY-EIGHT: IF YOU ARE GONNA START A FIGHT YOU THROW THE FIRST PUNCH AND MAKE IT COUNT

There was a strange lack of screaming when the attack started. It was the sort of thing which you just always tended to assume- that when a camp is suddenly threatened the night will be split apart by yelling. That didn't happen, not at first.

It was long since darkness had fallen after all, the soldiers no doubt sleeping heavily from having marched so far over the last few days. They were confident in the fact that they hadn't met much resistance until that point. It's the trouble with arrogance. The longer it continues, the more it begs the fates to prove you wrong. Waring your ass to taunt a hungry wolf. It was a lesson which you only ever had to learn once. Provided you survived the teaching.

Perhaps that was why I had still been awake. I would like to think so. My brain hadn't been letting me rest, not really, ever since Tabitha's forces had crossed the border. There was an ever-constant pain in my head, an itch in my limbs. It was the all-pervading sense that something was about happen; that I was standing on what could turn out to be the wrong side of history. That wasn't the sort of thing that I normally cared about; in fact it was a trait which had been most forcibly repressed over the years. It didn't stop the feeling crawling up my spine and into my mind.

So yes, I hadn't been sleeping.

I had been telling myself that I was on guard duty, in my own way. Tabitha's tent was of course the most protected in the encampment, soldiers posted all around the place where the precious leader slept. And, so I had observed, took the time to compose long letters to her wife. I had never realised just how much somebody could write about walking through the countryside, even if you were strolling with a few thousand people. Maybe they were really in love. Whatever, not my problem either way.

My version of guarding was therefore rather more circumspect, consisting of sitting by the banked fire which had the best line of sight to her quarters as well as a wide area of the camp. The coals were low enough not to ruin my night vision, so I at least had noticed when there was a sudden uptick in movement around the tents.

Screaming would have tipped people off at once, naturally, that is why we scream in the presence of danger in the first place. I will give credit to the invading force for maintaining their quiet for as long as possible. The bloodbath began with relative peace and quiet, no warning shouts or alarms being raised. Just a strange collection of darkened figures moving through the encampment with a deceptive level of purpose. Once again the concept of pretence to fool perception was being proved. Even to me. Sometimes you can kid a kidder it seems.

It held true in this instance. At least, right up until one of Tabitha's soldiers came stumbling out of his tent and directly into one of the people creeping around. The impact sent both men stumbling into the pool of light cast by a slightly more lively fire.

At first, I found myself staring at the dark figure, head tilting to one side of its own accord as I tried to figure out what was bothering me about its silhouette. It took longer than I want to admit. I will blame that on being tired.

The cut of the clothes was wrong. Well... right? As in- it was the style which belonged to the actual inhabitants of Tartyn. Including the army. It was the sort of uniform which I had seen every day for years. The very same which I had worn on more than one occasion.

It was the sort of outfit which most certainly did not belong in the heart of an invader's camp.

The soldier who had literally bumped into the infiltrators finally gave voice to a yell, no doubt noticing the same thing which I had. Or maybe he was just startled. The sound died rather abruptly, as did the man making it. A length of steel to the throat will tend to do that. Even as his tent mates began calling out in confusion, in turn rousing their neighbours, my own ears chose to zone in almost exclusively on the gurgling rattle of a windpipe struggling through copper.

Movement exploded around the camp now, with the sounds of mounting panic and surprise swiftly taking over. Men began staggering from their tents, still pulling on helmets and whatever pieces of armour they had managed to wiggle into whilst responding to the yells of their officers. It was almost comical as a man with stirpes of rank on his arm tripped over his unlaced trousers, all but falling on the sword of one of the attackers. Magda once told me that there was a fine line between comedy and tragedy, to which I had said that comedy was tragedy happening to other people. Maybe we were both right.

I found myself reluctant to move from my spot by the fire.

It seemed that Clarisse's forces had sent out a covert mission of scouts, a splinter group of which had decided to make a strike for the heart of the enemy and so disband the invasion before it could reach the capital. At least, that was what I guessed had happened. Purely a professional hunch of course. Nothing to do with the light mental exercise which Magda and I had indulged in on more than one occasion of coming up with worst case scenarios and responses. I, for one, had definitely not thrown out some ideas of how to train such a strike force.

And now I just sat where I was. I don't know why. There was a battle literally breaking out around me. Steel was clashing against steel and in turn sliding through flesh. Now there was screaming. Now there were yelled orders. Now there was chaos and fear and rage thick and heavy on the night air.

And still I stayed where I was.

One of the infiltrators came running in my direction, weapon raised into a perfect strike as he took down one of Tabitha's men just a few paces away. There was blood splattered across his face as he turned his half wild eyes to look at me. His cheekbones were surprisingly sharp beneath the grime. I knew that expression on his face. They had known that this was going to be a one-way mission for most, if not all of them. They would have volunteered for this. For the guts and the glory or simply from the desperation to stop this madness before it could spiral any further. Or maybe just because they were given their orders.

I don't know what he saw on my face. Or what he read from the fact that I was making no move to defend myself, let alone attack him.

I breathed in slowly, he blinked in confusion.

He turned away and darted off after a more active target.

A sharp cry from the right drew my attention. It is something so deeply ingrained in my instincts, carved into my very soul, to respond to one particular sound. One certain pitch of scream. It's the inevitability of a fish on a line, the undeniable truth that I will always respond to that primal call.

Sure enough, my eyes found Tabitha on the battlefield.

She had clearly run from her tent when all the commotion started. I suppose it made sense- no point in sitting in the middle of a clear target waiting for somebody to wander in and finish you off. That would just be narratively unsatisfying in so many ways. There was a sword in her hand, a smudge of ink across one cheek, and a shriek of pure fury on her lips.

I suppose one unfortunate side effect of her rather dramatic entrance to the fray, was that she had all but painted a 'kill me' sign on her forehead. The men who had invaded the camp had no doubt been well briefed on the priorities of their mission. Namely, to take down anybody that seemed to be in charge.

They swarmed like a pack of wolves.

In some ways it made the Tabitha's soldier's job a little easier. After all, when your enemies all bunch together it makes it far easier to make sure that you attacking the right people despite it being dark and you all being only a few minutes free of sleep. The strike force began to fall, rather quickly. They took a fair few along the way. Is that a credit to them? These days I can't really tell.

Between one blink and the next Sir Enhani materialised at Tabitha's side, trying to push her behind himself as some sort of human shield. There was the ring of steel, sparks flying as the blades clashed. That was not the right way to use those weapons. He was going to damage it with such technique. He didn't. The mace which went sailing overhead and smashed his face to splintered bone and pulp meant he didn't live long enough to.

It was strange. Being a spectator on a battlefield. The fighting seemed to ebb and flow around me. And all I could do was watch. I couldn't find it in me to stand and get involved. In truth I could barely feel my hands to hold a weapon. My whole body in fact felt as if was out of key with the rest of the world at that moment. I imagined that I was almost outside of myself, watching over my own left shoulder perhaps? I don't really know.

And then someone slashed downwards with their point heavy sword.

Oh. So I could move. Apparently. And fast.

I rolled out of the way, coming up and around to face them. A soldier. I couldn't really see the colour of the uniform beneath the grime. And at last things began to slide back into place in my brain.

Do you know what I have been taught? It is a question I like to ask people sometimes, when they bother to listen to what I have to say. Some reckon I was forged to protect. Others that I am simply made to die- at the right time of course. But they forget. All of them.

I was made to kill as well. In some ways first. Take blood from those who would threaten me and mine. No different to this pre-emptive strike. Except that it is far mor focused. And vicious.

There were blades in my hands, flicked free from the holsters at my wrists. A shriek from the person who had struck at me as they stumbled back with half their face gone. A moment later the steel lengths were buried in a pair of throats. New knives took their place. I spun to the left, ducking low beneath a strike, lashing out in turn, and licking the resulting spray from my lips. It was bitter-sweet and oh so familiar.

That's the thing you see. There is a darkness inside all of us, mine had simply been better raised, honed, directed. And then it had been starved. For far too long. Now it was free, hungry. These people had drawn it back out and were therefore fair game. If I am honest, I didn't entirely know which sides I was striking at. They were just people in my way. There was not my side and their side. There was me and my target. That is all. It is a beautiful simplicity. A clarity that for a blissful moment actually makes sense.

Don't get me wrong- I don't enjoy it. In so far as it doesn't make me happy. But there is a certain relief in finally knowing what you are supposed to do. In knowing that you can do it at all. So what if it would come crawling out of the corners of my mind in years of dreams to come? If I survived for it to have the chance to, then that was the price.

I guess the only way to re-find yourself in a battle is to give yourself over completely to the madness that lurks beneath your skin. Anar embrace and guide my hands.

But then, that was what I had always been trained for.

Tabitha was trying to weave through the surging crowd of struggling bodies, now shifting closer to where I was dancing through the mud. Bodies were milling around, and the wounded were starting to join the chorus, and all of a sudden all that I could see was the glint of steel at her back.

There was someone there, half edged in the gap between two tents, sword ready with full attention homed in on the woman heading his way.

It turns out that I could move faster after all.

The sound that I made was a strange one, now that I think about it. At the time I couldn't really hear myself over the general cacophony, but I am pretty sure I made a noise like the time the knights had accidentally plucked a feather from the wing of one of the castle geese.

I still think that it was a valid response to the fact that there was a foot of steel sticking out of my mid-section.

Tabitha at least turned at the noise. Another flash of metal, the brief impression of wide eyes over high cheekbones, another body on the grass. And then my knees were dropping to the same red soaked ground. I didn't feel that impact. In truth I still hadn't really felt what was going on in my general torso area. Or perhaps it was more the stomach? I mean I hoped not, those sorts of wounds were a real bitch to try and get over. If my guts had been nicked, then I was in for most likely a long and painful death. That would really put a dampener on things.

Someone's hands were on my shoulders, and my eyes tracked along their wrists, up their arms, finally meeting Tabitha's face. I think I tried to smile, to bare my teeth at least. I wanted to laugh a little, comment on how inconvenient this was. I am allergic to swords- at least when they are poked into me. Such an annoying health issue.

She was trying to say something, but it sounded like I was under water to my blurred ears. Now she was yelling, looking all imposing and impossible. She had always been good at that. It must be a pre-requisite for ruling.

More hands, a stretcher perhaps, but my attention span was really waning now.

The last glimpse I caught of her before the jostling of the stretcher sent my consciousness fleeing, was unmistakable. My eyes flickered shut to the sight of her profound satisfaction.

CHAPTER TWENTY-NINE: MEDICAL MIRACLE OR MISERABLE MORON?

It's easier than you think to sneak out of a military hospital set up just behind battle lines. Mostly because there is so much general chaos at such places, and medics tend to figure that if you are moving under your own power then you can wait to be seen. There are plenty of bodies in worse condition. A lot of them dripping unfortunate things onto the floor. Or else just lying where they fell. So, if you are able to at least shuffle on your own two feet you barely warrant a second glance.

Not to mention- who would be stupid enough to head back into certain danger when you have been dropped off into a safe space to recover?

Answer: me. I didn't think that you would be surprised by that.

If I am honest, I don't actually remember how I got to the med station in the first place. I was pretty busy being unconscious due to blood loss. It is an unfortunate habit of mine to pass out when I get too much of my insides on the outside. According to the gossip which I managed to hear whilst I was being stitched up, Tabitha herself had accompanied my stretcher. I guessed that was why I got seen so quickly despite not being in immediate danger of dying.

She didn't stick around, no doubt busy with running the upcoming campaign. Whilst Clarisse's forces had made the first strike, Tabitha would be getting ready for the full-on assault and the proper launching of her little war. There was a city to be taken, and now a fair load of rather pissed off soldiers to do so. In which case I could completely understand why she wasn't there when I first woke up.

Somewhat annoyingly for me, there was a nurse nearby who noticed the second I tried to sit up. I swear she took an element of grim amusement at how thoroughly I swore when the motions pulled on my stitches. At least she hadn't been fast enough to stop me from lifting the bandages to get a look at what I was dealing with. The surgeon had done a pretty good job considering the circumstances he was operating on. The stitches were certainly neater than when I did things myself- mine tended to slant depending on whichever way I was twisting. These were far more precise. With proper rest and recovery there would no doubt only be a faint scar left to show where I got stuck like pig at feasting time.

The nurse proved herself an even more experienced professional, in that she clearly had a sixth sense for when her patients were planning to slip away. She got me with another dose of the good stuff before I could even swing one leg over the edge of my cot. I fell back to sleep giggling. It was most embarrassing.

The next time I awoke, Tabitha was back. I was feeling distinctly stranger that time, and judging by the slight frown on the doc's face when he checked me over, I was running a bit of a fever. I hate that. Even if I wasn't necessarily developing an infection, the sheer pain and trauma often made the body do some weird shit. Recovery was never easy.

Whether or not Tabitha and I had much of a conversation... I honestly don't remember. I think I remember her saying something about gratitude, and I truly hope I stopped any of the responses that I wanted to make from falling out of my mouth. But come on- taking a blade for someone? Thank you should be standard. Even for monarchs.

If her slightly annoyed expression was anything to go by, I might not have managed to hold it back. Thankfully the moans of those far worse off in cots along the rows of the tent were enough of a distraction for my social lapses to be overlooked.

The one part I do remember, was the way that she clasped my hand in hers. She leaned in, all earnest sympathy and brave smile, telling me about how the great battle was nearly upon us. That she would fight in my name. That she wished I could be protect her back as was always meant to be, but I needed to get well... that when it was all over, I would once again take my place at her side.

She helped me take a mouthful of water which tasted faintly metallic and after which my blinks rapidly became longer. Between one and the next, she was gone.

Now I was awake again. A quick feel around was my first move to figure out what I had to work with. Alas, it seemed that they hadn't left any food nearby. At least they had kept my boots by my bed, with my blue coat even stashed next to them, my pack almost getting missed before I reached back further. The half-choked scream was worth the effort when I realised that I still had everything. I guess being obviously close to Tabitha had its benefits. The last time I had woken up in a place like this I had been robbed of everything I owned.

War is always about profit to somebody after all.

Lacing up the shoes brought tears to my eyes, pulling my arms into the sleeves left bile in my nose. A quick run of my hand through my hair to pull it back and tie it had me pointedly ignoring the dried blood which matted the strands.

I didn't doubt that if I had a mirror the reflection would have looked like something which had... well... crawled off a battlefield.

Judging by the general darkness of the tent, night had fallen. That by no means meant that the place was quiet or peaceful. Combat hospitals don't have such concepts. Night simply means that the doctors and nurses are too damned tired and continue their duties anyway.

That's why it is the best time to sneak out. Also, by that point they are less likely to try and stop whichever ungrateful bastard is choosing to skip out on their room without paying. Hopefully the empty cot would give a bit of comfort to some other poor sod who needed it more. I certainly didn't. I was absolutely fine. I could walk... after a fashion... and I most certainly did not feel the overwhelming urge to throw up whatever they had managed to get down my throat in however long I had been there.

Stepping out into the night, I took a heartily welcome breath of the cooler air. There is always something about medical places of any quality which seeps into your lungs.

So there I was, half leaning against a stack of crates outside the medic tent. I had boots on my feet, a pack on my back, and the suspicion that if I moved too quickly then I would end up leaving pieces of myself all over the ground. I had been worse. Surely. This wasn't even in my list of top five worst days.

The sounds of battle were ringing clearly across the deserted camp, matching the glow from beyond the tents which spoke of barely restrained fires. It was of course coming from the direction of the city.

No doubt about it. The main offence had begun in earnest. No wonder the med tent was relatively deserted. The medics would be out on the battlefield, dragging more people from the jaws of death. Surgeons and nurses would be preparing for the incoming wounded, busy, busy, busy. No rest for the wicked, which may be why only the good die young.

They would definitely be glad of the spare cot when it got

discovered. I was doing them a service really.

For a moment I paused where I stood in the dark. I have always had an annoying tendency to consider all my options whenever possible. And right now, the part of me which was logical and driven by the concepts of 'survival' and 'instincts' wanted my feet to turn me further into the camp. It was possible- I could hobble directly away from the battle, and just keep going until I reached a point where the events unfolding were just rumours of troubles in some foreign land.

I really wanted to. Like, really, deeply, wanted to be able to do it. I was tired. I was hurt. I was swaying on my feet. A battered facsimile of a person held together by thread and stubbornness.

Even walking out of the tent had been painful enough. I wanted to scream. I wanted to cry. And I hated myself for being so pathetic. It didn't matter. None of it did, or so I kept trying to tell myself. It was just pain, happening only to me, so why should it be of any consequence in the grand scheme of things? There was somewhere I needed to be. Who cared if every step was going to have me choking on my own vocal chords and the bile stubbornly crawling its way up my throat? At least if anybody saw me, I could claim that the tears were a result of the smoke rolling over the area.

Hell, I was beyond tempted go back into the medic tent, lie down, and let myself heal as instructed. When all this was over I would either be at Tabitha's side when she ruled as queen, or I could claim that I had been held prisoner all this time when Clarisse's forces came through the camp searching for spoils after their victory.

To put it simply, I could do nothing and be fine. I could turn my back and be more than fine (provided that I lived long enough to make it far enough...).

Let's be honest though, as we have already established, I am not always sensible. Less so when feelings got involved, such is human nature. And you want to know something? I was angry.

For once, on my own behalf. I was pissed. Because I had been lied to, by either or both of the women who I had laid my life on the line for far too many times. Sure, that was my job, but it wasn't one I had ever asked for. I hadn't questioned it. That hadn't been my place, hadn't been my *right.* But now? I was damn well going to get some fucking answers even if I had to wring it out of both of them at the same time.

Another deep breath, I pulled the straps of my pack just a bit tighter and spat the bitter taste from my mouth. I was going to war. Anar would watch my back. Anybody at my front had better clear the way. One way or another, this bullshit was going to end.

CHAPTER THIRTY: DEADMEN TELL NO TALES

If there is one rule which has always served me well about working in and around castles? It's the fundamental truth around the inability of the builders to not be overdramatic. Well, I guess when it comes to building edifices to a country's legacy it is probably the right amount of dramatic. Perspective and all. What I am trying to say, is that as part of some unwritten standard practice, castles always have quite a few secret passages.

I intended to make good use of the one which led from the city graveyard to the Royal Crypt. Cliché, but needs must.

By the time I managed to find a way into a quieter section of town, the assault on the citadel was well under way. I don't remember having ever seen the streets so empty. Avoiding what was becoming the front line, I instead skirted my way around downtown, weaving my path between still and dark houses. Most of the people had probably left when news came of the approaching army. With all the refugees who had fled before the advance they would have known what was coming. How much they would have believed is hard to say. It was the sort of situation which would have been almost completely out of the blue. Unless you knew what was going on behind the scenes, the sudden invasion made no sense.

Hell, I knew what was going on and still found it all hard to swallow.

The graveyard is on a hill to the western edge of the city, intended to be far away from where people would live, but over time the boundaries of those areas had encroached upon the dead's territory. Some even said that the hill hadn't existed when the city was first founded. But then the amount of space to bury people had shrunk and well... stacking is effective...

Macabre thoughts aside, the slope of the ground did at least help me keep track of whereabouts I had gotten to, despite the depth of the dark. By the time I had scrambled to the right statue I was swallowing hard against bile once again. I kept shoving the pain away, hoping it would fade out of my awareness. My body was frankly refusing to cooperate with that plan. Perhaps the knowledge that I still had the chance to back out was refusing to let me just focus on my mission.

Whatever.

The monument I was heading to was one which most did not realise existed. The monarchs of course have their personal crypt, their own vast vaults beneath the castle. So that their souls could watch over the home of their descendants, their spirits roam the halls and whisper advice to the next generation. It made for some great ghost story material to tell new squires. Everyone else got buried in this plot.

Basically, no royal would be caught dead around here. Get it?

This statue, the one at which I finally gave up and puked over the bottom of, was of a woman with a covered face. The stone was well weathered to the point where you couldn't tell if the obscured features were from a skilfully crafted veil, or simply that they had eroded away too far. Probably a bit of both. She bears no message, no markings to tell you who rests at her feet. If you know, you know.

Long ago I had sworn to protect their secrets, their spirits, their stories. In return they would watch over me until the day when I joined them.

I rested my hand in hers, lacing my fingers through her stone digits. Even in the relative silence of the deserted section of town it was impossible to hear the catch release. I could however detect the slight grating of shifting stone as the entrance to a passage opened in the side of the statue. I didn't need any light to know that as I slipped inside, I was being watched by the empty skulls which lined the catacomb.

The first time I had come this way the day that I had been officially claimed by Tartyn. Led from the black pit where I had been kept for long enough that my mind and memories had run like paint left in the rain, heavy hands had finally held me in place. Removing the blindfold had made me whimper in pain despite it being night. The light of the stars had never burned so brightly into my eyes before or since.

By the time I had it in myself to dare turn and look around myself, my handlers were already gone. I think I knew I was in a graveyard. It is hard to know. It just felt like a blissful quiet to me, the night air cool on my skin and the silence a balm to my soul. It was the truest peace I had known.

I don't remember why I took the statue's hand. Perhaps I wanted to pretend that someone was really reaching out to me. Could have been I was just a bit beyond delirious at that point. When the door had opened, I definitely remember stepping into the darkness. I can't forget however hard I try the noise which the entry way made when it snapped shut at my back.

There are reasons why no lights are allowed to be carried into the tunnel. Purely scientific ones as well. Basically, there is a very unique type of moss which grows in the tunnel. It had somehow managed to find a way to survive there amongst the bones. More things do than people realise in truth. The difference with the moss is that it is bioluminescent. It glows with a blue green light from the hollows which had once held eyes.

You can imagine the impact which such a sight had on my

younger self the first time.

When I had finally managed to make my way through the passage, I had shredded my vocal cords, what little had been left of them anyway. My fingertips had been torn up from where I had tripped and caught myself on the rough ground… and from where I had clawed at the walls as I begged for release.

I wonder if the moss fed on the blood which I had shed all those years ago.

Magda had been there at the end of the route. She had watched me come tumbling out of the tunnel, managing not to fall flat on my face. A claw like hand had gripped my cheeks, forcing our eyes to meet. I could barely make out her features. My body was a few feet below my soul, and I could have sworn that I was watching everything from a corner of the room.

Whatever she was looking for in my face must have been there. I began my formal training as the Queen's body guard the very next day.

After that first visit, I could not find it in myself to be afraid of the tunnel again. It had done its worst. People fear the unknown after all, and it was from then on something I could quantify. I think it was the first time I had directly learnt, faced, and conquered a fear in one go.

Even on my worst day I did not fear death. She had walked beside me for far too long, enough that I had grown fond of her company. And these skulls belonged to my people. Just as the royals had their sheltered halls for their dearly departed, so too did their generations of body guards have their hallowed ground. And in death as in life, it was geared to the protection of that which we were sworn to uphold.

It was one of the only truly secret ways into the castle. The one which we were forbidden to share with anyone except our own successor. Knowledge is power after all.

As I made my way along the passage, the sound of my own

footfalls echoed back to me. With how unsteady my gait was, the reverberations were rather disconcerting, almost making my head spin. That might also have been due to the fact that I was still a couple of quarts short of a full tank in terms of blood volume.

I blame that for how long it took me to realise that every now and then the whole place shook ever so slightly. A fine trickle of dust went skittering across one of the skulls, covering the moss briefly until it looked as if the soul light had winked at me even as the jaws grinned on.

Once I did, my ears perked up of their own accord, finally registering the muffled crump which preceded each tremor. I had to be getting close to the castle then- I was no doubt hearing and feeling the effects of a catapult attack on the main citadel. Now more than ever I hoped that people had the sense to evacuate the city whilst they still could. If not, then that they were finding places to hunker down and ride this out.

At least with the noise I knew roughly when to start feeling around for the end of the tunnel. The moss didn't grow this close to the finish line, what with the destination having a habit of being illuminated. The last time I had come this way I had walked straight into the door at the end in the dark. Magda had laughed at the resulting nosebleed for far too long in my opinion. As the portal swung open, the faint light from the lantern which remained ever lit in the crypt was almost blinding.

Luckily for me there was nobody around. I guess even when under heavy fire some places were considered off limits for commoners to shelter. Because of course protecting these bones was a vital use of resources. Imagine if it took a direct hit and the bodies of regular people got all mixed up with those of their betters. That would give nightmares to any self-respecting courtier.

I left the door open as an easy escape route should I need it. First rule of life- always have an exit ready.

Climbing the first set of stairs made me want to just go and lie back down with the corpses behind me. Their ghosts might not even begrudge me if I argued that I was guarding them. In truth I was almost sure that I had in fact already died and was only moving because I was too stupid, too stubborn, or both, to realise that I was done. Sod it. In that case I had nothing to lose anyway and so should just pull myself together to keep moving. That is exactly what I did.

The next corridor I came into was apparently busier than the ones I had been creeping through. There were a couple of pieces of evidence for this hypothesis. The first: I could hear voices coming from the end of the hallway in what I knew was one of the siege food storage areas. Hopefully they had managed to stash some supplies- you know in case this turned into a protracted conflict. Or at the very least they better be using it to shelter civilians from whatever was getting thrown over the walls.

The second bit of evidence for this area being occupied, was the fact that Hanson was staring at me with eyes so wide I was genuinely worried that they would fall out of his head. It took me a minute to figure out what he must be seeing from his point of view. I had most likely been declared dead. I mean- what other conclusion could everyone have possibly drawn? And now here I was all but crawling out of the sacred crypt, looking rather worse for wear.

Hell, with all the dust I had scrambled through I was probably even paler than just the blood loss could account for. That and the no doubt obvious damage I was sporting... yeah a walking corpse wouldn't be too great a leap of the imagination.

I am honestly impressed that he didn't start screaming. But then, I had trained him far better than that.

"You... you..."
"Surprise?"

"You are supposed to be dead." There was a squeak on the end of his words which at any other time would make him flush crimson in annoyance.

I tried to shrug, swiftly aborting the motion when it pulled at my... well, everything. "Yeah, it didn't stick. Sent me back for being annoying. Never mind that now- what are you doing here?" now that I thought about it, the question was a damned important one. He was still a kid. Sure, he was training as a squire with dreams of becoming a knight, but that was long in the future. For right here and now he was a kid. Just a child. Why the hell was he still here and not yet evacuated out?

He gripped his sword a little tighter. It was the same one I had given him on his last birthday. He had been ecstatic even when I pretended that I had been planning to throw it away or something, then figured that he could maybe make use of it. The fact that it was perfectly balanced for his grip meant nothing. He had hugged me hard enough that I had to stop myself from forcefully breaking the hold out of habit.

Judging by how white his knuckles now turned there was more than a little tension running through him. "I'm guarding the others."
"The others?"
"Servants, most of their kids. The lords and ladies all left with their people, but the rest of us..."

I grit my teeth against words which would only waste my already short breath. Of course. The rest got left behind. They were no doubt told that it was their duty to stay at their posts until the last moment. The army was here to fight, but their needs had to be met between battles. There was always the call for spare hands to feed the soldiers, fix the walls, tend to the wounded, keep the infinitely complex machinery of life running.

Perhaps the Queen truly had intended to get them safety and simply ran out of time. That would be more palatable to believe at least. And then they had been trapped when the army came faster than they had expected. Sure.

My mind darted back to promises I had made about protecting the spirits of my predecessors that they would in turn protect me. I heaved a sigh between my teeth. "Gather up everyone you can. There is a way out- the way I came in. Take them through the crypt- there is a door open which leads to the tunnel. Use the Everlight Lantern to light the way and lead them all out." I wondered if the moss would survive so much illumination exposure. Then again if the whole castle came down it would all be wiped out anyway. "When you get to the graveyard you head for the city limits and then keep going. You hear me?"

He was pale again, and yeah, I had just recommended a mild form of heresy, but come on it's all about priorities. And sure, I had probably also just invoked ages of curses down on my head for sharing that which must not be spoken of. Hopefully I would live long enough through all of this for that to be a problem down the line.

"But I…"

I stepped forwards, clapping one hand on his shoulder. Hanson flinched at the sudden contact. I wondered if he had half thought that I was some sort of apparition up to that point, a spirit who had dragged itself back across the divide from sheer determination to pass on a message. For the record, when I go, I will not be haunting anybody. I will be enjoying my well-earned rest. Once again, I pulled my attention back to the matter at hand. The inability to focus was going to very likely be the death of me. More than me if I couldn't persuade him to listen to me. "If you can get out of a warzone, then you go! This route won't be open forever, not if the attacking army moves further through the city and reaches the graveyard. Grab whoever you can and lead them to safety."

"But I want to stay and fight!"

Me? I wanted to flinch. I wanted to cry. Inar's grace the look in his eye. Yeah, there was fear there, only an idiot would not be scared and no way I would have trained someone without a lick of sense. But there was also that damned innocence. The belief that if their cause was just then they would inevitably prevail, and that the struggle was worth his life. And he had so much more of that life to live before anyone should dare to ask for it in exchange of any ideal. The image flashed across my mind, of him lying at my feet having gone through half of the things that I had in the last week.

No. Not him. Not yet. There would be plenty of time. I would make sure of it.

Softening my tone, I leaned on him a little heavier, making it clear that he was helping to hold me up where we stood in the dim corridor. The floor shook beneath our feet with another impact, dust trickling from the ceiling onto his hair and staining it grey.

"I need you to do this. No one else can." I was begging him in my head to listen, to understand what I was saying, "It is a nobler thing to save lives than take them. The people here? They are frightened, not ready for what a war really means. They will need someone to protect them if the enemy finds them. That will be your job. Hopefully this will end here, in our favour. In which case you will be called home and you will know that you helped save their lives when nobody else could or would. But if it doesn't? If the citadel falls?" somehow, I dredged up a dangerous grin, bringing a sense of roguish camaraderie, "Then you are going to need every able body you can scrounge to fight back when the time comes."

That seemed easier for him to understand, or at least to palate. A new steel entered his eyes and he nodded. "You said through the crypt?"

"That's right."

"Alright, we will round up everyone in the storage areas and..."

"*You* will. This is your mission. I can't come with you. I have other duties I need to carry out."

He ran an evaluating eye over me, one brow raising almost of its own accord at what he saw. I resisted the urge to stick my tongue out at him. Poor kid had been through enough shocks today. "Don't give me that look as if you think I can't. This is nothing. Remember who you are talking to."

It was my best performance, or at least as good as I could manage. No doubt the smile was too wide, the tremble in my hands too obvious. But any port in a storm.

It is the great thing about the confidence of youth- they are willing to believe much more easily than adults. Hanson half turned to go and start rallying the people hiding, hesitating at the last moment. He swivelled back, seeming to be trying to figure out what he wanted to say. After a second, he lifted his chin, straightened his spine, and offered me what might have been the sharpest salute I had ever seen.

There was no denying the fond smile which I knew was stealing over my face. For once I didn't pretend it was for any other reason than pure pride in what this young man was becoming. I nodded in response.

Another crunching impact somewhere above us. The moment broke. He turned fully and began to hurry back to gather up survivors to lead them out. Part of me wondered how much convincing he would have to do to get them to leave through not only sacred ground where they no one aside from the monarch and her priest were meant to step, but also through what was to many the literal embodiment of their worst nightmare. Then again, the fact that there was battle brewing at the backs? Survival instincts were thankfully very good at getting people to overlook certain civil niceties.

Hanson would get them out, even if he had to drag the first few through to safety with his bare hands. And he would do it as well. That boy was damned good at getting things done once he set his mind to them. One day he would be a fine leader.

And me? Well, I cursed myself for six shades of a fool as I began to haul myself up yet another set of stairs.

CHAPTER THIRTY-ONE: IF ONLY I HAD LEFT A KEY UNDER THE MAT

It is one of the most surreal things, breaking back into your own castle. The territory was so familiar, every path and stick and stone an old friend. I barely needed the light from the moon to guide my way across the courtyard from the store houses and kitchen area to the main keep. Considering the fact that there was a full army launching everything that they had at the front gate and a good portion of the wall, this route was relatively quiet.

You know- aside from the occasional harsh crash of stone and shrapnel from a strike gone wide.

If there was one thing which I was pretty sure of, it was that the ruckus going on around the main entrance was at least a decent distraction. Literally the oldest trick in the book, but tropes exist for a reason. Also, the attackers in this situation knew what they were getting into. Tabitha would no doubt soon be on my tail, using her own memories as a guide. Just as I knew of one way in, no doubt she had a similar route in mind. Perhaps even one steeped in just as much tradition and mystique.

Of course, it would be her leading the infiltrators. No way she would be able to resist the opportunity to deal out death and judgement personally. But I liked to think that I had the upper hand since I had been living here for the last seven years. Things change in that time.

"Stop! It's a spy!"

I cursed in every language I could think of, mentally, as I whipped around with my hands raised. The action sent fire lancing down my core and I was pretty sure that whatever skin tone I had regained from the exertion of moving had rapidly drained away again. I could just about make out two figures in the corridor, one of them definitely a guard, the other half hiding behind him.

"Don't shoot! It's Nina!" my voice was far scratchier than I remember hearing it.

Even in the dark I could see how the guard's figure stiffened, outrage seeming to bleed along his every line. A brief squint at his companion made me think that he was paired up with a servant girl. I guess it really was all hands-on deck. There was a distinct snarl to his response. "Liar! She died as a hero saving our Queen. Don't sully her memory in such a way."

Well... damn, that put a bit of a kink in my plans. At least now I knew that Clarisse had in fact made it back. Part of me couldn't help but be slightly flattered that Clarisse had apparently given me a bit of credit to her triumphant return. Or perhaps she didn't, and my distinct absence made people draw their own conclusions. At least this man didn't seem to think that the Nina he knew would have just betrayed my post and oaths and joined up with the enemy.

Either way, this was already taking up more time and energy than I could afford to give it. The fact that my mind kept wandering off on tangents was singularly irritating. But I mean, I couldn't blame them. He was a guard, she was a servant, their job was to stop people and ask their business, and with a literal army raging outside the front gate they were doubtless more than a little bit stressed. Besides, in the low light they could probably only see my silhouette- as in the fact that the cut of my uniform was wrong. Bloody stupid trousers with their close ankle design.

And it was only then that my treacle thick thoughts picked up on the fact that I recognised the voice of the person who had spoken. It was Jeremy. It had to be. Defending my memory to what he thought was a random infiltrator. And dammit I suddenly wanted to cry. That would be highly awkward for him if I did though. Not to mention, I was pretty sure that I had pulled some of my stitches and so was starting to bleed. Dehydration from pointless tears was not a complication I could afford.

"Wait, Jeremy, it is me and I can prove it."
He scoffed, drawing his bow a tough tighter, "How?" he didn't even ask how I knew his name. probably expected it was some sort of intelligence operative magic or something.
"Just let me show you."
"You are not to take one step closer. I know your type, get close to bring us down. No sudden movements now."

I huffed an aggravated sigh, "I'm not being threatening, I swear, I just want to show you my cloak." It was the best form of identification I could have. As I reached up to undo the clasp of my pack, I could hear the girl hissing at him that they needed to report this in. Another near miss on the crying as I realised that it was Serafina. The other escape ship had made it. She had survived. A corner of my heart sang a brief praise to Inar for sending my friends to me in my time of need. I just needed to persuade them not to kill me right away.

A quick rummage in the pack, and I managed to get a grip on the cloak. The one which I had carried with me since I had left home oh so long ago. Shaking it out a little was clearly a bad idea judging by how much it sent agony racing down my spine. Resigned to it not looking its best, I turned the fabric around, letting the threads gleam in the moonlight. I knew it was a distinctive pattern, the only one of its kind in the whole court, as was the way.

Jeremy ran his eyes over every inch. He took a step closer. I could see him properly now, every unshaven, rumpled, exhausted inch of his face. “How dare you steal the cloak of a friend and try to use it against us.” His voice was colder than a midwinter frost. “Oh for the love of the Inar! Jeremy, I don’t have time for this bullshit. It’s me- Nina. It’s a long story but I didn’t die, I am here, and yes- I am in a different uniform but how else did you expect me to get through the enemy lines?” not quite accurate, but close enough to the truth. “And if I weren’t me, how could I know that you asked Captain Haris out when she was at the pub out of uniform, and you didn’t recognise her?”

His bow was lowering, the tip of the arrow finally pointing away from my chest. Serafina was staring at me with wide eyes. “I laughed so hard when you told me, asking for advice so as not to be killed when you reported for duty, that I snorted a cerus seed up my nose.” I walked closer as I spoke, stepping into the ring of torchlight. I didn’t know if the gasp of shock was at the fact that it was indeed my face they saw, or the general state of said face. “We told everybody the resulting nosebleed was due to a training mishap. Hanson worshipped you for a week for thinking that you had bested me in a fight, until you felt bad and told him the truth.”

For a second nobody moved, nobody spoke, and then Jeremy dropped his bow as Serafina let out a small sob. Thankfully the nocked arrow only skittered along the flagstones. They both tackled me into one of the biggest hugs I can ever remember receiving. Also… the most painful. I think I just lost another stitch. For a heartbeat I just held still, soaking in the feeling of a truly friendly touch for the first time in far too long. At last, I could really admit to myself just how much I had missed home. These were my people.

And time was running out to protect them.

Reluctantly I broke the hug, doing my best not to flinch as

Serafina's fingers ghosted over the purple bruising on my cheek. She looked far more horrified when she realised that there was a slowly growing stain on my side which had partly seeped onto her clothes. My attempt at a reassuring smile was probably far more horrifying than I intended. It was only then that I realised the dressings on my nail bed had long since fallen off along the way.

"Nina, what in the world happened to you?"
"No time for all that. Listen, where is the Queen? I need to get to her urgently. We don't have a moment to lose."
"You need to see the physician first- bodyguarding can wait until we make sure you aren't about to drop dead or something. We will send her to you-"
"No! you don't understand. They are already sending people in."

Jeremy looked at me with something pained, pitying, "Did you…"
I gave him my best offended face, burying all the memories of the last few days under the deepest pile of outrage I could dredge up. "I didn't give them an Anar damned thing. They have someone on their side, an old member of court with a grudge who is helping them." Again, not exactly accurate, but I figured the whole 'the Queen is an imposter and the original is storming the keep' wouldn't go down so well.

He nodded as Serafina gave me a sharp look. "Alright, Sera, you take her to the Queen and spread the word for everyone to be on the lookout for intruders." A brief smile, "After all, the servants know this place better than anyone, as well as everybody who lives here. I will report in to the captain of the guard." He clasped my shoulder, grip lightening at my barely suppressed wince. "Do your duty, but stay alive you hear me? I can't go through thinking we had lost you again."

Without further ado, he nudged me towards Serafina before jogging off to update his superiors. I stared after him for a moment, emotions swirling in my chest and tightening in my throat. It had been so easy to forget how much of a family we were, to tell myself that I didn't really matter in the grand scheme of things, since I was unlikely to live that long. Seems I had gotten attached and been pulled in without even noticing.

Serafina was still giving me a side eyed stare as we began hustling through the corridors. I shot her a crooked smile, "I know, this uniform feels as strange to wear as it does to look at. Don't think I have time for a quick costume change, do you?"

She laughed a little, the line of her shoulders finally easing a fraction. "It is unusual, but it actually works for you."
"Thanks."

I quickly realised that we were heading for the throne room. It wasn't exactly what I had expected. Procedure demanded that in the event of an enemy at the gates, the Queen would be taken to the council chambers. Partly because it would be her role to direct the battle and that was the place with all the maps and dioramas and such, but mostly because it was the most heavily fortified room in the castle. In contrast, the throne room was only a symbolic power centre, decorated and imposing but in truth not particularly secure.

We slipped in through the side door which sat just behind and to the right of the throne. The other occupants of the room didn't notice our presence at first. Lizzie was pacing like a caged lion, hand tapping anxiously at the sword on her hip. I got the feeling that it was due more to the fact that Sir Gavin would no doubt be up on the walls to defend, rather than the imminent threat to her own life. She was body double to the Queen after all; if a melee were to break out, a case of mistaken identity was not out of the question.

Delilah was at the window with a telescope, no doubt scanning the keep's surroundings. She kept muttering things to a scribe perched behind her for him to write down. Ever the historian. At least if we made it through what was to come the official embroiderers would know which scenes to immortalise later on.

Magda was the only one to react as Serafina and I slipped in. No doubt she was there to act as bodyguard to the Queen, being the only one fully qualified after all. Retired or not, she could still give most a run for their money. I wondered what she had been thinking when she took the mantle up once more. For all of her vigour, she would know that her skills were not at the same level as they used to be. I get the feeling that duty wasn't the first thing on her mind when she saw me and all at once it was if several years had been shed from her face.

Apparently, she was still pretty fast, as it seemed to be between one blink and the next that she was across the room and folding me into her arms. So, hugs were the new standard form of greeting it would appear. I blinked back the salt in my eyes. It would only sting the marks on my face if they fell.

She led me around the dais, and I finally saw Clarisse. The Queen was on her throne, dressed practically for battle with her chest plate and greaves over her battle dress. The crown upon her head was all sharp spikes and dully gleaming metal. According to legend it had been forged from the sword of the last king who had tried to invade. Rumours said that the record of the battle was sown onto a vellum of particular delicacy.

It was the perfect image of a monarch on the eve of a war. Pride. Steel. Determination.

I had never felt so tired as I did then.

She rose when she saw me, one hand flying to her mouth. "Thank the gods." It was a hushed whisper, even as a smile broke out wide across her face. "I thought they had killed you. When they were chasing us and you..."

The others had turned their attention back into the room as she spoke, and a sharp squeal from Lizzie broke the hushed atmosphere. From the way that the scribe was suddenly scratching things down at high speed, I had the feeling that I was in danger of being immortalised alongside the rest of this mess.

"How did you get here?"
"Are you alright?"
"What happened to you?"
"Why are you in one of their uniforms?"

The last was from Clarisse, and the slight tension in her tone was enough to make the others hesitate. Magda spoke up before any of them could start spiralling into paranoia, "Oh for the sake of the gods how else did you expect her to dress? Even if her clothes had still been fit to wear after the last few days, they weren't the best choice if she intended to make her way through that bloody mob at the front door."

I never realised just how much I loved her no-nonsense attitude. Her arm was still wrapped around my shoulder, a comforting weight, a reminder that she was a steadiness I could hold onto.

"Of course." A reassuring smile from Clarisse and the rest of the room eased back into their relieved smiles and quick-fire questions. I held up my hands, "No time for the whole story, Your Majesty, we need to move. The enemy has almost certainly already infiltrated the grounds. The army is the distraction whilst a small strike team makes its way to you directly."

A round of cursing started up from the maids but I ignored them as I bored my eyes into hers. "They are being led by someone who knows this castle well." I was watching her closely as I delivered my report and felt the inching suspicion at the back of my mind as she didn't respond with the confusion I had expected. "But you already know who that is, don't you?" Of course she did. I stepped slightly away from Magda, turning now to look at her too. "Your reports have informed you of *her*, haven't they? And don't waste time on pretence. We all know you are the head of intelligence."

At least she didn't try to pretend otherwise, simply sighing heavily in the same way as when I had done something foolish as a child. "Yes. It's Tabitha. She is the one who had orchestrated the whole thing."

"Tabitha? She's alive?" Delilah's voice was faint, telescope hanging from numb fingers as she turned away from the attacking army to stare with horrified betrayal at her Queen.
"It would seem so. She faked her death rather than return to court."
"That makes no sense. We were her friends, her family! Why would she run from us?"
"Perhaps the fire drove her mad, whatever reason she is alive and coming for us."

The maid turned to Magda, "how long have you known that she is alive?"
"I was as stunned as you. I believed and mourned with the rest of you. It was only in the last few days as reports began to come in that she had been sighted leading the invaders that I dug deeper into the tragedy."

It was my turn to fix her with a hard gaze, "and what did you discover?" the understanding and answering pain in her eyes was all the answer that I needed.

Clarisse finally came down the steps, "Right, so the rumours are true. In that case I believe that it would be safer for the rest of you to evacuate the keep. It was one thing when we thought there was a chance that this was the diplomatic incident gone out of control. Given what we now know… well this is clearly a personal attack. As such, anybody near to me is going to be in danger." It was such a perfect act, so noble, so concerned for the wellbeing of her maids. I felt something sharp and bitter curling through my sternum.

"All of you need to get below to the catacombs. We don't know how far her revenge is going to stretch, so focus on getting those who can't defend themselves to safety whilst the rest ferret out any infiltrators and deal with them. I will stay here." She raised a hand to cut off the protests of the rest of the room. "That is an order from me, as your Queen."

I moved to stand behind her, falling into my customary place on pure muscle memory. "Do it. I have Clarisse, you do what you need to in order to resecure the castle and protect as many as possible." It was gratifying, in a way, to see how they trusted my judgement on the matter, nodding as they each moved to leave the throne room. There were a couple of backwards glances, but for the most part they left with renewed confidence.

Magda gave me a last, lingering hug before she too departed. I got the feeling that she simply couldn't bear to see what would happen next. It was the unspoken agreement between us, the mutual respect of those who knew that the events about to unfold had been a long time coming even if nobody else had known about them.

As the door finally clicked shut once again behind the last of them, I turned to fully face the Queen who I had protected for so many years. I didn't bother resting my hand on the hilt of my sword or anything so gauche.

Instead, I took a deep breath. "Now, I think it is time that the three of us have a talk, don't you agree, Tabitha?"

The burned queen stepped out from the shadows of the secret escape tunnel which led from behind the throne. The fact that Clarisse didn't even flinch at the sudden appearance spoke volumes about how she had been anticipating this entire situation to unfold. I wondered if she had been secretly suspicious, planning, for all these years.

"Alright then, speak and be heard."

CHAPTER THIRTY-TWO: I'M TOO OLD FOR THIS

"You were a friend, a sister! You betrayed and tried to murder me!"
Clarisse actually stamped her foot, all petulant child as her regal grace dissolved in the face of her intended victim. "Stop saying that- it makes it sound like I failed, and I don't take that well."

I seemed to have been forgotten as they stared each other down across the dais.

Tabitha was cold fury, clutching the hilt of her sabre in white knuckled hands. "I am the rightful Queen. I swore my oaths- it was meant to be my throne, my crown."
"Well I'm the one who's been running things for the last nine years, and you know what? I think I have done a damned good job overall." Her voice had risen to near a shriek, its pitch matched by the other Queen.
"So you are claiming my crown through… squatters rights?!"

Well, that was uncalled for. I cleared my throat, mounting the bottom step of the dais with both hands raised placatingly.

"Can I just interject here?" Both women fixed me with eerily similar glares. Damn, despite the scarring it was beyond clear as to why Clarisse had been the best body double back in the day. The resemblance was uncanny. For a moment I thought of how every member of the royal family was adopted in, and allowed myself the flight of fancy that perhaps Tabitha's statement of sisterhood wasn't so far off the mark. It was possible. And it would no doubt have been one hell of a joke to their Pantheon. Or maybe celestial beings would declare that the better punchline was if there was no such connection at all. That fate was simply that cruel.

Shaking my thoughts back into order, I took another step. "Well, technically you are both wrong. I mean, Tabitha" I gestured to her, "did swear the *original* fealty oaths at her coronation. However, she never swore the five-year reaffirmations so according to the constitution she has rescinded her claim to the throne." I ignored the resulting sputtering, "Clarisse meanwhile *has* sworn the five-year oaths, but as she didn't take the original the reaffirmation doesn't actually count, since she had nothing to reaffirm."

Tabitha blew a hard breath through her nose, clearly trying to dredge up some patience. "What are you saying?"

"Just that, purely theoretically, according to political science as we understand it, neither of you has any claim to the throne. So..." I couldn't help but wonder what the fallout of all this would be. Perhaps the council could sort it all out? Figure out which person should take over next? Maybe this would call for some sort of vote, similar to how the Rhean government decided things. Thank Inar that did not come under my job description.

"For the sake of all the gods, nobody cares about any of that!" Clarisse snarled at me, turning with her blade quivering. The sudden motion made Tabitha flinch in response, her own sword jerking up into a ready stance. They were both tense, posturing, a hairs breadth away from unleashing all that rage and pain upon each other.

I took another step, standing now between the both of them with a hand raised to each. Was it just my imagination, or did the tip of Tabitha's sword graze the palm ever so slightly?

The woman herself was staring at me in dumbfounded frustration. "Why are you protecting her? You don't even like her."

I shrugged, helpless in the face of my own reluctance to do what I felt I had to. "True, but you both seem to forget, that I also swore an oath."

Her face twisted into something bitter and hard. "Was this your plan all along? To betray me as well? So much for your protestations of loyalty."

From the other side I could see Clarisse's lips twisting into a mocking sneer. I think that is what did it really. Not just the last accusation, but the fact that the woman who had lied to me for so long seemed to automatically assume that I had retaken her side. I snapped.

"Hey! Shut it, both of you." I pointed at them each, willing my hands not to shake in rage lest they mistake it for fear. "Don't scoff and declare my actions as treachery. It is not my fault that I have no one left to be loyal to. Or for that matter, that neither of you ever asked exactly *what* I was sworn to do." They both looked puzzled for a moment. "You think I have just always been there, that I was made into what I am purely for your own advantage. And perhaps some of my predecessors have fallen into those roles. But me? I take my word seriously. As a wise old woman once told me, who you are can only be proved by what you do and where you hold your lines."

I was panting as I deliberately stomped my feet into the wooden boards, planting myself firmly. "This is mine. I was brought into this palace and earned my place through trials that neither of you could ever imagine in your worst nightmares. You think I would do all that for the sake of a single person?" I gave vent to a derisive snort, and part of my brain realised that I was saying a lot more than I had intended to when I first started speaking. "Get over yourselves. I swore to protect the crown. The throne. The ruler of this land which has become my home. Neither of you are those things. Not anymore. So now... well... I guess I fight to protect the ideals on which they were based."

For a moment there was silence in the throne room. A sense of freedom was filling my chest, as if by saying all of that out loud to the people at the heart of the issue, I had finally managed to settle my own doubts and confusions. It was clear now. My role. My place. As chosen by me, no matter what the original intentions of my moulding may have been.

The pair of queens before me seemed to digest my tirade at the same rate. Tabitha spoke first. "That might be the stupidest thing I have ever heard."

Clarisse was actually nodding in agreement with her, and if that didn't just take the cake in this absurdity. "This is why bodyguards aren't asked to consult on political matters during council meetings."

There was something burning, sharp, right in my throat. "There are people dying at this very moment. On both sides. Real people. With lives, with families, with dreams and hopes and fears and YOU-" I pointed at each of them, unsure anymore and frankly uncaring as to whether my hands were shaking, "YOU both made them promises. They are fighting, they are dying, for you. Do you not care?"

But of course they didn't. Because they were both queens. And all at once they looked terrifyingly alike in the flickering shadows.

Tabitha rolled her eyes at me. "They are soldiers. That is what they do." A raised brow, a slightly mocking tilt to her lips, "if only all were so dedicated to their duty."

Now it was my turn to stare at them in stunned silence. That was all they had to say to me? I had just poured my heart out and that was all they could respond with? I had always had a sense of attachment to these women, the obligation blending over the years with genuine fondness, a softening of a constricting bond until the ligature was a welcome grounding. It had been fraying. For the past few weeks, it had been picked at and sawn and unwoven with every twist and turn. The once strong braid had been steadily tweezed to pieces. I could almost feel the tug in my chest as the last thread finally snapped.

I let my hands drop although I somehow managed to keep my chin high. “Fuck it. I give up. Kill each other if you want. Just try not to make a mess on the rug.” I stepped back, leaving them once again with steel bared to each other’s throats.

They took me at my word, springing towards each other with twin shrieks of rage. I just slouched backwards into the chair behind me as my legs finally gave way under the weight of everything that had happened. It took me a good minute to realise that I had sat on the throne itself. It wasn’t particularly comfortable.

In front of me the queens were in full combatant fury. It was clear that even though they had the same initial instruction in the blade, Tabitha had picked up a new style over her time in a different country.

Sparks flew as their swords clashed against one another. I tilted my head to the darkened ceiling, gaze catching on the faintly fluttering cloaks which still lined the walls. My guts gave a dull throb as if remonstrating me for not remembering that I was wounded.

And all at once, Serafina was there. The torch in her hand added illumination to the room which had always faced the wrong way to catch the dawn’s rays. “What are you doing? Why aren’t you stopping them?” she was wild eyed, attention flicking between my lethargy and their prideful fury.

If I had nails I would have made a show of examining them. “Why should I? I tried; they did not wish to listen to reason. The throne room makes for a sufficient duelling ring. Let them at it. For honour and all that nonsense.”
She pulled me up from my chair with a surprisingly strong hand. “You have to end this!”
“You do it if you are so keen.”

The light was growing now. Red and gold starting to fill in the colours of the throne room. A blood dawn? Rising from the wrong direction? And when I turned my attention to it, through the windows I could hear the shouts about invaders turning to pleas for water and buckets...

I tilted my head as I looked properly at Serafina, and her torch. "Who do you think should win?"

She was all but trembling with adrenaline, with anger, with a righteous fury which I had never seen on her usually calm face. "How can you have any doubt? Tabitha is our queen, always was our queen. That imposter stole her crown out of sheer greed for the throne, for the power and acclaim and... and I have had to pretend to be her loyal servant!"

It was starting to make so much more sense. "You knew."
"Of course I knew! As soon as I saw her parading around in Tabitha's dresses on her return to the castle, I knew." She was watching the fight fully now, even as she spoke to me. Her breath kept hitching as if she was bracing herself to dive in and help but didn't know how. Her voice dropped to a distracted murmur. "I went to her, you know. Tabitha. I went to her as she lay sick and delirious from her wounds."

I had been brought to the court so long ago filled only with pride and rage. These people had stripped me of the former. All I had been left with for too long was the latter. And now I felt the stealing cold as those flames flickered and died in the face of the yawning apathy of my own existence.

"It wasn't a minister that sent word of her death. It was you."
"Lord Henry's signature was always the easiest to forge."
"Why didn't you..."
"Say anything? Who would have believed a lowly chamber maid? Clarisse had just tried to kill the Queen herself; do you really think that she would have had any qualms taking me out of the way should I prove a nuisance?"

She was panting now, remembered anguish twisting her features into something hungry and manic. I wondered how I could have missed it for so long.

"You loved her. Didn't you?"
"Yes."
"And you still do."
"Forever."

It made so much more sense now. She had been Tabitha's eyes in the court all these years, the person feeding her information and helping her plot out her revenge for all this time. I could see the oldest form of madness in her eyes. I connected another piece of the puzzle.

"You were the one who set the bomb on the airship, weren't you?"
"Of course."
I couldn't understand it. "But that could so easily have killed all of us, including you. Was that what you wanted?"
"It was a risk I was willing to take."
"By Inar's tears." A half-whispered curse.
The fire in her eyes matched that in her hand. "Please, neither your gods nor mine had nothing to do with it. They lack the creativity."

A sharp cry reminded us of the fact that two women were currently duelling with deadly intent just a few paces away. It was Clarisse. She was on her back on the floor, having apparently tripped over the edge of her cloak. The one which had originally been Tabitha's. The one which held the history of both of their reigns. It was pooled beneath her now, tangled in her legs as Tabitha stood over her in manic triumph.

She raised her sword high overhead. It was such a dramatic flourish. Highly unnecessary. Wasteful.

I don't remember throwing the knife.

Between one blink and the next I found my arm extended in front of me, knees bent in the classic position best suited for stability which had been drilled into me from childhood. My eyes tracked the extension of my limb, all the way to where Tabitha was staring in shock at the small blade now embedded into the meat of her sword hand. I wanted to throw up again.

It took a full breath before she remembered to scream at the pain.

The sabre fell from her hand, clattering to the floor a scant breath away from Clarisse's head. Tabitha was clutching at her wrist as she slowly turned to look back at me with stricken eyes.

Now it was Serafina screaming.

The tip of Clarisse's sword was suddenly protruding from Tabitha's stomach. The burned Queen looked down at the length of steel which seemed incongruous sticking out from her body.

The blade was withdrawn.

Tabitha turned back, apparently ignoring the growing flood of red, which was spilling down her stomach, across the fabric of her trousers.

Clarisse died with her triumphant grin still on her face when the burned Queen's knife went straight through her heart. It turned more to a grimace as the muscles relaxed. All I could think was that at least Tabitha had learned her lessons about always keeping a backup blade, and this time remembered to no waste motion.

The women crumpled to the ground.

Serafina was still screaming.

There's supposed to be that moment you know- the best bit in any story. When the person who has been pushed too far, seen too much, throws their head back to scream at the sky. And at that moment, with that release, their true power is unlocked and suddenly their enemies are destroyed. It is always so powerful and cathartic. It hurts, you bleed with them, but it feels somehow justified and righteous and as an audience you can tell yourself that it was necessary. The pain had a purpose, and it was beautiful in its tragedy.

I never got that. I watched them die, and my world fall apart around me, and some small part of me thought- this is it. I reached for all my rage and pain and power... and it just... didn't happen. There was a hollow where I had always been told that the tumult hid, an empty void of mocking apathy. I was left in the complete destruction of everything I had known and loved, and all I could do was stand and stare.

There was no scream of might and fury. My vocal cords had seized up along with any air that I could draw in. I could taste smoke on the inhale, along with what I could almost tell myself was roast being prepared for a feast. My left hand was shaking, my right was numb. It seemed I had dropped my weapons, for all that I couldn't remember doing so.

Instead of a scream, there was only silence. Well, except for something that was possibly a faint laugh, but perhaps more likely was my own shaky breathing.

Serafina had stopped her noise. She dropped her torch on the dais, all but flying across the room to cradle Tabitha in her arms.

I too moved down the dais steps as the flames began to lick curiously at the wood of the throne. Unable to hear, unwilling to listen, to whatever the maid was whispering to her Queen, I instead moved over to the open window.

Below, in the courtyard, I could see people running around in barely controlled panic. Whatever uniforms they were wearing, they were coming together to form bucket chains. It was only then that I realised just how much of the castle was already burning.

I will blame the crackling flames, the general pandemonium, my own utter exhaustion, for the fact that I didn't hear Serafina creeping up behind me. Or perhaps I did, and simply didn't care. Perhaps I thought that I deserved it.

Falling isn't so different from flying. I was back in the state where this mess had begun unspooling. The air was whistling in my ears, my hair flying back like a pennant. My cloak wrapped itself around me as I twisted through the abyss. There would be no water at the bottom. Just another type of oblivion.

I caught one last glimpse of the dawn rising on the other side of the castle, beyond the smoke.

I closed my eyes.

CHAPTER THIRTY-THREE: HEAD TOWARDS THE LIGHT

I had always been told that there would be a light to guide you to eternity, provided that you had done enough good in your life. Inar would usher you to her oasis with a soft caress to your cheek and a whisper of welcome.

Or else there would be darkness, the endless plunge into the abyss of Anar's throat.

For a while I was pretty sure that had been my fate. It would only be fair. I had fallen, that much I knew, from the window of the throne room and no doubt been swallowed by the aspect of the goddess to whom I had always pledged my actions. Inar would never have accepted them after all, but Anar had always understood. It was only natural that she would claim me in this the final offering.

So, I was surprised the first time that light cracked back into my reality. It was only for a moment, but it felt like an eternity. A flicker and then it was gone.

Another, and this time I could feel that it was in fact my own eyelid twitching. My lashes brushed my cheeks. I had cheeks. I apparently had a body. As if waiting for that recognition, existence came slamming back into me harder than whatever ground I may have hit.

Something came crawling up out of my throat. It might have

been a scream, or a whisper, or a couch, or a piece of my internal organs... but it sent shockwaves through every piece of me. And apparently there were still a fair few lying around. Enough that there was definitely white light exploding now within my brain, as if somebody had pried apart the bones to see what exactly I had been thinking. That might not even be much of an exaggeration.

There was something else, not part of me. It was moving, gentle against what I was pretty sure was my head. A hand. It was a hand. Strong, cool, bony... familiar.

I wanted to see, to understand, but forcing my eyes to try and open only afforded me a flash of light on glass before they slid shut once again. The hand was back, pressing into my own. It took as much energy as the creation of the universe, but I managed to get my fingertips to twitch. A victory. There were too few of those around these days. The hands which I somehow knew that I recognised squeezed back.

The ringing in my ears slowly dissolved into the muffled sounds of someone's voice for all that I could almost believe that I was underwater. That would explain why I couldn't really hear them, why my limbs were so heavy, why I suddenly couldn't breathe... I was in the water. Back in the water. Sinking in the lake, or the moat. My chest creaked. No- that must have been the wood of a ship passing overhead. That would be why everything was going dark once again.

I couldn't remember how to swim. Didn't have the energy to try. I would let the current take me.

When I surfaced the next time, it was a far sharper awakening. Awareness fanned the low-grade fire smouldering in what had once been my left leg, to a raging inferno of acid and flame. It coursed through my veins, lit up every nerve ending, sent embers rising from my throat until I choked on them and tried to empty the lava from my stomach.

New hands, one on my back, another on my shoulder, and all

sense of direction span out of my tenuous control as I was rolled to one side. Whatever had been scorching through my body finally found an exit through my mouth. There was enough of my ears left to hear the splatter on the ground.

To my back again, and I finally realised that it wasn't just my lack of sense which was making the world sway ever so slightly. There was a cadence to it, the well-known and remembered crunch and rumble underlying reality. I knew it from somewhere.

Voices around me speaking a language which I knew, found comfort in, and I wanted to speak it back before the chance was once again lost. I only managed some harsh gasps. My consciousness retreated in embarrassment.

The next time that I managed to slit my eyes open, I found myself blinking up at canvas stretching overhead. There was firelight bouncing from the fabric. *Had the whole castle burned?* Turning my head sent lightning shooting through my neck, my back, pooling and simmering in the left side of my body. Something wet was rolling down my face, salt stinging my lips.

It was blurry, but I could just about make out the sight of a campfire, of large shapes in the darkness, of bodies sprawled around. A battlefield? A graveyard?

One of the figures made a sharp sound, leaping up and rushing over. I lost track of them as my eyes tried to follow the motions only to get muddled up in a series of blurs. My eyelids wanted to flutter shut again, but this time I had enough awareness to fight it, to hold on to whatever this was for a few more moments.

I knew the face which was hovering over my own. There was a palm on my cheek, urging me to stay with the person it was attached to. Her lips were moving but I couldn't quite make out what she was saying.

Amara. It was Amara. I was in her caravan.

Had it all been a dream? Some terrible nightmares or

premonition of what was about to happen? Was Clarisse... Tabitha... lying just to my side and not snoring for once?

The pain wreaking havoc on my body said that was unlikely. But how had I gotten back here? It made no sense, and that alone was vaguely terrifying. I was supposed to do something... protect... no, that was wrong... it was all wrong, and confused, and jumbled up in my head.

Glass in the sunlight. Firelight on stone. On canvas. On glassy eyes that looked at nothing.

A vial pressed to my lips, bitterness flooding down my throat and yet somehow soothing the sting in its wake.

Amara made to move away, and with vague desperation I managed to latch one hand onto the sleeve of her shirt. The use of my limbs nearly sent everything spiralling away once more, but the blossoming panic forced my brain to stay with it just a little bit longer.

My lips were moving but I couldn't tell if any sound was coming out. I kept it simple, one word repeated over and over, the same plea.

Hands back on my cheeks, and then one moving back to stroke at my hair. A touch memory, soothing a calm forcing my muscles to relax ever so slightly. Or perhaps that was whatever I had been dosed with. Some part of me registered that those fingers weren't trailing through masses of lengths as they had once done. Where was my hair?

A slow blink, and when I forced my eyes open things were ever so slightly clearer. When had the sun risen? I could have sworn that it had been night only a breath ago... there was enough awareness now for me to realise that I was moving. I was in the back of a wagon. Turning my head this time was less agony inducing, and I managed to half prop myself up on my elbows. My arms shook like leaves in the wind with the effort, but I gritted my teeth and made myself hold the position.

A bracing breath which made my entire chest cavity scream in protest before I transferred the weight to one arm for just long enough to pull back the blanket covering me. Thanks to Inar I managed to catch myself before I fell backwards completely. I was pretty sure that trying to pull myself up a second time would have proved largely impossible. I didn't want to wait for that strength to return. I had to know.

For the first time in I didn't know how long, I looked down my body. What was left of it.

There were a lot of bandages, was my first impression. In truth they seemed to cover almost every inch of what would have been exposed skin considering that I wasn't really wearing any clothes. It seemed that I had recovered enough blood volume to flush at that realisation.

Judging by the bindings around my ribs, it was pretty safe to assume that I had broken most of them. Even so, it was the sight of my legs which caused me to finally lie back as my strength gave out. The right one was in some sort of splint, no doubt cracked at the very least. But the left? That was a far worse sight. Even from my brief glance I had noted the layers of bandages which were vaguely spotted with red. It too was splinted, but even I could tell that it wasn't sitting exactly right.

Once again safely on my back, I raised one hand to feel around my face and head. There was the unmistakable ridges of stitches running from my eyebrow. I followed the line upward and back to where it disappeared into my hair line. Or what would have been my hair line. There was only stubble beneath my fingertips.

I think that was what finally made the tears slip free.

I covered my face with my hands despite how much they shook.

A slight thump as someone jumped into the back of the wagon. I didn't have it in me to look at them. There was no curiosity, barely any registering of their presence. At least until they gently pulled my hands away, holding one in her own even as she wiped the tears from my cheeks.

Amara smiled softly down at me once again. At least there was no pity in her eyes. I think that was what gave me enough determination to try and say something. Anything. It took a few tries to try and get my mouth to move. I could feel every muscle in my face stretch and groan as I finally forced out a harshly whispered, "What?"

There was meant to be more. I wanted to ask what happened, how I got there, where was everyone else, what had become of the castle... so many questions. All I could choke out was one word slurred around an uncooperative tongue.

She seemed to understand. "You are safe." Her voice was still slightly muffled to my ears, but there was no mistaking that musical lilt which had always accompanied my mother tongue in her tone. "The battle ended with no winner for now. A friend arranged for your evacuation with the wounded and contacted us to take you further." An amused glint in her eye, "Your 'Mags' it seems can be very persuasive."

I wanted to laugh, to agree, to run all the way back whatever ash and stones may have been left even on my apparently shattered legs and talk to her for myself...

Instead, I half squinted against the dim light seeping through the canvas and didn't fight as the contents of another small vial were poured down my throat. The effect was pretty quick, numb heaviness seeping through my wrecked body and blending the edges of my mind and reality. For now, I would sleep. Perhaps with enough time I could even heal. What would come next? That was for Inar and Anar to fight over. Hell, maybe Mags would even figure out a way to load the dice.

Darkness called. And for once I knew what the right answer was.

www.ingramcontent.com/pod-product-compliance
Lightning Source LLC
LaVergne TN
LVHW091255150826
845673LV00006B/1429

9798846367487